COLLABORATORS:

ELIA KAZAN, ARTHUR MILLER &

MARILYN MONROE

by
Richard A. Schwartz

To Holly

I'm greatly looking forward to
talking about books with you.

all the best,

Rick

Richard A. Schwartz
ras1951@bellsouth.net

Cover art by Richard A. Schwartz

ISBN: 9798633042511

CHAPTER 1

Marilyn

I was one of Elia Kazan's girlfriends, we called him Gadg, when he fixed me up with Arthur Miller, the famous playwright. That was in January 1951. They were throwing a bash at Charlie Feldman's house to honor the great writer who'd just arrived in town. Art had recently won the Pulitzer Prize for *Death of a Salesman*, which Gadg directed; so this party was a big deal. I was just twenty-four then, an unknown, aspiring starlet who'd scored a few bit parts and was under contract with Columbia Pictures for all of seventy-five dollars a week.

Showing up as Gadg's date at a high-brow affair like this was a terrific chance to advance my career; so I was crushed when I phoned him on the afternoon of the party, and out of nowhere he tells me, "I have to work late," that night. When had he been planning to let me know? If I hadn't phoned, I would have just shown up in a cab and stood around waiting for him all evening, with everyone wondering who the hell that girl with no date was.

Gadg said he was casting for his next movie, *Viva Zapata!* He didn't mention that his casting involved making out in a parking lot with Jean Peters -- you know, Howard Hughes' girlfriend -- at the break-the-set party for *As Young as You Feel*. But that was Gadg. He could be like that. Fully self-absorbed.

"Look, Baby, I'll do you one better."

"Yeah, sure. Who's better than you?"

"How would you like to go with the guest of honor instead?"

"Arthur Miller?"

"That's right, Art. It's not every day you get to show up at a party with a Pulitzer Prize winner. You'll be on the front page of *Variety*. Maybe even in the *L.A. Times*. Wear that low-cut gown of yours and no one will even remember whether Willy Loman was liked or well liked. All the talk around town will be about your tits."

How could I turn *that* down?

"He'll pick you up at eight."

"*He*'ll pick *me* up? That's a switch."

"That's right. The guy's got class. That's why he'll never survive in Hollywood."

I thought about it for a moment. Gadg was right. Appearing as Art's date might give my career the shot in the arm it needed. But I didn't give in easy.

"You still owe me, Gadg. You owe me big time. *Viva Zapata!* my ass."

"Thanks for understanding."

"Don't forget, you owe me!"

"I've got to go now. I'll meet you at the party later on, after I finish up with *Zapata*."

"Save something for me."

3

"I always do, don't I?"

And that's how I was corralled into being Art's arm candy for his fancy fête. I didn't know much about him apart from his serious expression and his big ears. He was tall, and some people thought he looked like Abraham Lincoln, who, along with Einstein, was one of my personal heroes. And, of course, I knew Art had gotten the Pulitzer for *Death of a Salesman.*

Earlier Gadg had told me a little about him, but not much. We had other things besides talking on our minds back then. But Gadg did mention that Art was intense and uncompromising when it came to his artistic vision, and that sometimes they'd almost come to blows when they disagreed over how to interpret a scene or present a character. He also said that Art was married to a Catholic woman; Art was Jewish. Mary struck Gadg as harsh, with a lot of suppressed anger.

"Maybe she's entitled to her anger. Writers can be very self-absorbed."

Gadg just shrugged. "Maybe. Maybe not. Some people feed off their martyrdom. Either way, it's making them both miserable. And it's probably not great for the kids. He has two of them. Jane and Bobby."

"Now I know."

"Not your type anyway. He's too bookish, and he takes himself too seriously."

4

"Don't sell me short. There are depths to me you have yet to plumb."

"I'm content with the ones I have plumbed." He slid his hand between my thighs.

"No one's ever questioned your plumbing skills." I dragged my fingernails lightly over his belly, which was still firm and tight in those days.

"You're right. They haven't." And then our conversation shifted away from Art and from words.

So, I didn't know much about Art when we first met. But I did know he was married, had kids, was a little nerdy-looking in an Abe Lincoln sort of way, and was assuredly out of my league intellectually. I'd seen *Death of a Salesman*, and I agreed with the critics. The writing was incredible. I hadn't encountered anything else with such insight into family dynamics or the characters' feelings and motivations. To tell you the truth, I was too much in awe of Art even to flirt with him – although I've been told it came naturally to me.

CHAPTER 2

Art

Marilyn hit me like a ton of bricks that fell from a clear, blue sky. She took my breath away the first time I saw her. And she felt the same way about me too; that was even more amazing. Here she was, a twenty-four-year-old knock-out actress, sex oozing through her pores; and there I was, worn-down, henpecked, and thirty-five, the father of two, trapped in a marriage that, already chilly, had become outright frigid after I confessed to Mary that I'd been attracted to another woman. But I never acted on it. And never would. I told her that too.

In January 1951, Gadg and I had an artistic collaboration that was the envy of everyone. Charles Feldman, the big-time Hollywood producer, had lent his posh house to Gadg while Gadg worked on some late alterations to *A Streetcar Named Desire* for Feldman. That was the movie where Gadg "discovered" Brando. Gadg could write his own ticket in Hollywood back then, and everyone outdid themselves trying to keep him happy. Why not? His movies made them fortunes. Gadg's wife, like mine, had stayed behind back East, and he'd set up his own bachelor pad in Feldman's house.

I came to town to work on a screenplay Gadg and I were collaborating on. *The Hook* was going to be about racketeering on the New York docks, and we were both excited about it. In fact, much to Tennessee Williams' displeasure, Gadg had pulled out of directing *The Rose Tattoo* to work on *The Hook* with me.

When I finally showed up at Feldman's doorstep, bags in hand, Gadg was happy to see me, but he noticed right away that my spirits were low. It didn't take me long to open up about my problems with Mary.

"I guess it's her Catholic upbringing," I sighed. "She equates desire with the act."

"And you don't?"

"Of course not. No one can control what he desires. But we all can control how we act on those desires. That's how we determine who we are."

"Spoken like a true existentialist. Triumph of the will and all that."

"I'm an existentialist, not a Nazi."

"What's a Nazi but an existentialist without a moral compass? In any case, I think it's our desires, themselves, that determine who we are. Did you ever consider that? You make it sound like desire is some dangerous, out-of-control force that must be suppressed at all costs. I disagree."

"Not all desires. But some of them, sure. Otherwise we'd all kill each other sooner or later. How many times when we've been up all night arguing over a scene have I wished you dead? Or you me? Suppression of desire is the basis of civilization, for God's sake."

"But it's the *libido*, the passion, the sexual desire that fuels life," Gadg insisted. "Tamp it down too hard and the fire goes out. Read Freud."

"Give it free rein and everything explodes. Read Freud."

Gadg shrugged. "Everything explodes either way, but that's how life evolves."

"All I know is that Mary sure exploded. *KABOOM!* Right in my face. What new creation will come from *that* eruption, Heaven knows."

This wasn't how I wanted to start my trip out West. The ostensible purpose, of course, was to work on *The Hook* with Gadg, and I was very earnest about that. We both were. But I must admit I savored the thought of escaping Mary's critical eye and her silent – and sometimes not-so-silent – accusations.

I looked around and took in the expensive furnishings, paintings, and artifacts that filled the room. "It was awfully nice of Feldman to let us stay at his place while we work on the movie."

"And to leave the bar and bedroom so nicely stocked."

Almost on cue, a pretty, young actress wearing a bathing suit and flip flops sashayed into the room, smiled at us, and proceeded to the bar.

"I've noticed you haven't had to keep your desires too much in check."

"Not at all," Gadg replied. "Want a refill?"

"From the bar or from the bedroom?"

"Your choice."

I looked again at the young woman stirring her gin and tonic. "Don't tempt me. My resolve is weakening. It could lead to the end of civilization as we know it."

Gadg laughed. Then he called to the girl, "Honey, make me a whiskey on the rocks." He looked at me.

"I'll have a whiskey too. Straight up, please."

She poured our drinks and served us, showing off her ample cleavage as she bent over to place our tumblers on the coffee table. "Enjoy," she said, clearly referring both to the drinks and the view she was presenting.

"Thanks, Baby," Gadg said. I thanked her too; then she retrieved her gin and exited the room like she was auditioning for some sexy part in a film.

I removed a thick, heavily marked manuscript from my bag and tossed it onto the coffee table. "What do you think of these revisions I made on the train? Movies are so different from plays."

Gadg picked it up and silently flipped through the pages. He'd read the uncorrected draft earlier, while I was making my way to California.

"It's still too long. After two hours movie audiences get antsy."

"OK. So where can we cut? I don't want to lose anything that shows Marty Ferrara as a fundamentally moral man caught in an untenable situation. I want this movie to provoke people to think about what it means to be a person of integrity. To see the nuances involved. And the costs."

"I'm good with that. But how about shortening some of those opening scenes on the docks?"

"Sure. What else?"

"Well, I like those additions you made in Marty's speech to the longshoremen, where you play the rats on the wharf off the rats running the union. But then you lose it right after that, when he says –" Kazan flipped through the manuscript until he found the passage he was looking for. "Yeah, here it is: 'If this fink can take from me the bread and butter from my mouth, then I'm a slave in a chain.'"

"What's wrong with that?"

"First, the prose ain't natural: 'Take from me the bread and butter.' Who talks like that? A grammar teacher, maybe. Not real people. Certainly not a longshoreman."

"OK, that's an easy fix."

"But the real problem's in the next line: 'I was born in Italy, but *this* is fascism.' Too heavy-handed. Plus, it won't fly in today's climate. No studio is going to back a movie that complains about fascism. Not when Joe McCarthy and his pals on HUAC are crucifying the Abraham Lincoln Brigade for being *prematurely anti-fascist* back when they fought Franco in the '30s."

"The House Un-American Activities Committee." Just saying the words left a sour taste in my mouth like curdled milk. "What a joke. Since when is it a crime to be un-American? What's an un-American activity, anyway? Cockfighting? Camel racing? Chinese checkers?"

"And French kissing. I get your point, Art, and I'm with you all the way. Nonetheless, the fascists aren't our enemy today. The Reds are, and that's what audiences care about."

"Coming from you, that's a mouthful."

"I was a Communist for a reason back then. It didn't take a visionary to see that Franco, Mussolini, and Hitler were bad news. And that capitalism was a joke during the Depression. A cruel, heartless joke. Breadlines. Bums huddled around campfires trying to stay warm when they couldn't find work. Children sleeping in the street. It was disgraceful. There was nothing premature about my anti-fascism."

"Nor mine."

"But the Reds aren't any better. Look at Stalin. How many millions of innocents died in those sham purge trials of his?"

11

"They were an anti-Semitic pogrom disguised as politics." Stalin was a sore point with me. "He eradicated all the old-time Jews who'd been the backbone of the revolution."

"And then he gave Hitler *carte blanche* to invade Poland and start a world war. Millions more dead. How could anyone call himself moral and still justify all that?"

"They can't, of course."

"Well, the American Communists are as bad as the Russians; they just lack power. Otherwise they'd be as despotic as Stalin. Everyone would have to grovel before them and beg for Party discipline. Or be sent off for *rehabilitation*. That's the main reason I quit. Plus, they were taking their orders from Moscow. I never signed up for that."

"That's why I never joined. I won't have some Party hack telling me what to write. But don't you fear the fascists taking over America now: McCarthy, Hoover, McCarran, Nixon?"

"Of course I do. But I fear Joe Stalin and his atom bomb even more. And Chairman Mao and the hordes he's unleashed in Korea. More important, they're who our audience fears, not Hitler. We eradicated him and crushed Mussolini. Franco's off by himself in Spain. No one worries about the fascists anymore."

"I do."

"But that's not going to sell this screenplay to the studio heads. Hell, half of them are fascists themselves. So, cut the line."

"No. I want to keep it.

"Look, you can have all the social conscience you want, so long as the movie makes a healthy profit. But anything that turns audiences off loses money for the studios. They're already taking a beating from this new upstart." Gadg stood up and walked across the room to the large box with a small, round screen standing against the wall.

"What an invention," he sighed. "It will be the death of us all."

He switched on the television set, and before a picture resolved on the screen we heard a voice say, "LSMFT: Lucky Strike Means Fine Tobacco."

"Listen to these inane commercials," Gadg sneered. "Talk about manipulating the masses."

"And this just in," the television continued as a man behind a desk materialized before us in black and white. "The trial of Julius and Ethel Rosenberg has been set for March 6. The couple maintains their innocence; however, federal prosecutors insist that the self-avowed Communists stole the secret of the atom bomb. According to FBI officials –."

Gadg abruptly turned off the TV. "Bah! That's just what I was talking about. Those 'self-avowed Communists' want to

13

destroy this country. That means you, me, Mary and your kids too! You want to tell me they aren't more dangerous than HUAC?"

"It's not either/or. Both are dangerous. But it seems we're no longer permitted to acknowledge the threat from the Right. Just the one from the Left."

"Well, those Reds sure scare me. And they scare away paying customers too."

"It's not the Communists who are silencing today's writers. It's HUAC and the studios and the threat of blacklisting. Everyone is frightened by his own shadow, afraid to write anything that's even a little socially-minded, lest they end up ostracized and out of work. You've read Ayn Rand's *Screen Guide for Americans*."

"Of course, it's the Bible out here."

"'Thou shalt not smear industrialists, success, or the free enterprise system.'"

"'Or deify the common man.' It's awful."

"And now HUAC's starting a new round of Hollywood hearings in just a couple months."

"So I've heard." The disgust on Gadg's face was palpable. Did I also perceive a tinge of fear? "Look," he continued, "I agree, HUAC *is* totally cynical. So let's not give them any more ammunition to go after *us*." He gave me a knowing look. "Cut the line about the fascists."

14

I wasn't ashamed of any of the political stances I'd taken in the past. For me, fascism always represented a greater threat to America than communism, and, like the ancient Athenians who invented democracy, I believed it was each citizen's duty to become politically engaged. That's how I lived my life, and I was proud of it. Nonetheless, who wants to have his career needlessly trashed and his personal life wrecked by vindictive, self-serving political hacks?

"I'll think about making that change," I told him.

"This script still needs revisions. The ending is too ambiguous. It equivocates too much. Marty sells out at the end, but not really."

"I've always liked ambiguity. It's more provocative, more like real life."

"But this ain't real life. It's Hollywood."

"Alright. I'll think about that too."

Just then, the phone rang. It was Marilyn making her first appearance in my life. Even then, she was unknown to me and unseen, simply an offstage presence whose being I had to infer from Gadg's utterances into the phone.

"Hi, Baby. What's up?" Gadg was mostly silently after that, interjecting a *Yes* or *Of course* or *Uh huh* every now then to show that he was listening. Finally, he interrupted Marilyn's monologue. "Look, Baby, something's come up. There's been a change of plans for this evening. I can't make it until late."

15

Gadg winced as he absorbed her reaction. "It's for work. *Zapata*. Hold on a second."

Gadg covered the phone with his hand and turned to me. "Art, I need you to do me a favor. I invited this broad I've been schtooping, Marilyn Monroe. She's just a bit actress, but she's sexy as hell. I've got a date tonight with a girl I'm casting for *Zapata*. That'll take a while. Can you fill in for me with Marilyn? She'll take a taxi. You can meet her here."

"Fill in?" I was taken aback.

"Be her date for the night. Just until I get back; then I'll take over. She'll be flattered to be seen with someone of your stature. The publicity shots might help out her career. What do you say?"

At first I hesitated. I was, after all, a married man, and I knew that when Mary saw the inevitable pictures of me with a much younger starlet, she'd go off her rocker. Nonetheless, call it fate or what you will; maybe it was just a perverse act of defiance, but something possessed me to accept.

"OK. Sure. But I don't want her to take a cab. That's no way to treat a lady. I'll pick her up."

"As you wish, Art, but you don't have to. She's no lady. She's used to it."

"No. I'll get her."

Gadg removed his hand and spoke again into the phone. "But look, Baby, I'll do you one better. How would you like to go

16

with the guest of honor instead?" There was a short pause, and then, "Arthur Miller. That's right, Art. It's not every day you get to show up at a party with a Pulitzer Prize winner."

After a while Gadg hung up and then wrote on a piece of paper and handed it to me. "Here's her address. Have some fun. She's a great lay. And very available since her agent and one true love, Johnny Hyde, died about six weeks ago." He paused a moment. "She tried to kill herself after the funeral."

"My God, *that's* who you're fixing me up with? A suicidal sexpot! What if she goes off the deep end while they're honoring me? Mary would never let me hear the end of it."

"Don't worry, I know her. She won't."

I thought about it for a while. Finally Gadg punched me lightly on my shoulder. "Come on, Art, please."

I brushed my shoulder. "How?"

"'How' what?"

"How'd she do it? You know, try to kill herself."

"Barbiturates. Her roommate found her passed out on her bed with about thirty pills stuffed in her mouth. She couldn't swallow them because her throat had dried up. She was devastated by Johnny's death, and she felt lost without him. It wasn't long after she got out of the hospital that we met up, about a month ago, I guess. Not even."

"How did that happen?"

17

"Actually, I was visiting the set of a film where Marilyn had a small role, and the director was complaining that they were always waiting on her because she couldn't stop crying and her puffy eyes were ruining the shot. That was already three weeks after Johnny croaked, and she was still broken up. After they finally got the scene to work I followed Marilyn into a large, empty sound stage close by, where she was sitting in the dark, crying. I told her I'd been a friend of Johnny's, in fact a client, and that I'd liked him very much, but she just turned her head away and said nothing. I sat with her, silently, until they called her for her next scene. After the next take, I got the director to introduce us, and I asked her out to dinner.

"'I won't say a word if you don't want me to. I'll just be with you while we eat and then take you home.' At first she refused, but finally she came around. Later I learned that was because I'd sat with her in the dark like that. Plus, she thought I had a kind face."

"Quite a story."

"I give her the moral support she needs. I lift her spirits." Gadg looked down at his crotch. "She sure lifts mine."

"You know I would never exploit someone's suffering like that."

"Who's to say she's not exploiting me? I take her mind off her sadness and protect her against the pack of Hollywood wolves that's been circling ever since they planted little Johnny

18

in the ground. I give her status. She appreciates it." He looked back down again at his crotch. "All of it."

"In any case, I wouldn't cheat on Mary."

"Of course not; civilization would collapse. Well, have a good time anyway."

CHAPTER 3

Marilyn

That's true. I did try to kill myself after my Johnny died and his family treated me like I was a whore. You know, he went to his Maker calling out my name. I was in the corridor in the hospital, listening through the closed door because the family wouldn't let me in. Then they were outraged at the funeral when I threw myself over Johnny's casket, screaming hysterically over and over, "Wake up, Johnny, please wake up!" They thought it was all for show, but it wasn't.

Johnny changed my life. He wasn't just the agent who put my career on track. Johnny inspired me to read good books and enjoy fine music, and he got me to start talking again. I'd figured out early in life that if I didn't speak, I couldn't be blamed for anything. But Johnny showed me how unfair I was to myself when I surrendered my voice like that. He brought me out of my shell. What would I do now without him? Who would guide me? Not just my career, but my life?

I'd just lost my closest friend, and his family made me feel like shit. My heart was broken because I loved Johnny, and now he was dead, and they made me feel like shit. So a few days after the funeral I took a handful of barbiturates and passed out on my bed. Turns out I'd only been able to get down a few; the rest were still drooling from my mouth when

Natasha, my roommate, came home early and found me unconscious. She called the medics and changed the course of history, because, when you think about it, the modern world would never have been the same without Marilyn Monroe.

They called me Johnny's whore, but the funny thing was Johnny left me nothing in his will. Nothing at all. The only things I ever got from him were six bath towels, six sheets, and three pillowcases. So, if I'd been his whore, well I certainly got the bad end of the bargain. You see, sex with Johnny never did anything for me. I tried and tried, but he never could make me come. That's the bottom line. I liked Johnny, and admired him, and he was always so good to me, so protective of me, although he could also be cold and callous. Still, Johnny was my only real friend in all of Hollywood. I'd had so few of them in my life, and I truly loved him. But what can I say? Johnny just never turned me on. He wanted me to marry him. Before he died he became desperate for it. But what would have been the point? The same was true for Joe Schenck. He was one of the richest, most respected men in Hollywood. After Johnny died, Joe came on to me. He told me he'd give anything for me to marry him. He didn't have long to live, and I would inherit a fortune. I could even take lovers if I wanted, so long as I never went with the same guy twice in a row – a rather strange restriction when you think about it. But Joe was seventy-one years old, and I was twenty-four. I mean, really.

21

I've come to recognize that the single biggest challenge for my entire life was to overcome a deeply rooted belief that I was a piece of shit. I put up a good fight. No one can complain that I didn't, but Johnny's family confirmed all of my worst thoughts about myself, and I no longer wanted to live.

Art picked me up that night in a rented convertible. He was even taller than I expected and looked very dignified in his tuxedo. When I opened the door he made an imposing figure, towering over me as he stood there with a corsage in his hand.

"Thank you for agreeing to be my escort." He seemed a little timid as he handed me the flowers. "Otherwise, I would have had to go alone." He spoke this with such sincerity that I almost believed him, even though I knew he was covering for Gadg. Johnny had never given me a corsage. Gadg neither.

"I'm Art Miller," he said as I accepted the gift. He seemed at once totally self-confident – a Pulitzer Prize winner, after all, and the guest of honor – and at the same time shy and tentative. The tiny bouquet brought a spontaneous smile to my face. It was so delicate and Art's gesture so kind. My grin must have been contagious, since right away Art lightened up too. He offered his arm, which I gracefully accepted, and then he escorted me to the car, opening the door for me and making sure my dress was all-the-way inside, and I was comfortably seated, before he closed it again. That was a far cry from the taxis my dates usually had me take – and pay for. Art was so gallant, so polished, and I savored the attention this serious man of letters lavished upon me.

Art seemed absolutely sprightly as he hopped into the driver's seat and started up the engine, not at all the stiff and formal man who'd greeted me at the door just moments before.

"You have the most infectious smile," he told me as he backed out of the driveway, and I thanked him. A swing band was playing on the radio, and I told him how much I enjoyed a hot wind section while riding beside a handsome man with the top down on a cool, cloudless California evening.

I don't recall what we talked about for the rest of the drive; it was only about half an hour to Feldman's house. But I remember feeling more comfortable with Art than I had with any man in a long, long time. Perhaps ever. I felt comfortable with Gadg too, and I'd been at ease with Johnny, of course. But this was different. Art touched a different part of my being. He was witty and engaging, passionate about his beliefs and full of all sorts of interesting, esoteric facts and stories, but never condescending. He actually asked me questions about myself: my career, my interests, my aspirations. Not only that but he listened seriously and responded thoughtfully, with consideration. What other man did that? His words were kind and never suggestive or faintly obscene like so many of my Hollywood dates.

23

When we arrived, the party had already begun. Feldman's living room had been transformed into a dance floor, with couches and chairs lined up against the walls. A five-piece band played Glenn Miller in the far corner. The sliding glass doors separating the living room from the patio were open, and several fashionable guests mulled around a poolside bar, while aspiring starlets in show-and-tell bathing suits giggled and laughed as they splashed each other, much to the delight of onlookers.

As soon as Art walked in a voice in the back yelled out, "Here he is, the man of the hour."

"Where have you been, Art?" another voice demanded.

"Picking up my escort," he shouted back. "Everyone, this is Miss Marilyn Monroe."

That announcement sure created a stir. Neither Art nor I had expected that. I caught snippets of several snide remarks. I should have been prepared, but they hurt nonetheless. "Used to be Johnny Hyde's squeeze." "Guess she's moved on." "That didn't take long." "Look at that dress," a high-pitched female voice flew over the din. "If her tits stood out any farther, you'd think they were the prow of a pirate ship."

"Ramming speed ahead!" her jovial male companion replied.

"I hear she's Gadg's girl," another she-cat declared. "Art's just filling in 'till he returns from an evening *casting call*."

24

"Nice life that Gadg has."

"Silence!" Art commanded, and the room fell quiet. Not a soul moved. Art was outraged. You could hear it in his voice and see it in his face. "How dare you insult Miss Monroe in this way. Does it even occur to you that words can hurt people? It doesn't take a Pulitzer Prize to figure that out. I have half a mind to walk out of here right now."

"No, don't." I whispered.

"Sorry, Art." "Sorry, Art." "Wasn't thinking." "Standard Hollywood sniping." "Won't happen again."

Art proudly took me by the arm and escorted me to an empty couch across from the band. We had that part of the room to ourselves, and after Art's speech everyone gave us plenty of space.

"I'm so sorry for what they said," he apologized. "It's tasteless. Rude. Unforgiveable. I should leave and take you with me and not come back."

"No, don't. They're honoring you, and I don't want to ruin that. But thank you so much for standing up for me. No one has ever done that, and I can't tell you what it means."

I kissed him on the cheek. Art blushed, but he didn't resist. Waiters drifted by and brought food and drink, and we settled in comfortably on that couch. The harsh remarks directed at me were soon forgotten, and we became increasingly oblivious to the party around us. At some point there was a little honoring ceremony and Art gave a short, thank-you speech. He spoke a while with well-wishers and glad-handers but then excused himself and returned to our couch in that darkened corner. I told him how proud I was of him and impressed by him, and he glowed. I slid a little closer and held his hand. Art didn't let go.

"It was awfully considerate of you to pick me up tonight. You know, you didn't have to. At most of these Hollywood parties the 'dates' arrive by cab. Fewer complications for the guys at the end of the evening."

"You deserve better than that. Anyone can see that."

"That's the nicest thing anyone has said to me since Johnny died."

"How sad."

"Johnny's death *was* terribly sad. He wasn't just my agent, he was my best friend. Johnny was the first man in Hollywood who was truly nice to me. You're the second."

"Again, how sad. You must feel very lonely and unsupported now."

"Gadg has been good to me… Johnny wanted to marry me, you know. Even during his last days in the hospital he wanted us to get hitched, just so I'd be taken care of after he died."

"So why didn't you?"

"Johnny was special. He really was. I cared for him so much. But I just didn't love him. I guess he never really excited me. You know what I mean. How could I marry someone just for money?"

"It's been known to happen."

"I'd feel so cheap. I thought about it, but I couldn't do it."

"I applaud your integrity. Johnny Hyde was a wealthy man. I think most people in Hollywood; hell, most people in the world, would have succumbed to that kind of temptation."

"Well, what's the point if it makes you feel like a whore?"

"You're an extraordinary woman, Marilyn. A truly extraordinary person. I feel privileged to know you."

These words left me flabbergasted. That such an imposing, dignified, accomplished, and brilliant man would feel privileged to know *me*. The very thought swept me off my feet.

"Thank you. Coming from you, I'm speechless. Thank you so much. I'm so honored that you would say such a thing."

Art looked deep into my eyes. "To meet a person of such integrity – the honor is mine."

"You know, when Gadg first told me you'd be taking me instead of him, I was pissed off. Not surprised but pissed. But I'm not anymore."

"I thought we only called him *Gadg* on the East Coast."

"No. We call him that out here too. But I never understood why."

"It's short for *Gadget*." I looked at him, puzzled. "He can fix anything."

So much for small talk about our mutual friend, Gadg.

"You know," I placed my other hand on top of his, "in this town a pretty girl is never appreciated for anything besides being pretty. It's terribly demeaning, but if you don't play along you never get anywhere in your career. Even then all they ever give you is nitwit roles, and how far can an actress advance a serious career that way? Sometimes being pretty can be such a curse. Do you think I'm pretty? Sometimes I worry that my breasts are too large."

I know that was a silly thing for me to say. But I was a flirt; sometimes I just couldn't help myself. Plus, I admit it, Art was starting to turn me on.

"You're beautiful, large breasts and all."

"You can touch them if you want."

I could see the desire in Art's gaze as it slid from my face to my chest, and I anticipated the feel of his fingertips gently brushing my nipples. But he surprised me.

"As tempting and as generous as that offer is, I'd better not." Art looked wistful. We sat silently for a moment, then he continued, "I always had the opposite problem."

"Tiny breasts?"

"No. Well, I do have tiny breasts. But that's not the problem. People have always admired me for my mind but dismissed my physical prowess. Such as it is."

"I think you're very manly. You look like Abraham Lincoln."

"I've been told that. Thank you."

"You know, Abraham Lincoln was the only famous American who seemed like me, at least his childhood." I rarely discussed my early life with anyone, but here I was opening up about it to Art.

"Those years must have been very hard."

"Yes, they were. I'm glad they're over."

There was an awkward pause, as though we'd run out of things to say, and my heart sank. He saw through me so quickly. He could see how shallow and ignorant I was. What on earth had led me to believe I could hold a conversation with such a learned man, an intellectual genius like Art?

But then he spoke up. "I confess I peeked inside your door when I picked you up, and I saw a volume of E. E. Cummings on your coffee table. Do you like him much?"

"Oh yes. Some guy I knew left it behind by accident. Or maybe not by accident. He bought it to impress a girl. Not me. But really, he doesn't like to read. *I* thought the poems were delightful. I love the one about the lame balloon man with goat

29

feet. The boy and girl are feeling their first sexual attraction to each other, "And it's spring!"

I giggled as I delivered that final line. I couldn't help it. It's so joyous. And Art's face lit up.

"That's one of my favorites too. The goat-feet link the balloon man to Pan, that randy troublemaker who pops in and out of Greek mythology. He was practicing his old black magic on those kids; you can be sure of that."

"I've never read any mythology but I'd like to. Can you recommend something? I just know that poem makes me smile. All his poems do: "Buffalo Bill's defunct. How do you like your blue-eyed boy *now*, Mr. Death?"

"If only Cummings could see the expression on your face when you recite his lines. You'd make him a very happy man."

"I bet I could, if I wanted. I could make you happy too."

"Alas, I'm married. No one is allowed to make me happy."

Art looked away into the distance, and his face became so forlorn. The poor man was truly suffering. But he soon pulled himself together and returned his attention to me.

"Why don't you check out *Bullfinch's Mythology* sometime? Of course, Ovid's *Metamorphoses* gets closer to the original stories. There are some good translations. I'll find one for you."

"I'd love that. There's so much I want to learn about, but I don't even know where to start. My education stank. Like the rest of my childhood."

The mere mention of my childhood must have made me regress, because without even realizing it I kicked off my shoes and sat cross-legged on the couch, like I used to do when I was a teenager and I wanted attention. I got it too. My gown had slipped up my leg, and Art couldn't take his eyes from my thighs.

"You don't mind, do you?" I asked in my most innocent inflection. "All that talk of goats' feet reminded me of my poor, pinky toe. I stubbed it on my way out of the shower when I was getting ready for you to fetch me."

"Not at all. Which toe is it?"

I pointed to my left foot, and Art began to caress it. He kept on caressing it the whole time we talked.

"Oh, that feels so good. Do it some more."

"Your wish is my command."

"I've never had a toe massage from a Pulitzer Prize winner before."

"We give the best foot rubs. It's one of the conditions for the award."

I laughed at that. "Gadg told me you were too serious. All work and no play. But now I see that's not true, is it?"

"I hope not."

31

"How well do you guys really know each other?"

"We're friends, but mostly we talk about business when we're together: theater and politics. Sometimes our marriages."

"From my experience," I offered, "I'd say that theater *is* politics. Marriage too."

"From my experience as well. And these days politics has become theater."

"I don't really follow politics. Except for civil rights. I think it's a shame the way colored people are treated in this country. That's one of the things I admire about Gadg. *Pinky* is the only movie I've seen that really takes on discrimination."

"Yes, I admire that about him too. And *Gentlemen's Agreement* takes on anti-Semitism, which strikes close to home for me."

"You're Jewish?" I pretended I didn't know, even though Gadg had told me.

"Born, raised, and *bar mitzvahed*."

"Maybe that's why I like you so much. We're both outsiders."

"*Auslanders*, yes. Are you an *Auslander* too?"

"I was raised in nine different foster homes. I never knew my daddy, and Mama was locked up in a mental institution when I was just a little girl. So I was always on the outside looking in. Even here in Hollywood I never feel like I fit."

"That seems so sad."

"But I'm not sad now. Not with you. You make me feel secure and well cared for. Like I fit."

"I'm happy I can do that for you. Here with you, all my troubles seem far away."

"What kind of troubles could a Pulitzer Prize winner have? The world must be at your beck 'n' call."

"You might think, but that isn't how things work. There's always the next project to get funded and made. Deadlines to meet. Lectures to prepare. And to my wife I'm not a celebrity. I'm just that familiar face she sees every day. Sometimes it's too familiar."

"Yes, wives can be like that. Taking for granted the good thing they've got."

I snuggled against him and Art put his arm around me.

"Husbands too," he sighed. He held me silently for a while, just smiling down at my face as I purred upon his chest. At last he said, "Come, let's dance."

It was already late by the time we hit the dance floor, and many of the guests had left. They'd been discreet enough not to interrupt us with their good-byes. So we had the floor mostly to ourselves as we slow-danced through one song and then another. Then Gadg showed up. I noticed him across the room talking to Feldman.   He caught my eye and started toward me, but right away he could see there was something happening between me and Art; so he turned around and quietly walked back the other way.

Finally the band stopped playing and the lights went out. Art thanked Feldman for a wonderful party. Feldman looked me over and told Art that he was glad he enjoyed himself so much. And then Art drove me home. The late-night air was chilly, and I snuggled beside him as we wended our way back to my place. The radio was playing a love song, the stars were twinkling down upon us, the wind blew against my face, and I'd never felt so much at home in all my life.

After we pulled into my driveway Art got out and opened my door for me. He was such a gentleman. I gave him my hand and stepped out delicately from the car. He kept hold of me as we walked to the door. On the top step I turned and kissed him quickly on the lips.

"Thanks for a wonderful evening."

"No, thank *you*.   The pleasure was all mine."   He squeezed my hand.   "I enjoyed tonight more than I ever imagined I could. You are wonderful. Good night."

Art released my hand, turned, and walked back to the car. I was stunned as I watched him go; I expected him to come inside, and then, perhaps, to come inside. Instead, I waved when he backed out of the driveway, and he waved back. Then I let myself in, ran into my bedroom, and threw myself onto the bed. I felt giddy for the first time since I was a little girl.

CHAPTER 4

Gadg

Although Art swore that he and Marilyn had never, you know, *made it*, Art spent most of his time with her when he and I weren't working on the screenplay, and she wasn't shooting a scene. Often I joined them. Art would drive, and Marilyn would sit in the middle with an arm around each of us, and we'd go riding along the beach with the top down, laughing and singing. Or we'd walk through bookstores and see which one of us would get recognized first. We were having a blast, and Art looked like a very different man from the one who'd shown up at my door just a couple weeks before.

Finally Art and I got *The Hook* to where we thought it was sufficiently presentable and politically correct that we could shop it around; so I set up an appointment with Harry Cohn, the president of Columbia Pictures. I'd worked with Harry before. He was an old-time studio head, crude and crass but we understood each other. He and Art had never met.

Marilyn brought out a playful side of Art I'd never seen before. Of all people, he was the least likely to become a prankster. But the night before our meeting with Cohn, Art came up with the idea of dressing Marilyn as our stenographer, Miss Bauer, and bringing her along with us to record the meeting. "In order to avoid misunderstandings later on."

Marilyn already was on Columbia's payroll, but her roles had been so small she was sure Harry wouldn't recognize her in her disguise. So she borrowed a wig and a pair of eyeglasses with thick black frames from the prop room and sat between us as we waited to be admitted into the inner office. A sexy receptionist in a low-cut dress sat across the room, absorbed in filing her nails.

"You're sure Cohn won't remember you?" Art asked.

"I don't think so. I'm small potatoes around here. However, I *did* meet him once a while back. He interviewed me right in this same office." A pained expression flashed across Marilyn's face, but she cast it off immediately.

"How'd it go?" Art asked.

"It didn't take long." She pointed to the girl manicuring her nails. "His receptionist escorted me into the executive suite and closed the door as she left. Harry sat behind his fancy mahogany desk looking very smug, like he was totally in command of everything, which he was. He gestured for me to sit in the chair across from him, and he leered at me as I sat. Of course, I couldn't really blame him: I dropped a pencil and made a point of bending over to pick it up, so he could peek at my tits. That's how the game's played around here. Harry was smoking a cigar and his underarms were stained with sweat. It's funny that I remember that; however, between the tobacco smoke and his body odor, the aroma in the room turned my stomach. But I fought that down and managed a perky smile."

I just shrugged. Stories like this were a dime a dozen in Hollywood, but Art's face showed his disgust. I'd never really thought much about it until then. It's like Marilyn said. That's just how things were done in Hollywood.

"'So, you'd like a contract with Columbia,'" Marilyn said in her best Harry Cohn imitation.

"'Yes, Mr. Cohn. I think my body of work speaks for itself. If you've seen the clips from *Asphalt Jungle* and *All About Eve*, you know that I have a strong screen presence.'

"'Your body certainly does speak for itself.'

"Then Harry did the strangest thing. He stood up, walked around the desk, and sniffed me: my hair, my forehead, my cheeks, my breasts, my stomach. He almost fell over trying to stick his nose close enough to my crotch to get a good whiff."

"That's outrageous!" Art was halfway out of his chair before I restrained him. The receptionist looked up from her fingernails and asked if everything was all right.

"Everything's fine," I assured her, and Art sat back down, still upset.

"Finally, Harry stood erect and announced his conclusion," Marilyn was intent on completing her story. "'Your body *does* have a strong presence. I like that.'

38

"While I sat there in shock, trying to assure myself that what happened had really happened, Harry walked behind my chair. Then he cupped and squeezed my breasts, like he was sizing up a couple of honeydew melons. The produce must have been satisfactory because next he propositioned me, although it was more like a command.

"'I tell you what, join me on my yacht this afternoon, and I'll give you all the attention you deserve.'

"This wasn't why I had come here, why I'd been so excited because Harry Cohn, the president of Columbia Pictures, was going to interview me in person, why I thought this moment would be my big chance. I should have slapped his face and stormed out. I wanted to. But I restrained myself. One phone call from Harry Cohn would destroy my career forever, and I didn't want to burn any bridges. So I answered coyly, 'And will your wife be accompanying us?'

"'My wife? Hell no. What? Are you crazy?' Then he began muttering to himself, 'My wife! What the hell would I want my wife for?'

"'Thank you for the invitation. It's very kind.' I spoke in my best Little Miss Innocent voice. 'But I'm afraid I have a previous engagement.'

"'A previous engagement? What the hell. Break it.'

"'I'm afraid I can't.'

"'What do you mean, you can't? I'm Harry Cohn for Christ's sake! The head of Columbia Pictures. Do you want to work in Hollywood, or don't you?'

"'Very much. I want to be in the movies more than anything. But I'm afraid I just can't break my appointment.'

"'Then get the hell out of here, you little cock tease. I'm Harry Cohn! I never want to see that those tits of yours again!'

"And *that's* my Harry Cohn story," Marilyn concluded.

Art was furious. "How can I do business with a man like that?" he fumed. But I just shrugged. "This is Hollywood. This is how things work."

"Is that abuse of power any different from the docks in Red Hook?" Art pointed to the manuscript.

"Yeah, the sex is a lot better."

Art was about to take the bait, but Marilyn calmed him down. She caressed his cheek and stroked his head and told him the whole incident was in the past and she hadn't suffered from it. "It's not worth ruining your chance to make *The Hook*. Playing our prank on Harry will be my revenge."

Just then the receptionist walked over to us and announced that Mr. Cohn would see us now. We stood, and she led us into his inner sanctum.

The setting was much as Marilyn had described. Harry Cohn, now sixty years old, still sat regally on a cushy office chair behind his fancy desk, smoking a cigar. A large Columbia Pictures logo filled the wall behind him. The chair was slightly higher than the ones his visitors used, so he had the advantage of looking down at us. Harry stood to greet us and stepped forward. He gave Marilyn a salacious once over before he turned to me.

"Gadg, good to see you." Then he stuck out his hand to Art. "You too, Mr. Miller."

They shook hands briefly; then Harry returned his gaze to Marilyn. "And who is this beautiful young thing?"

"This is our stenographer, Miss Bauer," Art jumped in. "If you don't mind, she's going to take notes for us. I want to make sure I don't distort any of your suggestions."

"Sure thing," Harry answered, but he never removed his eyes from Marilyn's chest.

"Nice tits," he complimented her as we sat. "Haven't I seen them before?"

Marilyn pretended to blush. "Oh, I don't think so."

Harry sniffed the air around her. "You sure? A rack like leaves a strong impression." Before Marilyn could answer, he returned behind his desk and resumed his seat on his throne. Then he spoke to me. "Now, about *The Hook*. It has potential but it carries a lot of risk."

"Risk?" Art demanded. "What risk?"

"I showed the manuscript to Roy Brewer."

41

"Since when does the head of the stage workers' union approve screenplays?" Art was already beginning to fume. "Why does he get a vote?"

"Because I asked him. If I'm going to invest in a movie that bashes union leadership, I want to make sure I don't get any shit from our own unions. I can't afford the headache."

"*The Hook* is about longshoremen, not stagehands and movie projectionists."

"The point is that I showed it to Brewer and he has serious reservations. He says that racketeering isn't a problem for unions today; it's the Reds trying to take them over."

"A union president who runs his own stable of goons *would* say that."

Cohn ignored Art's jibe. "Roy thinks that if we make a movie about corruption in the Longshoremen's Union, the Reds will find a way to exploit it. And I refuse to be responsible for anything that will help those bastards. The unions are a big enough pain as it is, but at least I can deal with someone like Brewer. If the Commies take control, they'll throw the whole industry into chaos. Every goddamned movie we make will need approval from Moscow."

"So, instead you beg for approval from the likes of Roy Brewer?"

"If the Reds control the docks, they'll be able to halt the flow of supplies to our boys in Korea. We could lose the war.

42

Shit, they can bring the whole country to its knees if they shut down the ports."

"Yes, but – "

"I, for one, will not play into their Commie hands. Roy's contacted someone he knows at the FBI to see what they think."

"The FBI! It's a movie, for Christ's sake, not an atom bomb. What the fuck does the FBI have to do with it?"

I placed my arm on Art's shoulder. "Calm down. This is just the way things work out here nowadays." Then I spoke to Harry. "We can introduce some scenes that make the Reds look bad. But we can't make them the main villains. The whole story is about confronting corruption at the top. And the Reds ain't at the top."

"Brewer says there is no corruption in the Longshoremen's Union. And he should know. He's close to Joe Ryan out on the other coast."

"You mean Joe *it's never been proved* Ryan? What about Malcolm Johnson's *Crime on the Waterfront* series? That's what we based our script on. It won a Pulitzer."

"So maybe you don't have to change the story wholesale. But at least show the Reds lurking in the background, ready to pounce at the first opportunity." Harry picked up the manuscript and thumbed through it. "Look here. Brewer thinks that after your man, Ferrara, starts to make a

43

name for himself by calling out the bosses, you could insert a scene where a Commie tries to ingratiate himself with him. Make Ferrara think they're his ally, that they'll back him up. But Ferrara just tells the bastard to go to hell. The American worker doesn't need help from any damned Reds. A scene like that could go a long way to making this script acceptable."

"Yeah, we could do something like that, couldn't we Art?" I just wanted to get the fuckin' script approved and funded. Nothing we said here really mattered anyway. We would take back control of the story once the shooting started and Columbia was financially invested. Then we could just throw them some sop to appease Brewer and his crowd, everyone would be happy, and we'd all get rich.

But Art wasn't from Hollywood and he didn't know how the system worked. "Forget it!" he raged. "I'm not going to compromise my screenplay just to satisfy the likes of Roy Brewer. I won't tell him how to run his union, and he shouldn't try to tell me how to write a movie. I'm withdrawing the manuscript!" He stood and turned to Marilyn and me. "Come on!"

"Be reasonable, Art. Compromise is what Hollywood filmmaking is all about. It's a collaboration."

"I'm willing to make compromises, Gadg. You know that better than anyone. But I won't kiss Roy Brewer's ass. Let's go!"

He grabbed Marilyn's arm, nearly pulled her from her chair, and escorted her across the room. I waited behind. Maybe I could still salvage something. It was a good story and would make a good movie. But Harry wanted nothing more to do with Art.

"It's interesting how, the minute we try to make the script pro-American, you pull out," he yelled to Art's back as he passed through the doorway. Then Harry turned to me. "You're just a good-hearted whore like me. We'll find something else to work on. But I never want to see that sonofabitch again, you understand?"

"I don't think you need to worry about that. The feeling seems mutual."

Harry grunted, and I left him scowling at his desk. I walked into the next room where Art and Marilyn were waiting for me, talking.

"I hope you got all that down, Miss Bauer."

"You were fantastic in there, Art. It was wonderful to see you stand up to Harry Cohn like that. I bet no one's done that in years."

"At least not since you told him you had a previous engagement."

We rode back from Columbia Pictures mostly in silence. Art and Marilyn dropped me off Feldman's house, where I was

45

still working on *Zapata!* and *Streetcar.* Then Art drove Marilyn to her apartment. He stayed there throughout most of the evening, and I was already asleep when he returned.

I hoped that Marilyn would get him past his anger and that I could talk some sense into him. But the next morning when I got out of bed Art was standing by the front door with his suitcases on the floor beside him.

"What's going on?"

"I'm waiting for the taxi. I'm going home."

I was stunned. I'd never known him to be a quitter. "Art, don't be this way. Harry Cohn offends you; I get it. Roy Brewer offends you; I get that too. But that's no reason to just pack up and leave the next day."

"I won't have a baboon like Brewer dictating how I must write my scripts."

"We could have worked something out. We could have thrown him a crumb and done what we wanted to do anyway."

"Like writers in Russia? I'm an American. I love being an American precisely because I don't have to kowtow to petty people in positions of power. And I'm not going to start now. Hell, that's what *The Hook* is all about."

"No, instead you're going to silence yourself by throwing a tantrum, withdrawing your screenplay, and running away. Now no one gets to see your story about a man who stands up to petty people in positions of power."

46

We heard a car horn outside.

"It's my taxi." Art started to pick up a suitcase, but then he set it back down and put his hand on my shoulder. "Gadg, I hear what you're saying. I know how much work you've put into this project, and I deeply regret that it will come to naught."

His apology just made me bitter. "It doesn't have to. I gave up premiering *The Rose Tattoo* for this."

"I know you did. And I know how much that meant to you."

"Well, then, stay here, Goddamn it. Make this movie with me!"

The taxi honked again, this time more impatiently.

"Look, Gadg, we'll talk more about the script. Maybe we can shop it somewhere else or work something out. But I just can't stay here any longer."

"Why the hell not?"

This time the taxi driver leaned on the horn. Art opened the door and gestured to him. Then he picked up his bags.

"I said, 'Why the hell not?'"

Art turned to face me. "Because I'm in love with Marilyn." Then he walked out the door and closed it firmly behind him.

I stood there in shock. "Shit," I finally muttered to myself. "This is the end of civilization as we know it."

47

CHAPTER 5

Marilyn

So there I was in bed, Art's letter on the nightstand next to me and his photo looking down on me from a shelf above, and Gadg on top of me and inside of me. After Art left so abruptly without an explanation or even saying goodbye – and after all we'd shared the night before – what was I supposed to do? Become a nun? Sure, fucking Gadg with Art's piercing eyes staring down at us seems perverse. It was. To tell the truth, I think Gadg was turned on by it. After all, he was almost literally rubbing his rival's nose in his semen. Talk about primal male dominance! You don't get more primal than that.

And maybe I was turned on by it too. With each thrust of my pelvis I was showing Art that no matter how hard I'd fallen for him, *I don't need him! I don't need him! I don't need him!*

But even as I screamed my mantra at the top of my lungs, part of me knew it wasn't true. Part of me knew I needed Art very much. But I couldn't have him. He'd run back to his wife a continent away.

Like I say, what was I supposed to do? Become a nun?

CHAPTER 6

Art

Dear Miss Bauer,

I am a man torn between passion and duty. Such is the stuff of tragedy. I am Wotan, the chief of the gods who must accede to the slaying of his beloved bastard son, Sigmund, in order to appease his demanding wife and remain true to his word. The guarantor of sacred oaths, Wotan must either surrender everything he most desires and holds dear – the ring of power, Sigmund, and his favorite daughter, Brünnhilde – or abnegate his weighty responsibilities and destroy all that it is his duty to protect. To succumb to his desire and bring joy to his heart is to bring about nothing less than the destruction of human civilization and the demise of the gods.

In the end Wotan does what is right. He does what he must. He surrenders the ring and smashes Sigmund's sword, thereby allowing his son's foe to slay him. Wotan then banishes Brünnhilde -- never to see her again -- because she tried to protect Sigmund after Wotan ordered her not to save him. Brünnhilde willfully defied Wotan because she could not bring herself to do her father's bidding and thereby break his heart. Ah, families….

I left Hollywood and fled back East – yes, fled *is the word – lest I succumb to the greatest temptation I have ever known and rush into your arms. For I am a married man, and Mary is my Fricka: stern, moral, and demanding. I swore fidelity when we married, and I always keep my oath. For what is a man if he fails to abide by his word? His word is, indeed, his bond. And my marriage now feels so much like bondage. It ties me hand and foot and brings me little joy.*

CHAPTER 7

Gadg

So, there I am, screwing Marilyn in her own bed right beneath Art's watchful eye. That's the stuff of movies. I'm banging away and Marilyn is screaming, "I don't need him! I don't need him!" and a photo of Art is beaming down on us with an affable smile that seems to say, "Enjoy yourself; have a ball!"

Finally, we come. We lie there silently, catching our breaths, until Marilyn finally tells me, "Wow, Gadg. You're such a beast. There's no one like you."

"Not even your boyfriend Art?"

"I wouldn't know. He's too principled to let me find out. Here, listen to what he wrote me the other day."

Marilyn picks up a letter from the nightstand and I draw my fingertip lightly over her nipple as she scans through it. "Blah, blah. Wotan, Sigmund, Brünnhilde, whoever they are." Then she turns her head to me, "Umm, that feels good. Do it some more."

I comply and she returns to Art. "OK, here we go: *His word is, indeed, his bond. And my marriage feels now so much like bondage. It ties me hand and foot and brings me little joy.*

"I told her of my immense attraction to you – to a woman I'd met in California. I thought she would appreciate my

honesty and the depth of my commitment to her. But like Fricka, Mary flew into a jealous rage. She spurns me in bed and has only mean words for me outside it. I try to appease her, to comfort her, to love her. But she will have none of it."

"I've heard that story before." I turn over on my back and let out a sigh. "Some people don't learn from experience."

"Ummm. You sure do," Marilynn purrs. Then, "Here, listen to this: *And still I think of you.*"

Marilyn repeats the final words, *And still I think of you.*

"I want to cry," she declares.

"Don't use my shoulder to cry for Art. He's a big boy."

"Then cry for *me*." She pushes my hand aside. "You don't know what love is."

Before I can respond to *that*, Marilyn returns to the letter.

"What kind of marriage is it that I am protecting if she will have none of me, and I want only you? And yet I swore fidelity to my marriage for better and for worse. And a man's word is his bond, is it not?"

I drag my fingers slowly across her belly and Marilyn lets me. As the palm of my hand swirls her around navel and drifts towards her thigh she proclaims, "Wives, I swear! Look how they torture their men. Who else uses words like, *Is it not*?"

Then she shudders. "Oh, I love your hands. Between Art's words and your hands, I'm in heaven."

"That works for me."

52

"The poor man. He's so noble and sincere. I love that about him, but look where it gets him."

"Exactly, look where it gets him. He's in bed with a cold wife who forsakes him, and I'm here fucking you."

"Don't you believe in nobility, in principles?"

"I believe in principles more than you imagine. But I also believe in *real politick*. What kind of idiot tells his wife he lusts for another woman and expects her to thank him for his honesty? What kind of writer walks out on a movie deal because he won't make a few changes to satisfy the man who writes the checks? We could have gotten that screenplay to work without major compromises. But for Art, any sort of appeasement is like Chamberlain groveling before Hitler. Except for when it comes to compromising himself for his wife. He crawls on his hands and knees for Mary. What do you see in him, really? Apart from his misguided nobility?"

"Art takes me seriously. No man has ever spoken to me like he does, like I have a mind that he can appeal to, instead of just my body."

"Did anyone ever tell you, you've got a great ass?"

"As a matter of fact, yes. But it's always nice to hear it from a stud like you. Art knows I had a rotten education, but he never treats me like I'm stupid. Never. He tries to expand my knowledge, to teach me and help me grow. Who is this Wotan? And Fricka and Brünnhilde?"

53

"Characters from Wagner's *Ring*. It's based on a Norse myth."

"Yes, mythology. Art spoke to me about it that first night, when he held my pinky toe all evening."

"Some men have a strange way of wooing. I'd have held something else."

"Who says I would have let you? I offered to let Art, but he declined. He said he was tempted but he'd better not. I've never met a man like that before."

"You probably never will again."

"We were talking of E. E. Cummings and the balloon man with goats' feet. Afterward Art bought me a copy of Ovid. It's wonderful. I've never read anything like it. Art takes me places I've never been with anyone before. So do you. But his are places in my mind. Not even you or Johnny ever did that. He talks to me about politics and ideas and social justice, not Cadillacs and his latest conquests or his newest film. He takes it for granted that I am interested and able to understand. Here, listen to what he wrote last week."

CHAPTER 8

Art

March 4, 1951

Dear Miss Bauer,

I am indeed a tortured man. My thoughts of you consume me, and when they don't, my fears about the state of the nation do. McCarthyism sweeps through the country like the plague, bringing suffering and desolation to everyone it touches. Our greatest virtue as a society has always been our respect for independent thought and independence of action, but HUAC and McCarthy are crushing it.

It's become a witch hunt. Just like in Salem, back in the days of the Puritans. The only way for a person to deflect charges of sorcery against him was to point his finger at his best friend or wife or neighbor. Or else be hung. I'm thinking of writing a new play about it. It would be set in Salem but hopefully it will help Americans see what's going on today. What do you think?

CHAPTER 9

Gadg

She puts the letter down and asks, "Did you hear that? He asked me what I think. Art won a Pulitzer Prize, and he wants *my* opinion."

I just nod my head.

"Art thinks eventually he'll be summoned to testify. You too. He hopes he has the courage spit in their faces."

"Don't we all?"

CHAPTER 10
Gadg

Thank you, Mr. Kazan, for agreeing to testify before this executive session of the House Un-American Activities Committee. As previously agreed, this is a private session, and no transcripts of this hearing will be made available to the public. For the record, I am Francis E. Walter, chairman of the Committee and the Committee's sole representative at this hearing. The date is January 14, 1952.

And so began my first encounter with HUAC. Few people know that I testified twice. The first time was a private hearing that was never publicized. The studios arranged that for me, and if it had stayed private there never would have been any problem. But someone leaked it, and I had to testify again in open session. That's when the damage was done to me and to others. But here's what happened the first time.

KAZAN: Thank you for accommodating me in this matter.

WALTER: The purpose of these hearings is to ascertain the nature and extent of Communist Party involvement in the entertainment industry. As you know, worldwide Communism presents a clear danger to our nation, and any effort to support their cause by funneling money to the American Communist Party or by lending prestige to its efforts must be viewed with great concern, especially while our soldiers continue to fight communist aggression in Korea under the most severe conditions.

KAZAN: I share your feelings about the communist threat across the seas. Domestically, however –

WALTER: It is a well-known fact that the American Communist Party takes its orders from Moscow, and so any support of communism, at home or abroad, aids and abets Joseph Stalin and his efforts to achieve global domination. Moreover, Party members have committed devastating acts of espionage against our country, infiltrating the highest levels of our State Department and stealing critical atomic secrets. Alger Hiss and the Rosenbergs are ample proof of the seriousness of the domestic threat.

Now, down to business. You were a member of the Group Theater between 1932 and 1940, were you not?

KAZAN: That is correct.

WALTER: And were you a member of the American Communist Party while you belonged to the Group Theater?

KAZAN: Yes. I joined the Party in 1934 and left it in early 1936. I couldn't tolerate its efforts to dictate what writers should write or how actors should act or directors direct. I do not see how a true artist can conform to any party line.

WALTER: But you do confirm that the Group Theater was a Communist organization?

KAZAN: Not at all. There was a Communist contingent within the Theater, to which I briefly belonged. Its goal was to take control of the Theater, but it failed. For one thing, the people in charge were extremely egotistical. They knew what they wanted, and nobody shoved them around. They were not the kind of people who would ever submit to Party discipline.

WALTER: But other members of the Group Theater were Communists?

KAZAN: Yes. There was a Communist unit within the Group Theater.

WALTER: Would you identify its members for the Committee?

KAZAN: I don't want to answer that question. I don't take refuge in anything. I will not take the Fifth Amendment or invoke the First, and I am not hiding behind any immunity of any kind. It's a matter of personal conscience.

WALTER: And who recruited you into that unit?

KAZAN: Again, I respectfully decline to answer that question.

WALTER: Was Clifford Odets a Party member?

KAZAN: I prefer not to answer that.

WALTER: Have there been any individuals who have previously appeared before this committee who were members of that Communist unit?

KAZAN: Coming down on the train this morning I knew I would be asked this question, and I knew the risks I would run by not answering it. I am not taking immunity. I just made up my mind not to answer, as a matter of personal conscience. There were two names on the list you showed me.

WALTER: Would you care to identify them?

KAZAN: No, I wouldn't. I will say this. I believe that, in general, the Communists are a conspiracy and that in industries and institutions that affect national security they should be exposed. But for the life of me, I do not see how an actor saying someone else's lines can be subversive.

WALTER: Was John Garfield a member of the Communist Party?

KAZAN: I am not ducking you. I cannot remember. Julie Garfield was a kid from the Bronx. That's what I remember about him. I don't remember his having been interested in much of anything except girls and acting.

WALTER: What, exactly, did you mean when you said your position was a "matter of personal conscience"?

KAZAN: I feel that if I did give you the names you are requesting, I would badly hurt someone. And I choose not to do that.

WALTER: Several previous Hollywood witnesses were not penalized because they came here and made a clean breast of their past connections.

KAZAN: Well, I may be wrong, but I feel if this were an open meeting instead of an executive session, the plans I am working on as a director of a picture would be canceled tomorrow. The pressure groups are so strong. And I understand everyone's anxiety. God knows, I think you should investigate and what you are doing is right. But if this were known, if this were an open meeting, I feel that I would be out of a job.

WALTER: Thank you for your testimony, Mr. Kazan. These proceedings are now closed.

And that was that. Or at least it should have been.

CHAPTER 11

Art

In the spring of 1952, I finally made up my mind to go ahead with the play that eventually became *The Crucible.* I had my doubts that I could pull it off, mainly because I was such a logical and analytical creature, and I wasn't sure I could fully comprehend, much less accurately convey, a mass outbreak of such wildly irrational behavior. But as McCarthy and HUAC persisted in waging their vendettas against the Left, I became increasingly outraged at seeing men and women of good conscience being forced to choose between having their careers demolished and their personal lives decimated, on the one hand, or ruining the lives of people they'd known twenty years earlier, people who, like them, had joined the Party solely because they wanted to combat poverty, homelessness, malnutrition, and inequality, people who had committed no crime nor taken any steps to undermine the government. How were HUAC's showcased rituals of confession and atonement different from Stalin's purge trials of the '30s, except the price of atonement for Stalin was even more severe? And how were they different from the Salem witch trials in the 1690s? They all required good people to jettison their moral scruples in order to survive.

While reviewing the historical accounts, I became drawn to the story of John Proctor, a married Salem farmer and critic of the inquisition who became the first male convicted and executed as a witch, after a teenage girl, Abigail Williams, accused him. What if, I wondered, Abigail had been a serving girl in Proctor's house, and she and he had an affair, but Abigail had tired of him and called it off? But he won't let go! Like in *Carmen* or *The Blue Angel*. Finally, Proctor threatens her somehow if she refuses to come back to him, and the only way for Abigail to free herself before he does her deep harm is to name Proctor as a witch.

No. Better still. What if *he* has called it off and confessed everything to his wife and is trying now to get back into her good graces. But Abigail is desperate and will stop at nothing to snare him again. So, she accuses his wife figuring that after they hang Elizabeth, Proctor will come back to her. When that doesn't work, Abigail accuses Proctor, thinking in her deranged way that this will somehow make him love her again.

Yes, that could work. Their love affair isn't in the official history, of course, but it gave me a good premise to work from. One thing that so often becomes lost in all these shows trials is how they enhance the self-interest of the people pulling the strings and making the accusations.

63

After a few false starts I decided to begin my play shortly after Proctor has ended the affair and returned to Elizabeth, whose reception has been cool, to say the least. But in my notebook I sketched out a scene prior to the beginning, just to help me get a better feel for the dynamics between Elizabeth and Abigail.

ELIZABETH: Whore! Strumpet! Be gone! Be gone I say. One of the girls will bring you your things in the morning, but I want you out of this house right now. Do you hear me, harlot? Right now!

ABIGAIL: So that's the thanks I get for all I've done.

ELIZABETH: Thanks for all you've done? You bedded my husband! In my own house! In my own bed! That's what you've done!

As I wrote, I heard the voices of Mary and Marilyn speaking the roles of Elizabeth and Abigail.

ABIGAIL: I kept him alive. I made his juices flow again. John Proctor is a man still in the prime of his life, a succulent grape hungry to be plucked. But he was rotting on the vine from your indifference. I made fine wine from the fruit of his loins, while you were letting his seed splatter on the ground. Don't you know the Lord condemns such waste?

64

ELIZABETH (Slapping her): Blasphemer! How dare you!

ABIGAIL: He resisted me at first. You know, he really did. He wanted to be true to you. But later he told me that once you'd sensed I'd cast my spell, you turned your back on him He felt lost and alone, but you refused to let him in. Where else could he go?

ELIZABETH (Furious) That's enough, you whore! Be gone!

Elizabeth exits in a rage, leaving Abigail alone, smiling to herself.

Marilyn and Mary in a cat fight. Or a street fight. Either way the thought made me shudder.

In early April, after I'd sketched out some basic ideas about how I wanted to approach the characters and the nature of their dilemmas, I decided to drive up to Salem for a few days to review the court documents and other records from the actual inquest. The night before I was set to leave, Gadg phoned me from his home in Connecticut. He said he needed to talk with me. I detected some urgency in his voice; so I offered to come by on my drive up to Massachusetts.

I set out early, and even though it was damp and chilly when I arrived, Gadg insisted we walk through the woods that bordered his property.

"So, you're going ahead with the play about the Salem witch hunts," he began once we reached the trail. "Marilyn told me something about it."

"If I can pull it off. I'm still not sure. I was getting ready to drive up there to do some research when you called. Connecticut's on the way, so I figured I'd kill two birds with one stone."

"So now I'm a dead bird? More like a dead duck. What's the angle, apart from showing the obvious, that witch hunts are bad?"

"I'm focusing on John Proctor, a farmer who shows up in the official history. His wife was accused of witchcraft by one Abigail Williams, a serving girl Elizabeth had fired. Before my play begins, Proctor has confessed to Elizabeth that he had an affair with Abigail and is seeking his wife's forgiveness, but forgiveness has not been forthcoming."

"Strikes close to home, don't you think?"

"Mary hasn't had anything to do with me ever since I told her I left Hollywood to keep myself from betraying her with Marilyn."

"How can someone so smart be such a schmuck? What do you think your confession did to Mary's pride? To her sense of her own beauty. To her sense of herself as a woman? Did you really think she'd be overjoyed by your honesty?"

"But if we can't live honestly and openly, then what's the point? Socrates says -"

"I testified before HUAC in January. In closed session."

I stopped in my tracks. "I didn't know."

Gadg stopped too and faced me directly. "I'm being open and honest with you now."

"And were you open and honest with the Committee?"

"I didn't name anyone, if that's what you're asking."

Gadg started walking again and I followed. It had rained a few hours earlier, and it never occurred to me to bring hiking shoes; so sometimes I struggled to keep my footing as we circled around puddles and pockets of mud.

"Did you take the Fifth?"

"No." Then "Shit!" Gadg nearly lost his balance on a slippery stone. "I didn't invoke any claims at all to immunity. I admitted my own membership but didn't implicate anyone else. Strangely enough, that seemed to satisfy them."

"Lucky you! Clearly they don't want to expose you. You're too valuable to lose to the blacklist."

"Perhaps I was. But now someone has leaked my testimony, and it's going to go public any day. So the studio has *advised* me to volunteer to testify again, this time in open session."

"Gadg, I'm so sorry for you." I fought to keep my balance and keep up with Gadg at the same time.

"If I don't cooperate fully and name names, I'll never work in Hollywood again."

"At least you can still direct on Broadway any time you want. That's more than most people in your position can say."

"You don't get it. Live theater is too small a stage. I want to direct movies. I adore the big screen. The close ups and the jump cuts, the panning and tracking, the freedom to leap back and forth in space and time. The ability to splice incongruous images together. And then rip them apart again. I love the medium. It gives me such an expansive palette to work with. Movies open me up in ways the stage never can."

"To be honest, Gadg, you have a gift for directing movies unlike anyone else."

"I don't want to surrender that. But Skouras says that if I don't cooperate, I'll never direct another film. It's that simple."

"Do you believe him?"

"He's the head of Fox, for Christ's sake. Plus, he's my friend."

"It could be a bluff."

"What do you mean?"

Suddenly I became excited. "Look, Gadg, you're the most successful director in Hollywood right now. Your name is gold. Money in the bank. *You* could break the blacklist."

Gadg looked skeptical. "How?"

"Just do what you did in your first testimony. Talk about yourself but don't give them any names."

"They could send me to jail for contempt. I don't want to go to jail over this."

"So then take the Fifth. That'll keep you out of prison."

Gadg was exasperated. "I'd be blacklisted before Walter gavels the hearing closed."

But now I was even more excited. For the first time I saw a real opportunity to make those fucking studio heads back off the blacklist. They were all full of patriotism and bluster until real money was on the line. Then they turned tail and ran. Every time.

"That's the point!" I insisted. "Let them blacklist you. Then the studios will have to choose. They can do without your services and lose millions in ticket sales. Or they can release your films and trust the public to cross the picket lines and come through at the box office. Aren't you the one who told me that Hollywood is all about profits?"

Gadg spat on the ground. "They're too chicken shit to take the risk."

"Look, it's not like you're still a Communist. Talk about why you left the Party and why you don't trust it now, maybe even fear it. That will give you credibility. Do you think people will stay away from your movies just because you refused to be

69

an informer?   They won't.   They'll admire you for it.   Nobody likes a stool pigeon."

But Gadg would have none of it.   "Maybe.   Maybe not. But they won't ever have the chance because the studios wouldn't let me work.   And more than anything, I want to work. On movies."

"Gadg, listen -"

"No, you listen to me!   I'm willing to sacrifice for certain things, but I'm not willing to give up my career to protect a party that takes its marching orders from Moscow.   I won't sacrifice everything I've made for myself in this life for a bunch of self-righteous bullies who demand that everyone toe the party line, or else.   Who want to destroy America."

Gadg's voice rose with his anger.   "If they didn't insist on operating in the shadows, then no one would be caught in this dilemma in the first place.   I wasn't ashamed of what we were doing back then to help the poor.   Showing how the fat cats keep the little guy down.   So why all the secrecy?   Why not have open rolls, like the Democrats and Republicans?   Don't you see?   It's the damned Party and its cult of distrust that's causing everyone so much grief."

"But informing will destroy innocent lives!"

"And not informing will destroy mine!   Who would I be protecting?   To the ones who are still members, I'm a traitor. They'd stab an ice pick in my eye if they could get away with it.

I should give up everything for *them*? As for the people like me, those who saw through those cowards years ago and left, let them name names too. They can keep their jobs and be true to who they are now."

"I can't agree with you, Gadg. The American Communist Party isn't a threat to anyone. HUAC and the blacklisters are. Talk about having to toe the party line. You saw what they wanted to do to *The Hook*." Now my voice rose to match his. "Goddamn it, Gadg! You were in the room with me! And you, more than anyone else, can strike a blow against them. Maybe even knock them out."

Gadg shot right back. "But if I don't knock them out, then I'm the one writhing on the canvas, bleeding and crippled. And who will be there to pick me up? Not those Red bastards or their former friends and fellow travelers. No. I won't give up everything to save their asses."

"You can still write your own ticket on Broadway. It's not like you'd starve."

"No, I wouldn't starve. I'd only lose my chance to realize my greatness as an artist. For what? To protect something I don't even believe in anymore? To save people who'd like to see me dead?"

I could see I wasn't going to change his mind. "You asked my advice; I've given it to you." I kicked a stone, and we stood a while in silence as water from a tree limb dripped down before us.

"It's not the witnesses who are at fault anyway," I went on in a quieter voice. "It's the damned Committee. Those self-serving, sanctimonious bastards. They enjoy watching people like you and me twist in the wind while they pretend to be patriots. They already know who was in the Party back then. The FBI was all over it. Your testimony won't do anything to protect America. They just want to see you crawl. Your humiliation silences the Left and makes HUAC appear powerful and important. That's the only reason for these hearings. These rituals of public atonement come straight from Stalin's playbook."

Gadg had nothing to say to that, so I kicked another stone. "What about me?"

"What about you?"

"I was never a member. You know that. But I did attend some meetings of Party writers back then. Once I even gave a speech."

"I don't know anything about that. I have no first-hand knowledge that you ever participated in any Party activities."

"OK. We understand each other. We still have that. Don't worry about what I think. Whatever you do will be okay with me, because I know your heart's in the right place."

We turned around and hiked back in silence. He accompanied me to my car, and we silently shook hands in a heartfelt way.

"Poor Gadg," I sighed as I pulled away. Then I drove off to Salem.

CHAPTER 12

Gadg

WALTER: Thank you, Mr. Kazan, for agreeing once again to testify before the House Un-American Activities Committee. Although this is also an executive session, unlike your previous testimony the transcripts of this hearing will be made available to the public. For the record, I am Francis E. Walter, chairman of the Committee and the sole representative of the Committee at this hearing. The date is April 10, 1952.

KAZAN: I understand.

WALTER: Although you previously declined to identify individuals known to you as members of the Communist Party, as a "matter of conscience" as you put it, you have now voluntarily requested that the Committee reopen your hearing to give you an opportunity to describe their participation in Party activities. Is that correct?

KAZAN: I want to make a full and complete statement. I want to tell you everything I know. To that end, I have prepared a statement.

WALTER: Please proceed.

KAZAN (reading): I have concluded that I did wrong to withhold these names before, because secrecy serves the Communists, and it is exactly what they want. The American people need all the facts about all aspects of Communism in *order to deal with it wisely and effectively. It is my obligation as a citizen to tell everything that I know.*

I was a member of the Communist Party from sometime in the summer of 1934 until the late winter or early spring of 1936. During those years, to my eyes, there was no clear opposition of national interests between the United States and the Soviet Union.

It was not clear to me when I joined that the American Communist Party was taking its orders from the Kremlin and acting as a Russian agency in this country. On the contrary, it seemed to me that the Party had at heart the cause of the poor and unemployed people whom I saw on the streets about me. I felt that by joining I was going to help them; I was going to fight Hitler, and, strange as it seems today, I felt that I was acting for the good of the American people.

I was assigned to a unit of Party members who, like myself, were members of the Group Theater acting company. They were Lewis Leverett, co-leader of the unit; J Edward Bromberg, co-leader of the unit, now deceased; Phoebe Brand – I was instrumental in bringing her into the Party; Morris Carnovsky, who later married Miss Brand; Tony Kraber, who, along with Ted Wellmen, recruited me into the Party; Art Smith; Paula Miller, who later married Lee Strasberg and with whom I remain friends today. She quit the Communists long ago. She is far too sensible and balanced a woman, and she is married to too fine and intelligent a man to have remained among them.

WALTER: Is that all?

KAZAN: Clifford Odets. He has assured me that he got out about the time I did.

WALTER: Continue.

KAZAN (Reading): My unit's mission was four-fold. We were asked to "educate" ourselves in Marxist and Party doctrine, to help the Party get a foothold in the Actors Equity Association, to support various "front" organizations of the Party, and to try to capture the Group Theater and make it a Communist mouthpiece. As I testified previously, we failed in this final task. Nor did the Party come even remotely close to controlling Actors Equity.

I was instructed by the Communist unit to demand that the group be run "democratically." This was a characteristic Communist tactic: they were not at all interested in democracy; they wanted control. They had no chance of controlling the directors, but they thought that if authority went to the actors, they would have a chance to dominate through the usual tricks of behind-the-scenes caucuses, block voting, and confusion of issues.

This was the specific issue over which I quit the Party. I had enough regimentation, enough of being told what to think and say and do. The last straw came when I was invited to go through the typical Communist ritual of penance: groveling and apologizing and admitting the error of my ways. That was the night I quit them. I had had enough anyway. I had had a taste of police-state living, and I did not like it.

WALTER: Mr. Kazan, we appreciate your cooperation with this Committee. It is only through the assistance of people such as you that we have been able to bring the attention of the American people to the machinations of the Communist conspiracy for world domination. This session is now closed.

When it was over and I had offered up Clifford Odets, Tony Kraber and the others as human sacrifices to my career, Walter and his staff packed up and left the room. I remained behind, fuming in my chair, silently cursing the people I had exposed. Look what they put me through because they didn't have the guts to be honest about who they are and what they do. Now they wanted *me* to take the fall because they insisted on operating in the dark? *Well, screw them!*

CHAPTER 13

Marilyn

"A kiss on the hand may be quite Continental, but diamonds are a girl's best friend....Girls grow old and men grow cold and we all lose our charms in the end....And that's when those louses go back to their spouses."

I liked to sing in the shower. I liked the sound of my voice, even if I didn't have great range. And, a few weeks after Gadg testified, I'd landed the lead in a new musical comedy. Of course, Jane Russell got top billing, even though *I* was the featured blonde, Lorelei Lee. And she was going to be paid a lot more than me. That didn't seem fair, but then nothing in life is fair, especially in Hollywood. And this was my big shot at stardom. After all, Howard Hawks was going to direct. This was going to be big time!

I was feeling good as I toweled off and smiled at myself in the mirror. Things were starting to take off for me. I put on my robe and walked into the bedroom. A letter from Art had arrived earlier, right after my agent called to give me the good news about *Gentleman Prefer Blondes*. You'd think I'd have been delighted to hear from the man I loved and adored, but the hard truth was, I was already beginning to recognize that Art could be a real downer. Did *everything* have to be serious? Did *every* injustice have to be met with outrage? I recalled a poem by William Butler Yeats that Art had shown me in a Beverly Hills bookstore not long after we first met. I can still picture him pulling the volume down from the shelf, and I remember how special it made me feel that a Pulitzer Prize-winner was reading his favorite lines to *me*. "A Prayer for My Daughter" spoke about how the woman Yeats loved passionately had become so consumed by politics and righteous indignation that she'd become "an old bellows full of angry wind." Now I was afraid Art was turning into that woman.

I went to the nightstand, picked up the envelop and opened it.

Dear Miss Bauer, My work on the play about the Salem witch hunts continues. I have completed the draft, but I am still at a loss as to what to call it. I had been thinking of Harlot's Cry, *but right now I'm leaning toward* The Crucible, *which is a vessel made to endure great heat and pressure. It is also used to pulverize things. Mary says I should call the play* Death of a Salem.

"*Death of a Salem*," I repeated to myself. "That's funny. I didn't think Mary had it in her."

Mary says I should call it Death of a Salem. *I must admit that's very clever. For a long time I wasn't sure I could pull this play off, but Gadg's testimony last spring got my juices flowing. At first I was inclined to forgive and accept. After all, he was in an untenable situation. But Gadg could have broken the*

79

blacklist if he'd stood his ground. Instead, he groveled. And his groveling empowered those bastards even more.

My man Proctor is racked with guilt – not for consorting with Satan, which, of course, he has never done – but first for betraying his wife and then for humiliating her when his infidelity is made public.

"Again with the guilt. Art, you are becoming a Jewish cliché."

It's his guilt that provokes him to confess to witchcraft. At some unconscious level Proctor hopes his confession will bring forgiveness for his betrayal of Elizabeth.

"Don't count on it, Art."

Of course, it will also save him from hanging. For after he confesses, the officials will exonerate him and he can get on with his life. He can go back to farming or directing Hollywood movies. Whatever. Besides, what's the big deal, after all? As Proctor tells Elizabeth, "Nothing that was not already rotten long before is spoiled by giving them this lie."

"Well, he's got a point there. In the long run, futile gestures are just…futile."

But in the long run Proctor is a good man and can dissemble only so much. For it's not enough that he testify against himself. No, the inquisitors insist that he implicate others, even the saintly Rebecca Nurse. He must name names. But now he refuses to cooperate further.

80

"I can see the nobility in that. He's protecting somebody who's innocent. But what if she weren't so innocent? Would his refusal still be so noble? Answer me that, Mr. Playwright!"

If only Gadg could have been strong enough to take a stand like Proctor's, instead of just wanting to get on with his life. It was not his duty to be stronger than he was. The government has no right to require anyone to be stronger than he is. But still, one can only wish that Gadg had more mettle. This crazy period will pass, and Gadg may live to regret his testimony. So, Miss Bauer, what do you think?

"I think Joe DiMaggio is a lot less complicated and a lot more fun. People should just do what they have to do and then move on. I don't understand all this nonsense about guilt and remorse."

There was a knocking at the door, and Gadg entered.

"Your roommate let me in."

"I was just reading this letter from Art. It's about his new play."

"You mean the one set in Salem. He told me about it last spring." Gadg sighed and shook his head. "That was a lifetime ago. I take it the play is his penance to Mary for being tempted by the likes of you. Nothing like public atonement to purge the soul. Art should have been a Catholic. He'd have loved the Middle Ages. Instead of writing plays he could have marched through the streets wearing a hairshirt and whipping himself as a flagellant. His groveling is disgusting."

"I think so too. Say, I've got great news. I've been offered a starring role in a musical, *Gentlemen Prefer Blondes.* Howard Hawks is directing. Howard Hawks! Can you believe it? This is big time! I play Lorelei Lee, a dumb blonde with brains."

"Just like you. That's terrific, Baby."

"There's a great production number at the end, 'Diamonds Are a Girl's Best Friend.' It's funny and really sexy. You'll love it. I wear a hot, slinky dress and all these men are falling at my feet. I get to shake my ass and my tits and really put on a show."

"I can't wait. I'll help you rehearse. You can shake your tits for me."

"Anytime, lover." I shook them and Gadg grinned. "Would you really help me rehearse?"

"Sure. If I have time. I've had good news too. I've been talking with Budd Schulberg, my fellow *collaborator,* as Art's crowd calls us. He's got a fine idea for a story about a longshoreman who stands up to the Mob. I read the first draft last week. Schulberg's calling the movie *The Golden Warriors,* but I think *On the Waterfront* is better."

"Wasn't that what you and Art were going to do in *The Hook*?"

"There's some overlap, sure. But Schulberg's take is totally different. Art's guy, Ferrara, was going to be a martyr: Art's into martyrdom. It's his Catholic streak. The union bosses snuff out Ferrara for challenging their power. And nothing changes. The bad guys are still in charge and the workers remain under their thumb. It's a tragedy. Art's into tragedy. Because of his guilt.

"But Schulberg's story is about a man whose real act of courage comes when he repudiates the code of silence and informs on Johnny Friendly, the union boss who sold out Terry and killed his brother."

"Johnny Friendly. That's a funny name."

"Everybody on the wharf calls Terry a rat, a stool pigeon, after he testifies before a federal commission. But because he does, Terry makes his slice of America a better place, not like Art's schmuck, Ferrara, who just dies for its sins.

"Schulberg's story is about triumph and change; it's not a tragedy that celebrates impotent martyrdom, all in the name of Truth. Just like Art martyrs himself with Mary, and then nothing changes between him and you."

"That's for sure. You know, Joe DiMaggio's been after me. I never thought I could go for a jock, but there's something a little shy about him. I like that. He's very considerate. Plus, they don't call him "Joltin' Joe" for nothing."

83

"Joe DiMaggio? No kidding? He's no martyr. He's a winner."

"You and Art are really duking it out, aren't you? Art lands a blow with *The Crucible*, then you strike back with *On the Waterfront*. It's a regular knock down/drag out. And I have a ringside seat. All I need is a mug of beer and a hot dog to cheer you two heavyweights on. Norma Jeane never could have imagined it."

"My *Waterfront*'s going to pulverize Art's *Crucible*."

"You make it sound so virile."

"It is, when it's done right."

"Art would never describe it that way."

"Art feels he needs to suppress his virility. To control it and constrain it in order to be moral and civilized. That's where all his damned guilt comes from. That's why he's in New York now with Mary, who can't stand him, instead of here banging you. But me, I don't believe in holding back. In art or in life."

"Don't I know it!"

"By the way, your old friend Harry Cohn's on board, especially now that Art's out. 'Who needs that Commie pinko anyway?'" Gadg imitated Cohn's heavy Jewish accent. "'Schulberg's play is ten times better and a hundred times more American.'"

"Harry Cohn," I shuddered. "What a monster."

84

"It'll take another year before we even get to production. But it's going to be a winner. I can feel it."

"Gadg, that's great!"

"It'll give me a chance to tell Art and all his liberal pals to stick their sanctimonious superiority up their ass. Who the hell are they to judge me? The real act of courage is telling the truth, not hiding in the shadows. There's a part at the end where Terry screams at Friendly, 'I'm glad what I done. Do you hear me? Glad what I done!' Well, that's exactly how *I* feel. They can go fuck themselves."

"I love it when you get all righteous and indignant. It turns me on."

"Well then come on, Baby. Let's screw."

And screw we did.

CHAPTER 14

Marilyn

So, I ended up marrying Joe DiMaggio. It lasted all the way from January 1954 to October. I'd put him off when he first asked me out. The last thing I needed in my life was some arrogant jock. But I finally agreed to a date and was pleasantly surprised at how kind and considerate he could be. That was a nice change of pace from the self-absorbed Hollywood players I was used to. He'd retired from his legendary baseball career with the Yankees a couple years earlier but still had a lots and lots of fans.

My career started taking off about a year earlier; so, we were a celebrity couple while we were dating and were often in the news. The small but sexy parts I had in *All About Eve* and *The Asphalt Jungle* and even my role as Jack Benny's fantasy girl on one of his early TV shows had some impact; but, of course, it was *Gentlemen Prefer Blondes* that put me on the map. Plus, it didn't hurt that *Stars and Stripes* had earlier named me "Miss Cheesecake of 1951." I was glad to know I was helping to lift the spirits of those brave boys fighting in Korea. Sincerely, I was.

In '52, I'd starred with Cary Grant and Ginger Rogers in *Monkey Business*. And the next year my performance in *Niagara* provoked a lot of comments. That's because I was at the center of some of the sexiest scenes ever filmed in Hollywood, up to that time. Remember, there were decency codes back then that really limited what they could show, or even imply. In one scene they filmed me wearing nothing but a towel; in another, just a bed sheet. This was considered shocking back then, if you can believe it; but that just made people want to check out the movie for themselves, especially the men. The film didn't get great reviews, but I did. The *New York Times* said that the waterfalls and I were "something to see." Then, of course, *Gentlemen Prefer Blondes* came along, and after that *How To Marry a Millionaire.*

Those three films from '53 made me one of the top ten box office hits in all of Hollywood, but I was still stuck in my old contract with 20th Century Fox, earning a lot less than my co-stars. Since it was me who was the big draw, that was infuriating. Not only that, but I had no say in the films they cast me in or who I would work with. I yearned to be a real actress, but they were type-casting me in all these silly sex-pot roles. I wanted to do more than that. I felt like I was suffocating.

Everything almost fell to pieces when some nude photos that I'd posed for in the late '40s surfaced. I'd recently divorced from Jim and was practically penniless and needed the money desperately. Besides, really, what was the big deal? I never understood why everyone got so uptight about sex. I was paid all of fifty bucks for the photoshoot, and the guy with the camera kept the rights to the images. Back then those pictures could have ruined my career. But the studio and I decided to get ahead of the eight ball; so I held a press conference and explained how I'd been struggling just to pay the rent back then. That won me sympathy, especially among the men, and instead of destroying me, the nude photos made me even more popular. Then Hugh Heffner bought the rights, and in December of '53, he featured me on the cover on the first issue of *Playboy*. And as the centerfold inside.

That got *Playboy* off to a terrific start, but it almost destroyed my romance with Joe. He was so conservative, especially when it came to sex. And the thought of every man in America slobbering over my tits drove him mad. But he was slobbering over them himself – the real ones, not the photographs – and he didn't want to give them up; so, we got married the next month. It didn't hurt that our wedding deflected criticism over the *Playboy* spread, but I wanted to marry Joe, and I really wanted to have kids.

Looking back, I can see that Joe's jealousy doomed us from the start. He just couldn't accept me for who I was. He loved the fact that I was pretty and sexy and desirable, but once we got hitched, he wanted me to act like a typical, modest Italian wife. Hell, I was a movie star and a sex symbol. I was never going to be what he wanted me to be. He'd even go nuts when I'd walk around the house naked. But I figured that if the shades were pulled down and the doors were closed, why not? I enjoyed it. Being naked lightened my spirit and made me feel so free. That's why I rarely wore underwear. Joe didn't approve of that either.

Our marriage began to disintegrate on our honeymoon. Can you believe it? We went to Japan soon after we married, and while we were there the USO asked me to do some shows for the boys in Korea. The fighting had stopped by then, but still Korea was a tough assignment. How could I say no? After all, those poor GIs were living in the rain and sleet and snow for us, risking their lives because who knew when the North Koreans might decide it was a good idea to launch a surprise attack, like they did in 1950. Who knew anything about what the North Koreans might do? So, I gave the troops something to help them forget how dreary it was on the front lines.

They flew me in in a helicopter for the first show. It was cold and starting to snow, and I waited backstage in dungarees. After a little while someone came up to me and said I'd have to go on early because the soldiers were shouting and stomping and even throwing rocks onto the stage. "I don't think we can hold them any longer."

So I changed right away into my silk gown; it had a low neckline and no sleeves. I felt cold, but that didn't matter because the GI's loved it. And they loved me. I sang "Diamonds Are a Girl's Best Friend," and then I did a little solo dance that drove them crazy. I never heard so many cheers and screams and whistles in my life. Those boys were so worked up, I needed an armed escort just to get back to my helicopter.

Those performances left me all tingly inside. I was serving my country; the shows were packed, and for the first time I knew I truly was a real movie star. A hundred thousand horny young men cheered me on, loving me for how I made them feel. *They* made me feel so sexy and alive, but Joe hated it. Their undisguised and uninhibited lust for me drove him mad.

Then he went crazy that fall when I was filming that scene from *The Seven Year Itch*; you know, the famous one where a sudden blast of air blows up my dress. A huge crowd had gathered just to get a glimpse of my panties. Maybe two thousand people. Can you believe that? Joe was on the set. It was no big deal to me; the filming was exhausting, but also exhilarating and fun. All of New York adored me. But the whistling and cat calls drove him nuts. He kept saying, "What the hell's going on here? What the hell's going on here?" It was embarrassing. Each take made Joe more and more furious.

"Get a look at that snatch!" I heard one man shout. "I wouldn't mind stealing a couple of those bases," yelled another. "Or sliding into home. How 'bout it Joe?"

That really set him off. The assistant director tried to reassure him that it was just their hormones going wild, but Joe had no patience for that.

"Hormones my ass!"

"Face it, Marilyn has that effect on men. You know that better than anyone. But it doesn't mean anything."

"What do you mean, 'It doesn't mean anything'? You've turned my wife into a whore!" Joe almost took a swing at him, but I guess he was saving himself for me.

"Look at those drumsticks," someone from the crowd called out as my dress flew up again. "What I wouldn't give to bite into those?"

"Or that ass!"

"That's it. I've had it! I'm out of here!" And Joe stormed off the set.

I was exhausted by the time I got back to our hotel room. Joe was already there, waiting for me. He met me at the door, and as soon as I stepped inside, he slapped me across my face. Hard. I was shocked. And stunned. And hurt. I didn't deserve this.

"No wife of mine is going to prostitute herself like that. I won't have it!"

"I'm a movie star. This is what we do."

"This is my city. I was a hero to those people, and now you've turned me into a laughing stock. A dirty joke. A whore's lapdog."

"Oh, so this is all about *you*, is it? My career means nothing to you."

"Not if it turns you into a whore." Then he hit me again, even harder.

No man should hit a woman like that. Ever. So we split up. There's your dramatic irony for you. The movie that finally made me a star for real destroyed my marriage. At least I didn't have to worry anymore about what Joe would think every time I wandered around the house nude or winked at a sexy guy.

They released *The Seven Year Itch* in June of '55, and it took in over four-and-a-half million dollars at the box office, making it one of the most profitable hits of the year. That gave me the leverage I needed to take control of my own career. I declared that since Fox had refused to pay me the bonus they'd promised, my contract with them was now void. So I moved to New York and, along with my photographer friend, Milton Greene, I started my own movie company, Marilyn Monroe Productions. The press thought I was nuts, and Fox even made a movie with Jayne Mansfield to ridicule me. *Will Success Spoil Rock Hunter* is about a dumb blonde who starts her own production company. But going off on my own turned out to be a good move. Moreover, I'm proud to say, it torpedoed the Hollywood studio system, which fell apart not long after.

I wanted to excel in my craft, and in New York I was able to devote myself to honing my skills. I attended workshops on method acting at the Actors Studio, which Gadg had co-founded about a decade earlier. I became close friends with Lee Strasberg, the director, and his wife, Paula, whom Gadg had named in his HUAC testimony.

And I reunited with Art.

CHAPTER 15

Gadg

While Marilyn was making her mark in *The Seven Year Itch*, and Joe DiMaggio was making his marks on Marilyn, and she was setting her sights on Art, and Art was seething over *Waterfront*, I discovered James Dean. Well, Paul Osborn spotted him first when Jimmy was playing a homosexually seductive Arab boy in a stage production of André Gide's *The Immoralist*. Paul thought Dean might be good for the role of Cal that I was casting for *East of Eden*, my next movie after *Waterfront*. It was based on a novel by John Steinbeck, and Paul was writing the screenplay.

Steinbeck and I had collaborated on the screenplay for *Viva Zapata!* three years earlier, before my HUAC days, and we'd hit it off well. Between the meddling by Darryl Zanuck at 20th Century Fox and objections from the Communists in Mexico, where we planned to shoot the film, John and I worked hard together to fend off a lot of bad "suggestions" intended to make the movie more profitable, on the one hand, or more politically correct, on the other. The Mexicans' interference reminded me of how the Party had tried to force-feed its ideological talking points into my plays when I was at the Group Theater, and I assured John that I didn't back down then and I wouldn't now.

94

"This is how the Party works. I've been through it before. It's why I left."

This was news to John, whose own experience while making *The Pearl* was that everyone in Mexico, up to and including the president, could be bought. But these Mexican Communists were too ideologically pure for bribes.

I told John how, about a decade after my resignation, Albert Maltz published a piece in *New Masses* complaining that the Party's effort to use art as a weapon in the class struggle was counterproductive; it was a straitjacket that made writing clumsy, shallow, and unappealing. That term *straitjacket* really resonated for me. When I read Maltz's piece I thought, "Thank God. Maybe this will spur some big changes." Alas, just the opposite occurred. High-level party officials flew in from New York to "re-educate" Albert, and after a series of ideological meetings and kangaroo courts they demanded that he either recant or leave the Party, which by then was pretty much his whole life. So Albert recanted and went on to serve time in federal prison as one of the Hollywood Ten who told HUAC to go to hell. But he was never the writer he could have been. Budd Schulberg – my fellow *collaborator* with HUAC – later faced a similar situation with his novel, *What Makes Sammy Run?* But Budd told the Party where they could stick their revisions and, like me, he got booted out.

In the case of *Zapata!* it was John and I who got the boot -- from Mexico when we refused to make the changes in the script they insisted upon. So, although we badly wanted to film the movie there on location, we ended up shooting it in Colorado, Texas, and New Mexico, and employed Americans for the production crews instead of Mexicans, who desperately needed the work. Not that their Communist Party gave a damn about them.

So now John and I were working together again on *East of Eden*. Along with Tennessee Williams, John had been one of the few friends who stood by me during my HUAC days, and that meant a lot. He'd refused to condemn me, just as he refused to condemn Lillian Hellman, one of my harshest critics who had declined to name names. John believed our situations were difficult and complex, and he would not -- could not -- reduce our moral dilemmas to easy matters of right and wrong. Unlike the partisans on the Left and on the Right who would froth at the mouth at the first hint of ideological impurity, John and I both took nuanced positions on most of things. That was our view of the human condition.

Lillian did not share our view. She was shrill and self-righteous and absolutely certain of herself. She became an idol of the Left when she told HUAC, "I cannot and will not cut my conscience to fit this year's fashions." That's a great line, and kudos to her for coming up with it. But now that's all anyone

96

knows her for, certainly not for her plays or her love affair with the Soviet Union. And people forget that for all of her bravado, Lillian dodged prison by taking the Fifth. Art, at least, stood his ground and risked giving up Marilyn's bed for a prison cot when he refused to give names.

But I digress. I was telling you about Jimmy Dean. Paul Osborne sent him to my office in New York one day in 1954. He *was* his screen persona: insolent and irreverent with an attitude. He slouched into the reception room and plopped down on the leather couch, looking resentful for no particular reason.

"I don't need this shit," I thought to myself. So I kept him waiting to just to let him stew. Plus, I wanted to see how he'd react to that. When I finally admitted him into my room, he was no longer scowling; the chip appeared to be off his shoulder. So that was good, except Jimmy seemed incapable of carrying on a conversation. We sat there staring at one another until he finally offered to take me for a ride on his motorcycle. I said, "Sure," and off we went wending our way through the busy streets of New York City. Jimmy was trying to show off how this big-city traffic couldn't faze a country boy like him, and I didn't enjoy our outing.

That was his interview. When I got back to my office, I called Paul and told him we didn't have to look any further; we'd found our Cal. Then I sent Jimmy to meet Steinbeck, whose impression was that Jimmy was a real snotty kid.

"That's irrelevant," I answered. "He *is* Cal, isn't he?"

"He sure as hell is." And John was on board.

Jimmy and I both had a little, or a lot, of Cal in us. Maybe that's why we were able to work together. A lot of people found Jimmy difficult to get along with. All three of us -- Jimmy, Cal, and me -- had been rejected by fathers who were sure we'd never amount to anything and were not shy about telling other people about it. I met Jimmy's father once, briefly, and I could sense right away how much tension there was between them and how much Mr. Dean disliked his son. Poor Jimmy. My father used to complain to his customers that I would "never be a man." Poor me. And fictional Cal was always a failure in his father's eyes too. As Nietzsche said, "That which doesn't kill you makes you stronger."

Based loosely on Steinbeck's own family history, *East of Eden* is about two brothers who vie for their father's affection and respect. The parallels to the Biblical story of Cain and Able are obvious and embedded in the title. Jimmy played the younger boy, Cal/Cain, who whose efforts were never good enough for his stern, judgmental, and ultra-religious dad, aptly named Adam and acted by Raymond Massey. Massey sized up Jimmy right away as a rotten kid who was moody and unprofessional.

"You never know what he's going to say or do," Ray would complain.

Jimmy responded to Ray's antipathy by becoming even more sullen, which was great for the picture, because profound sullenness was exactly what his role called for. In fact, I'm not ashamed to say, I sometimes fanned the flames of their antagonism because it was perfect for conveying how Cal and Adam felt about each other, and their mutual contempt came across so well on camera. In addition, a love affair Jimmy was conducting with an actress from Sardinia, Pier Angeli, went bad during the filming, leaving him miserable and alone, a condition that was hard on Jimmy but ideal for Cal.

East of Eden was my first big budget movie with a lot of advance publicity. Still, I never expected Jimmy to become such an overnight sensation. Somehow his sullenness and sense of alienation and rejection really struck a chord with teenagers in mid-'50s America, and among the girls his repressed pain translated into tremendous sex appeal. I guessed at some gut level they needed to mother him. At our first preview in Los Angeles hundreds of girls started screaming as soon as Jimmy appeared on screen. And the commotion grew greater with each showing. Jimmy went from obscurity to stardom in an instant.

After *East of Eden* my pal Nicholas Ray cast him as Jim Stark in *Rebel without a Cause*. (The symbolism of the name is heavy-handed, like the rest of the film, don't you think?) That movie enshrined James Dean as an icon for an alienated and misunderstood generation, and frankly I regretted my role in contributing to that. This myth of a middle America overflowing with lost and lonely teenagers necessarily implied that parents were insensitive clods who couldn't understand or appreciate their children and that the misunderstood youth all had sensitive souls their mothers and fathers were repressing.

I'm sure it happened sometimes. With millions of families to choose from, of course it did. Hell, it happened to me. But it wasn't common in my experience, and I seriously doubt the James Dean legend truly represented the majority of parent-child relationships in America. I admit that in *East of Eden* I, too, contributed to the myth of the repressive parent and the rejected child, although Adam Trask is never as insipid as Jim Backus wearing an apron in *Rebel without a Cause.* Adam may be cruel and hard and unloving, but he's not a eunuch. He knows who he is and what he stands for, even if he is a sonofabitch. Me too.

CHAPTER 16

Art

Marilyn moved to New York at the beginning of 1955, but we didn't make contact until months later. I was living in rural Connecticut then, working at the farmhouse. So we weren't likely to run into each other on Fifth Avenue.

But that didn't stop Marilyn from trying. Before leaving California she sought advice from Gadg on how to reach me. It wasn't as though she could just walk up the front steps and ring the doorbell; she had to somehow arrange an encounter. Gadg and I had been estranged ever since his testimony, but he offered to help. Either he was playing Cupid by bringing us together, or he was trying to hurt me by using Marilyn to break up my marriage. Perhaps both. Or neither.

Four years earlier it wouldn't have been a problem for Gadg to tell her what to do and who to see. We had several mutual friends who could, potentially, act as go-betweens. But Gadg had alienated most of them with his testimony, including Hedda Rosten, a good friend of mine from college and, incidentally, Mary's roommate, and Hedda's husband, the poet and playwright, Norman Rosten, who was also my close friend at the University of Michigan. For a while we two couples made an almost inseparable foursome.

We'd all been neighbors when I lived in Brooklyn Heights too, and the Rostens still lived there. Gadg believed that if Marilyn could connect with them, Norman and Hedda might help her reach me. Under the circumstances, however, Gadg couldn't just pick up the phone and introduce Marilyn. So he suggested she could meet them through Stan Shaw, a photographer who, by coincidence, was friends with both with Marilyn and the Rostens.

And that's how it happened that, in January 1955, not even three months after she'd split up with Joltin' Joe and less than a month after she'd moved to the city, Marilyn and Stan set off on a walking tour of Brooklyn Heights. Ostensibly their purpose was to take photos, but the real reason was that they wanted Stan to be able to ring up Norman and Hedda, tell them he was in the neighborhood, and ask if he and "a friend" could drop by. It was a dark, wet winter day, and the miserable weather gave them an additional excuse: they wanted to get out of the rain.

Norman answered Stan's call and invited them up to his apartment, by all means. Marilyn was wearing dark glasses and casual clothes, and Norman and Hedda didn't recognize her at first. But when Hedda saw the bedraggled young woman standing before her shivering in her wet clothes, she took Marilyn into the kitchen to get her something warm to drink. And while the coffee pot percolated, the two women began what proved to be an enduring friendship.

The whole incident sounds like it could have been a scene from a movie. Or a comic opera. Or perhaps one of Lucy's schemes on *I Love Lucy*, which was still a top-rated television show back then. But, alas, although it did succeed in introducing Marilyn to the Rostens, Marilyn and I didn't meet up again until five months later, when I happened to run into her at a cocktail party Lee and Paula Strasberg were hosting. By then Marilyn and the Strasbergs had become good friends; so it wasn't surprising for her to be there. I didn't often leave my sanctuary in Connecticut, but I had to go the city that day for some reason, and I dropped by after I'd concluded my business.

My heart stopped when I saw Marilyn standing by herself in a corner, drinking an orange juice and vodka. I know that sounds like such a cliché, but that's what it felt like. It was visceral. Finally, I collected myself and walked over to her. She looked pleased to see me, but we kept our distance. She told me about her workshops at the Actors Studio, and I talked about a new play I was working on, *A View from the Bridge.* After a while we parted, and I hadn't even asked for her phone number. Of course, the next morning Paula was only too happy to supply it.

It didn't take long for our long-suppressed romance to blossom. Even though Hedda and Mary had known each other before Mary and I even met, and Hedda had covered for Mary when she and I would slip off late at night to screw on the front lawn of the Botany building, Hedda had been won over by Marilyn's charm. And, who knows, perhaps sharing an intimate friendship with a major movie star flattered her.

In any case, when push came to shove both Norman and Hedda chose Marilyn over Mary. They arranged rendezvous for us at their apartment and even let us borrow the guest bedroom from time to time. They provided an especially good cover for me because I could tell Mary I was going over to see Norman and Hedda, and Mary would think nothing of it. When we wanted to go out in public, Norman would be my beard, pretending to be Marilyn's date while I was along just as his friend. I never saw him laugh with such delight as when he read in Walter Winchell's column that, "Marilyn Monroe is cooing it in poetry with Norman Rosten." Other columnists who saw through our subterfuge referred to Norman as Cupid. In time Eli Wallach replaced Norman as my beard. Marilyn called him Tea House for some reason, and she delighted in a signed photograph of Albert Einstein that came in the mail one day, even after she learned that it was a prank and Eli had forged the signature. It remained one of her prized possessions throughout her life. Eventually Marilyn took her own apartment at the Waldorf Towers; so the Rostens' role in our deception diminished. Nonetheless, they remained good friends to both of us.

It didn't take long for the gossip columnists to notice that Marilyn and I were showing up at a lot of the same places at the same time. Even Walter Winchell finally caught on. He wrote that "America's best-known blond moving picture star is now the darling of the left wing intelligentsia, several of whom are listed as Red-fronters." I'm told that J. Edgar Hoover, himself, inspired that not-so-subtle reference to me.

I'm sure all that publicity and public speculation wasn't easy on Mary, but she never confronted me directly about it. Not until she finally had to. Maybe she just pretended that the accusations and innuendoes weren't really true, even though at some level she must have known they were. Instead Mary started taking classes in body movement. She thought the exercises were making her look younger. Was she unconsciously competing with Marilyn? I don't know.

My love affair with Marilyn, hurtful and unfair to Mary as it was, rejuvenated me. I felt more youthful than I had in years, more energetic and more excited to be alive. I regret that Mary had to pay the price for my rejuvenation, but I've never regretted loving Marilyn. If ever people were fated to be together, it was us. Here are a couple of lines from a poem I wrote to her a few months after we'd begun our affair:

"I will come again to the kitchen, pretending you are not there and discover you again. And as you stand there cooking breakfast, I will kiss your neck and your back and the sweet cantaloupes of your rump and the backs of your knees and turn you about and kiss your breasts and the eggs will burn."

That's how I burned for Marilyn.

CHAPTER 17

Mary

Finally, in October 1955, on Art's fortieth birthday, I threw the bum out. I felt bad for the kids, but it had to be done. Art and I weren't screaming at each other or anything like that, but by the end of summer you could cut the tension in our house with a knife. Art was no longer even trying to conceal the fact that he and that harlot were an item. The gossip columnists spotted them out together all the time, and their photos were plastered over all the scandal sheets. How could Bobby and Jane *not* be affected by that? I was a Catholic, albeit a seriously lapsed Catholic. So the decision to divorce didn't come easily. But a life of alternating between denial and simmering fury is untenable; so, finally I had to act. For my sake. For Jane and Bobby's sake. And even for Art's.

"Be gone! Go. Run off with that movie star slut you've been salivating over all these years. That's my birthday present to you; I'm giving you your freedom. That's what you've wanted all along, isn't it? But you were too chicken shit to ask for it; so you made us both miserable instead. Well, I've had enough. Someone will bring you your things, but I want you out of this house. Do you hear me? Right now!"

Art checked-in to the Chelsea Hotel on 23rd Street, and I took him for everything I could. After what he put me and the kids through for all those years, why not? Pretending to be devoted to me. Pretending to be in love. Pretending to care about us and our lives. *I* pretended to the press that the rumors about Art and his whore had nothing to do with our divorce. I needed to keep a shred of dignity.

After everything was finalized I moved with the kids to Gloucester. The press left us alone after that and we were happily free from public scrutiny ever after.

CHAPTER 18

Art

Not long after my divorce was settled HUAC caught up with me. I knew they would eventually, although by 1956 the worst of the red scare had already passed. The Democrats took control of the Senate in the fall of '54, and they censured Joe McCarthy for threatening other senators. That effectively emasculated him, and he died a few years later, in 1957, from liver disease caused by his drunken binges. That same year, on what the Right called "Red Monday," the Supreme Court issued four rulings that reversed and curtailed some of the worst anti-Communist legislation. Of course, those laws were still on the books when I was subpoenaed, but the mood of the country had definitely mellowed since Gadg underwent his ordeal in '52. Nonetheless, fear of the red menace remained, along with politicians' eagerness to exploit it; so if I refused to name names I would still face prison time for contempt of Congress.

I must say that Marilyn was wonderful throughout all this. The studios tried to get to me by going after her. "Either you get your boyfriend to name names or you'll never be heard of again," they threatened. She just told them to stick it where the sun don't shine, or words to that effect. Then she made a public show of support by coming down to Washington to be with me prior to the hearing, although she returned to New York before I testified. While she was still in town that SOB chairman, Francis Walter, offered to call the whole thing off if Marilyn would pose for some publicity photos with him. It would be, "a painless solution to your problem, Mr. Miller." I didn't even dignify that suggestion by passing it along to her. Marilyn probably would have agreed and then spat in his face during the photo shoot, while all the flashbulbs were going off. She'd have done it too. Just shows you how cynical that whole HUAC operation was.

The ostensible rationale for the Committee's latest round of witch hunting was alleged misuse of U.S. passports, which was no more a real problem than the unfounded allegations of voter fraud used to suppress African-Americans sixty years later. But it was an opportunity for more grandstanding and for the Republicans on HUAC to play to their base.

WALTER: Thank you, Mr. Miller, for coming to testify before this subcommittee of House Un-American Activities Committee. This is a public hearing. For the record, I am Francis E. Walter, chairman of the Committee. Also present are Representatives Edwin Willis, Bernard Kearney, and Gordon Scherer. The date is June 21, 1956, and the purpose of these hearings is to investigate the unauthorized use of United States passports.

MILLER: It seems odd for a Congressional committee to investigate the passport application of a single individual, a harmless writer at that. Or a performer like Paul Robeson, whose passport the State Department has denied, and I quote here, "Because of the applicant's recognized status as spokesman for large sections of Negro Americans." And because he has worked for the independence of colonial Africa. The State Department seems to forget that the United States was founded on independence from colonial rule.

WALTER: Please, Mr. Miller, this is not the place to comment on other witnesses or the work of this Committee.

MILLER: Can you enlighten me as to how any new legislation or governmental oversight can possibly come from these hearings? How do my travel plans possibly merit a federal investigation by a legislative body or an act of Congress? Or rather, please tell me what is the actual purpose of these inquiries, apart from intimidation and suppression of the free exercise of Constitutional rights?

WALTER: The Committee will be asking the questions here. Do you currently have an active passport application?

MILLER: Yes, I applied over four weeks ago, so I may travel to England in order to prepare for the opening there of my play, A View from the Bridge, and to accompany the woman who, by then, will be my wife. She will be making a movie, The

111

Prince and the Showgirl. *With Sir Laurence Olivier, I might add. Is that colonial enough for you?*

CHAPTER 19

Marilyn

Did you hear that? Did you hear it? Art just told the whole world he's marrying me. Me! Can you believe it?

You know, he never really proposed.

CHAPTER 20

Art

WALTER: And when you applied for a passport in 1947, did you then take an oath swearing that you had not contributed to the Communist cause, supported it, or been under its discipline?

MILLER: Why weren't former Nazi supporters ever compelled to take such oaths? We fought a world war against them. Why hasn't Lindbergh ever been hauled before this committee to explain his Nazi sympathies in the '30s?

WALTER: Mr. Miller –

MILLER: Yes, I know, just answer the question. I don't recall actually taking the oath, but in any case, I would have been willing to swear that I have been affiliated from time to time with groups that have since been cited as Communist-dominated organizations. I would certainly have also sworn I was never under the discipline of the Communist Party.

WALTER: And would you have taken an oath that you had never contributed to the Communist cause?

MILLER: I may have contributed a dollar or two in the past to some organizations. Those donations would now be called contributing to the Communist cause. They were not considered that then, however.

WALTER: To what organizations are you referring?

MILLER: Let me think…. I understand the Joint Anti-Fascist Committee has been cited. I contributed from time to time to their efforts during and after the Spanish Civil War.

WALTER: And were you aware that the Spanish Loyalists were supported by the Soviet Union?

MILLER: Yes, among others. And were you aware that Franco was supported by Hitler?

WALTER: I again remind again you that the Committee asks the questions here, not the witness. Did you not sign petitions and lend your name to causes that attacked the work of the House Un-American Activities Committee?

MILLER: Yes I did. I was exercising my Constitutional rights. Even if you make yourself out to be super-patriots, your committee is not above condemnation. It seemed to me that the then-prevalent, rather ceaseless investigation of artists was creating a pall of apprehension and fear among all kinds of people. And I do not believe that such an atmosphere is healthy for the state of art or the state of our democracy.

WALTER: Can you tell me why, given your insistence on speaking up on behalf of politically active writers, you did not, in 1945, support the poet Ezra Pound? In fact, in 1945, you criticized those who defended Mr. Pound on the same basis that you later endorsed those who defended the Hollywood Ten.

115

MILLER: In the first place, this was a time of war. Pound was literally and in every conceivable way a traitor. And there was no question about it in anybody's mind. Moreover, he threatened me personally. You know, I actually listened to his broadcasts on shortwave radio. With my own ears I heard him in his jolly, self-assured way call for the complete eradication of my people. I am a Jew. He was for burning Jews, and you will have to pardon my excitement at the time.

WALTER: So, in your view, it is permissible to condemn a fascist traitor who attacks Communism, but it is not permissible to condemn Communist traitors.

MILLER: I wouldn't characterize my position that way.

WALTER: Moving on. Did you not collaborate artistically with Mr. Elia Kazan?

CHAPTER 21

Marilyn

Now they're asking him about Gadg. Can you believe it?

CHAPTER 22

Art

MILLER: *Elia Kazan directed two of my plays.*

WALTER: *And in 1953, did you criticize Mr. Kazan as a renegade intellectual for testifying before this Committee and identifying members of the Communist Party?*

MILLER: *No. I have never made a statement about Elia Kazan's testimony in my life.*

WALTER: *And did you break with Mr. Kazan after he cooperated with this Committee?*

MILLER: *I would not choose the word* break*, but yes, I disassociated from him. I am not at all certain that Mr. Kazan would have directed my next play in any case. There were other considerations, private ones with absolutely no political interest, that affected our relationship. The fact is that he did not direct any more of my plays. As I have stated in the* New York Post*, it may be that in the future he will.*

CHAPTER 23

Marilyn

Of course I'm the *private consideration*. Can you believe it? Now I'm the subject of a Congressional investigation! What would Norma Jeane think?

Next time I'll try for the President. Well, maybe not. Doing it with Ike would be creepy. Guess I'll stick with Art.

CHAPTER 24

Art

WALTER: *The question is, did you attack Kazan because he broke with the Communist Party and testified before a Congressional committee?*

MILLER: I stated earlier, sir, that I have never attacked Kazan. I will stand on that. But if I had, would that be grounds for denying me the right to travel abroad?

WALTER: Moving on then. In 1940, did you apply for membership in the Communist Party.

MILLER: No, sir. I did not.

WALTER: But you did attend Communist Party meetings with writers in New York City?

MILLER: I understood them to be meetings with writers who were Communists, but they were not Party meetings, as such. I wanted to discover first-hand what Communism was really all about and where I stood in relation to it. The ability to pursue ideas freely, even unpopular ones, is one of the American liberties I cherish most, and I exercise it often, in many contexts.

Socrates maintains that the unexamined life is not worth living, and attending these meetings was one way in which I examined my own life. However, I did not find them particularly useful.

WALTER: Mr. Miller, please tell us who invited you and who attended these meetings.

MILLER: Mr. Chairman, I understand the philosophy behind this question, and I want you to understand mine. When I say this, I want you to understand that I am not protecting Communists or the Communist Party. I am trying to, and I will, protect my sense of myself. I could not use the name of another person and bring trouble on him. These were writers, and the life of a writer is pretty tough. I wouldn't make it any tougher for anybody. I will tell you anything about myself, as I have. But I will not identify other people.

WALTER: May I point out that moral scruples, however laudable, do not constitute a legal basis for refusing to comply. If you do not answer this question, you are placing yourself in contempt of Congress.

MILLER: All I can do is reiterate that my conscience will not permit me to name another person. I will, however, add that these meetings showed me that I am not a Marxist. Great art, like great science, attempts to see the present remorselessly and truthfully. If Marxism is what it claims to be, a science of society, it must be devoted to the objective facts more than all the philosophies it attacks as false.

Therefore, the first job of a Marxist writer should be to tell the truth. If the truth is not what he thinks it ought to be, he must insist on telling it anyway. But my idealized view of

121

Marxism does not conform to reality. In reality, the Marxist writer must alter the facts to fit the Party line. I could never do that. I have not done that. And I would not do that for any party or movement or government.

WALTER: We are about end this session. I conclude by asking why you do not use some of your magnificent writing ability to fight against well-known Communist subversive conspiracies in our country and throughout the world?

MILLER: I concur that it would be a disaster if the Communist Party ever took over this country. That is an opinion that has come to me not out of the blue sky but out of long thought. I believe in democracy. I believe it is the only way to live for myself and for anybody I care about. My criticism of our government, such as it has been, must not be confused with hatred. I love this country as much as any man. But the task of the artist is to speak the truth as he sees it.

Speaking truth is the ultimate act of love, even if the truth is painful – especially if the truth is painful – because it enables the society to perceive its own self-destructive hypocrisies and actions.

I am a playwright, so let me put this in dramatic terms. If a tragic hero were to gain insight into his flaws before he commits the acts that destroy him, he could avoid his tragic fate. Likewise, a nation that recognizes how it has deviated *from its core values can save itself by using this knowledge to rectify its self-destructive behavior.*

I would like more than anything else in the world to make my plays more affirmative, and I intend to do so before I finish. But this must be done on the basis of reality. Otherwise, I would be no better than the Marxist writers who distort their work to conform to the Party line. Otherwise, I would simply be contributing to our nation's self-deception and self-destruction, and that would be the most unloving thing I could do for my country.

WALTER: Mr. Miller, you are in contempt of Congress. This session is adjourned, but this is not the end of this matter.

No, it wasn't the end of the matter. Eventually a federal court found me guilty and fined me $500, which was a slap on the hand compared to the jail time that John Lawson, Dalton Trumbo, Ring Lardner, Jr., and the rest of the Hollywood Ten did for standing up to the Committee back in '47. They had insisted that the First Amendment protected them from having to answer questions about their political beliefs and affiliations: What right is it of the government to ask about any American citizen's political activities, so long as they are conducted legally, which they were? It took a few years for the appeals to work their way through the judicial system, and that at least put HUAC on hold. But finally, in 1950, the Supreme Court ruled

123

against the Ten, and they served prison terms ranging from six months to a year. Lardner, at least, had the satisfaction of being locked up in the same federal penitentiary as John Parnell Thomas, the self-righteous, super-patriotic, holier-than-thou HUAC chairman who'd raked Lardner and the rest of the Ten over the coals. Thomas was caught about a year later in a kick-back scheme. Some patriot he was.

After the Supreme Court struck down the witnesses' right to invoke the First Amendment, the only way anyone could refrain from naming names and still stay out of prison was to cite their Fifth Amendment protection against self-incrimination. But this meant looking guilty as sin, although there was never any law in America against being a Communist. *Fifth Amendment Communists*, as Senator McCarthy called them, were immediately blacklisted and became social pariahs. I can't begin to guess how many marriages were destroyed and children estranged. The ruling that affirmed the Ten's contempt conviction also set the stage for the new round of hearings in 1951-52 that ensnared Gadg.

Even though my fine was negligible, I appealed as a matter of principle. And though the court costs put a huge dent in my finances -- $40,000 was a lot of money in those days -- I finally prevailed. First, my lawyer, Joseph Rauh, Jr., somehow managed to get me a temporary visa, so I could travel to England with Marilyn as we'd planned. Then, the following year at the contempt trial, Rauh argued that the writers who attended those meetings were irrelevant to my passport application – the ostensible reason for the hearing. And when the prosecution accused me of traveling to a Communist country in 1947, Rauh pointed out that Czechoslovakia had still been a democracy back then. It didn't turn Communist 'till '48. Just shows you how sloppy those anti-Red crusaders could be in their zeal to harm their enemies. Not that the trial judge cared, but it made a difference when we won on appeal in '58.

My testimony before HUAC was a big deal, and the press was all over it. So, when the hearing concluded I was swarmed by journalists and photographers as I stood on the Capitol steps. Weighty matters of individual freedom were at stake in these hearings. I'd raised important questions that begged to be asked about governmental reach into private lives. So, naturally, the only thing anyone questioned me about was Marilyn.

Is it true you and Marilyn Monroe are getting married?

"I stand by my testimony."

But what if the State Department won't give you a passport?

"That would be a travesty of justice, an unpardonable abuse of power. I have committed no crimes. What have I done besides listen to what some people had to say, condemn a wartime traitor, and protest the cynical actions of a

125

Congressional committee?   Isn't that the prerogative of any American? Isn't that what we mean by freedom of speech?"

You didn't name names.

What if they turn you down anyway?

Or send you to prison?

"No matter. We will get married, and when Marilyn goes to London, she will go as Mrs. Arthur Miller."

CHAPTER 25

Lyle

I remember playing catch with my pal, Bobby Miller, one summer day when we were both about nine. He'd moved to Gloucester a few months earlier and was a Yankee fan. I, of course, lived and died with the Red Sox. Back in the mid-fifties I mostly died, although that year they actually had a winning season. Of course, New York took the pennant, and I had to listen all season long to how Boston was eating the Yankees' dust.

"Did you see that catch Jimmy Piersall made on Tito Francona yesterday? I watched it on television. It was incredible. He jumped over the fence and took away a home run."

I tossed the ball to Bobby.

"Piersall's a clown, not a baseball player. Mickey Mantle, *he's* a centerfielder. His average is even higher than Ted Williams'."

He threw the ball back to me hard, and it stung my hand inside the glove. Ted Williams was my hero, so his taunt stung even more.

"All I know is that the Yankees lost to the Senators yesterday. The *Senators*! And the Sox beat the Orioles."

My throw was low, but Bobby managed to scoop it up. He was a pretty good athlete. Finally, I did have to admit that Mickey Mantle was a better centerfielder than Jimmy Piersall. But I'd never concede that he was a better player than Ted Williams. Not then. Not now.

Looking back, Bobby was an interesting kid, although naturally I just thought of him as someone I liked to do stuff with. He was curious and bright, but he kept mostly to himself. Bobby didn't have many friends besides me. He didn't talk much about his life in New York, although one time he told me he went to an expensive private school in Greenwich Village with the Meeropol boys; you know, the sons of Ethel and Julius Rosenberg. That must have been weird. This was just a year after their parents had been electrocuted for stealing the secret of the atomic bomb, and I wish I'd asked him about the Meeropol kids, what they were like. But I was only nine, and I didn't think much about it.

We threw the ball around a little more, practicing fielding ground balls and catching pop ups. All of the sudden, out of nowhere, Bobby stated matter-of-factly, "My father's marrying Marilyn Monroe today." Then he tossed another ball in the dirt. I fielded it and made a pretend throw to first base to get our imaginary runner out by a step.

CHAPTER 26

Marilyn

"Be careful, Morton. I want to live to see my wedding day."

About a week after Art's testimony his cousin Morton was driving us through rural Connecticut on what was supposed to be the day before the day before our wedding. We'd promised to hold a press conference at Art's house later that afternoon, but Morton was driving his Oldsmobile like a maniac.

"Don't worry, Marilyn. I know these roads like the back of my hand."

Morton made a sharp turn around a sudden curve, and I was flung against Art in the back seat. Another turn in the opposite direction, and Art was flung against me. The story of our lives?

"Hey, Morton. Be careful. I mean it."

"Did you see that little white car back there? It's been following us for the past few miles. I'm trying to lose it."

"God, I hate those paparazzi. They're all leeches, feeding off my fame. Imagine the headlines if we crashed and died. They'd be in heaven."

"So would we," Art answered gently. "But I'd rather picture the headlines after we're married: *MARILYN MONROE*

WEDS ARTHUR MILLER. WRITERS EVERYWHERE TAKE HOPE."

"There's a fork in the road coming up," Morton called back to us. "I'll lose them there. They won't know which way we went."

"It gives us a fifty-fifty chance, anyway," Art looked at me and smiled.

I turned my head and saw the white car gaining on us. It was only about fifty yards behind us now, half a football field. Morton accelerated as we approached the fork, made a quick feint to the left, and then turned hard to the right. I grabbed Art's arm for support, but Morton really did know what he was doing, and a moment later we were in the clear. The other car had vanished from sight.

Then *CRASH!* Followed by the sound of breaking glass. Morton slammed on the breaks, turned around, and sped back the way we'd come. Soon we saw the white car, its windshield shattered and its front end crumpled against an old maple tree on the side of the road. Morton slammed on the breaks again, then threw the car into park and leapt out. "Stay here!" he yelled to us and ran to where a man was groaning.

Art wanted to go after him, but I held him back.

"Hold me, I'm scared."

Art looked conflicted, torn between his impulse to "do the right thing" by rendering aid and his need to comfort me. It was the first time I ever saw that conflict in his eyes, but it wasn't the last.

Art looked anxiously out the window, but he slid closer and wrapped his arm around me.

"There, there. There, there. It will be all right."

"How do you know?"

"I don't know. Just trying to say the right thing."

Morton ran back to our car. He was huffing and puffing and his eyes showed terror.

"We have to go for help. I think she's dying."

"Who's dying? Who's dying?" I felt frantic.

"The photographer. Her head smashed into the window. The driver seems OK, but I'm not sure. He's sitting on the ground, but he's mostly out of it. He moans now and then, but he's in a daze."

Art hopped out and took command. "Morton, run back to that fork in the road and flag down a passing car. I'll see what I can do to help. Marilyn, stay here."

"No, I'm coming with you," and I crawled out as well. I didn't want to be alone.

Art's legs were much longer than mine, so he got there first. I arrived in time to see him open the passenger door and then catch a bloody blond head as it slipped out.

"My God!" he said in a stage whisper as he cradled her skull. I suppressed an impulse to vomit.

"Help me! Help me!" cried a male voice on the other side of the car.

Art looked across at the driver on the ground, now writhing in pain.

"Help me!" he insisted even more urgently.

Then Art looked at me.

"Here," he said and gestured me forward. "Hold her head up like this. I'm going to see what I can do for him."

So, we changed positions, and I held Mara's head while Art ran off to render help. That was her name, I learned later, Mara Scherbatoff. She was a Russian aristocrat who'd escaped the Bolsheviks as a child and had been working as a photojournalist for *Paris-Match*. Now she was dying in my arms. On what would now become my wedding day.

But before she expired, Mara briefly came to. With great effort she raised her head and stared deeply into my eyes. Her ferocious gaze cut right through me. "Selfish woman," she accused me. "What made you think you can run from us. Your fans made you. You belong to us, as much as to him. More. How dare you!"

"But -"

"We made you and we can destroy you. I curse you! I curse your ridiculous marriage. My death is on your hands. You will never wash it off!"

Then her eyes closed again, her head sank back into my hands, and Morton came running up to me. He took one look.

"My God!"

Then took Mara from me and pushed her back inside the car.

"She's dead, isn't she?" I was numb. And then I started to cry.

Morton felt for a pulse. "Yes. She's dead." Then Morton yelled over the roof, "Art! Come here. Now!"

Art abandoned the driver and ran to my side.

Morton pointed to Mara, now slumped over in the passenger seat. "She's dead." Then he added, "I flagged someone down, and they're going for an ambulance."

Morton looked at me. I was still weeping. "Take Marilyn back to the car. I'll stay with the driver until the medics come."

Art put his arm around my shoulder and gently walked me back to the Oldsmobile. We both slid onto the back seat. Finally, I stopped sobbing.

"There, there," he whispered. "There, there."

"She looked into my eyes before she died."

"How awful."

"It was. It was awful. It was terrible."

Then I glanced down and saw my sweater was stained with Mara's blood. "My sweater. She bled all over my new,

133

yellow sweater!" The tears came back again, and I couldn't stop for several minutes.

At last I regained some composure. "She looked into my eyes. And then she spoke to me. And then she died. Why must it always be this way? Why am I never allowed to just be happy?"

"Sometimes I feel our romance is a Greek tragedy. But then I look into your eyes and all I know is joy. Our love can transcend even horrors like this one, terrible as it is."

He held me close until the police were done interviewing Morton, and we drove away.

Later we held our press conference as scheduled. Since we were in the middle of nowhere in rural Connecticut, Art figured there'd be only a few dozen reporters. He was wrong. It was a madhouse. A zoo. About four-hundred reporters, photographers, and cameramen pushed and shoved each other across the front lawn of Art's farmhouse. You'd think that a fatal car accident would make them at least a little more somber and respectful, but not even a tragedy like that could curb the voracious appetite of the paparazzi. Instead Mara's death was fresh meat to frenzied dogs.

Marilyn, how do you feel about this accident?

"Terrible."

Do you think it was your fault?

"No. Why would it be?"

You were running away from her, weren't you?

"Yes, but I didn't make her drive into that tree, did I?"

I don't know, did you?

At that point Art stepped in. "Of course Marilyn's not at fault here. Neither am I, nor my cousin Morton. We had nothing to do with that car, and it's disrespectful not only to us but to the poor woman who died to suggest otherwise.

Marilyn, do you still plan to go on with the wedding.

"Why wouldn't I?"

Out of respect for the dead?

Maybe it's a jinx.

"That's enough!" Art grabbed my arm and escorted me back toward the house.

Her blood is own your hands, I heard one voice call out as the door slammed shut.

"I can't believe those jackals." Art was furious, but all I could do was cry. This wasn't how I envisioned my wedding day. Not at all.

That was on Friday, June 29. Our wedding was scheduled for Sunday, but Art knew that the press would be insatiable until we were actually hitched. So that night we slipped out the back door to avoid the reporters camped out front. It was dark, but Art knew his way around the grounds, and we snuck into a neighbor's yard and then into his driveway, where Morton met us with the Oldsmobile. He drove us to the

Westchester County Court House in White Plains, where Judge Seymour Rabinowitz married us. Art borrowed his mother's wedding ring for the occasion, and that meant a lot to me.

Saturday was the deadline for Art to give the Committee the names they wanted or be formally charged with contempt of Congress. Naturally, he let the deadline pass, and on Sunday we got married again, this time in a Jewish ceremony at the home of Art's friend and agent, Kay Brown.

I'd converted for the wedding. I always identified with Jews anyway. Everybody was always out to get them, no matter what they did, like me. So, my decision wasn't as strange as many people seemed to think. Plus, I admired my rabbi so much. Robert Goldman was very smart and scholarly, and he detested HUAC. Moreover, he had the courage of his convictions: he'd faced down police dogs and fire houses when he marched for civil rights down south. I'd been raised by fundamentalist Christians who'd go to revival meetings under big tents and listen to stern sermons about hell fire and damnation. It was all so harsh and unloving, like the rest of my upbringing. But this rabbi understood what made sense in religion and what didn't.

So, my conversion was actually one of the most rewarding experiences of my life. Not everyone took it seriously, but the Egyptians sure did. They banned all my movies. I'm not sure how much my conversion mattered to Art, but I know it meant a lot to his parents, Izzy and Gussie. I liked them both, especially Izzie. I never had a family of my own, and they both welcomed me with such warmth. I wanted them to be the mother and father I never had.

Rabbi Goldberg had coached me in the basics, and I enjoyed my role as a traditional Jewish bride. After he pronounced us married, Art lifted my veil and offered me a glass of wine, which I consumed with pleasure. Then he wrapped the glass in a napkin, placed it on the floor, and smashed it with his heel in the time-honored practice. I believe that tradition has something to do with breaking the bride's maidenhead, but we didn't think too deeply about *that*. Afterward everyone rushed up to kiss me. Great merriment followed as the liquor flowed and the band played on. For the first time ever, I felt like I belonged.

CHAPTER 27

Gadg

So, yes, I prospered while blacklisted writers, actors, and directors scrambled to survive. Unable to work in the movies or on TV, many lost their careers. I can't imagine a worse fate for me than that. My art infused my soul. It was so much of my being and how I lived. I'd have been lost without it. I'm sure that was true for many of them as well. Writers, at least, could sometimes submit original screenplays through *fronts* who took the credit and pocketed a big chunk of the paycheck. Dalton Trumbo's *Roman Holiday* won an Oscar for best screenplay, but they gave it to Ian McLellan Hunter, who was officially credited. And Pierre Boulle received the Academy Award for *The Bridge over the River Kwai*, although Carl Foreman and Michael Wilson actually wrote it. That's how it was back then. At least Boulle, who'd authored the novel, had the good taste not to accept his Oscar in person.

Did I feel sorry for those who'd been blacklisted? Yes, of course I did. They'd stood on principle and paid a stiff price. That's the stuff of heroism. Who wouldn't admire that? But did I feel guilty because I'd named names? NO! Did I think they were better people than I was? NEVER!

It's funny how our lives progress. We can go for years comfortably, or not so comfortably, ensconced in the roles we have adopted or had thrust upon us. We are laborers or professionals or aristocrats of a certain kind; we are children, siblings, parents, husbands, and wives. We are respected as masters of our crafts, pillars of our communities. Then our circumstances change and our roles alter. Our parents die and we are no longer constrained by their judgment or our need to win their love. Our friends and siblings move away and we lose their support and companionship or their jealousy and endless competition. We divorce and begin to navigate our lives alone. We change careers and along with them our goals and aspirations. In short, we become different people.

Art and I used to argue about that sometimes. He thought that we all have an inner core that remains essentially fixed throughout our lifetime, and that our primary mission in life is to nurture that inner core so it may realize its fullest potential. I disagreed. I believed that a person is the sum total of the all roles he or she plays at any one time. Then, as the roles change, our essence changes too. Art would point to Socrates as his exemplar: "Know thyself." But I would counter with Socrates' most notorious student and lover, Alcibiades, a chameleon-like charmer who was the most decadent of Athenians, but when he literally had to jump ship and change sides, he could out-spartan all the Spartans in a life of deprivation. Then he got the queen of Sparta pregnant, bragged about it, and escaped to the Persians, with whom he

139

took up *la dulce vita* again. Alcibiades single-handedly shaped the course of the Peloponnesian War, fighting for both sides. Was there any core self for him to know?

According to my theory, when I joined the Communist Party and submitted myself to Party discipline in 1934, I became a new person. *Born again* in the Party, I was now driven by a cause, a central system of belief. I was an activist, a comrade-in-arms. Of course, I was also a theater director and a husband, but even those roles were shaped substantially by my identity as a Communist.

Then, after they "disciplined" me for placing my artistic integrity over their Party machinations, I quit and became a different person. Sure, I retained my progressive beliefs and my outrage over social injustice, but I was no longer an activist, no longer a comrade-in-arms. I became more of a loner. Indeed, now I was an outcast, a traitor to my Party associates; so my role as a theater director consumed even more of my being. After the war I began to direct movies, and that changed who I was too. Not only did this new, more fluid medium make me rethink how to tell a story, it transformed who I was as a director – how I coached actors, how I conceived of dialogue and narrative structure, even how I experienced time and space. The change in me was profound.

Moreover, movie directing brought me to Hollywood and that transformed my circle of friends, which in turn transformed what I talked about, what I thought about, what I cared about, what I desired in life and expected from it, whom I could fuck. After all, our identities are molded, at least to some degree, by whom we fuck, are they not? Would I still have been the same person had Marilyn never entered my life and had I not, literally, entered hers? I don't think so.

My second testimony before HUAC in 1952 was one of those events that changed not only the course of my life but also who I was. Whereas prior to my naming names I'd been a solid citizen of Hollywood's liberal crowd, now I was a *collaborator*, little better than the sordid Frenchmen and women who consorted with Germans during the war. Whereas before I was admired for addressing social injustices in my movies when no one else did, now I was scorned for being in league with HUAC, which, in turn, was in league with corrupt capitalists and fascists. Whereas I'd shared an artistic collaboration with Art that enriched us both and elevated our work to unimagined heights, now we were estranged.

So, I had to find new friends, new lovers, and new artistic partners. And each of those pulled and pushed and twisted me into still more new identities. How lucky I was to be able to activate so many of my potential selves, to experience so much diversity in what my life could be. If HUAC had been content with my first testimony in executive session, as they seemed to be, and if no one had threatened to leak it to the

141

press, then the bomb that blew apart my life never would have exploded, *KABOOM*, and I'd have lost out on experiencing my post-testimony self, a self I came to like and appreciate very much.

On the other hand, perhaps Art had a point. Diverse as all the identities of my lifetime were, they did all share a certain core. Political activist or loner, director of plays or movies, Communist or collaborator, fucker of East Coast intellectuals or Hollywood starlets, no matter what the role I played, no one pushed me around. I was a winner; and no matter what identity I assumed, I was determined to finish on top. I was not only going to survive, I was going to thrive. That's who I was, and I've never been apologetic for that. Not once. Why should I? All we really have going for us is the will to live, and while I may have betrayed friends and lovers and wives from time to time, never have I betrayed that spark of life, that energy of creation that courses through my veins and screams to the Universe, "I am!"

CHAPTER 28

Art

Did you ever read that poem by Stephen Crane from his *Blackriders* collection?

A man said to the universe:
"Sir I exist!"
"However," replied the universe,
"The fact has not created in me
A sense of obligation."

CHAPTER 29

Gadg

Screw you, Art. The meaning of life isn't a concept or an idea, it's simply the fullest possible experience of living. Who cares if the Universe gives a damn or not?

CHAPTER 30

Art

Actually, we agree on that.

CHAPTER 31

Gadg

Then perhaps there's hope of reunification after all.

After my testimony I doubled down. I took out a full page ad in the *New York Times* explaining why I thought cooperating with the Committee and blowing a hole in the Party's web of secrecy was the right thing to do. Art and his crowd dismissed the essay as self-serving, and after that they had nothing further to do with me. Art had been truthful when he told HUAC that he'd never denounced me publicly. He didn't have to.

Plus, of course, there was still the matter of me fucking Marilyn while he was in New York chained to Mary. Art never complained about that. How could he? He didn't have a leg to stand on, while I had three. Our copulations ate his heart out. We all knew that. Well, screw him.

CHAPTER 32

Gadg

The five-year period after my testimony was the most productive in my life: *Viva Zapata!*, *Man on a Tightrope*, *On the Waterfront*, *East of Eden*, *Baby Doll* and *A Face in the* Crowd all made a splash on the big screen. Well, *Man on a Tightrope* not so much, probably because it was released in West Germany. Tony Quinn got an Oscar for *Zapata* and *Waterfront* took eight of them, including best picture and director. The others garnered a lot of nominations and Golden Globes and things like that. During that time I was truly realizing my potential as an artist, and nothing could be more exquisite than that.

It's no coincidence that during this fertile period I was reviled by both the Communists and Art's crowd of liberals. The Reds still hated me for abandoning them, and now they hated me more for outing them. And the liberals detested me for selling out – although how many of my critics were put to the same test I was, really? Moreover, anti-Red crusaders like *Counterattack* still questioned my loyalty, even after I'd named names. All that collective vindictiveness me made me focus more intensely than I ever had before. I'd always been very focused, but the chip they placed on my shoulder made me doubly so. I vowed to be tougher than my enemies and harder working. And I firmly believe that the only genuinely good and original films I made came after April 10, 1952. My earlier films were adept; the ones I made after I testified were personal. They erupted from me fired by my resolve.

I was sorry *Man on a Tightrope* didn't receive more recognition. It's about a circus troupe that narrowly escapes from communist Czechoslovakia. My critics naturally claimed the movie was self-serving, that I'd made it just to make communism look bad and thus justify my cooperation with HUAC and reassure the hardcore right-wingers that I was sincere. Actually, that was *my* first response when Darryl Zanuck at 20th Century Fox offered me the script.

"Don't you think it's degrading to knuckle under to *Counterattack* and those other rightwing fanatics," I told him. "I've done all the crawling I'm going to do."

"But you'd be working with Robert Sherwood."

"Look, Darryl, Sherwood's a good writer, especially *Roosevelt and Hopkins* and, of course, *Best Years of Our Lives*." Then I tossed the manuscript onto his desk. "But this isn't worthy of him. It's dreck, a propaganda piece. The good guys are too virtuous, and the bad guys are all evil. There's no nuance. It runs against everything I've based my career on. I'd only be doing it to satisfy a bunch of red-baiters who want my ass."

148

"It's not such a bad thing to save your ass," Darryl gave me a knowing look. "Besides, this isn't propaganda, Gadg. It happened exactly the way Sherwood wrote it. Didn't you read those newspaper clippings I sent you?"

"They were in German."

"What about the pictures?"

I finally told Darryl that if the story was accurate, I'd make the movie. Otherwise, I wouldn't. So, Darryl agreed to pay for Bob and me to travel to Munich and meet the troupe.

The war had been over for only about seven years. Parts of the city were still in shambles, and the distrust of the war years remained on the street. I've often been told that I look Jewish, and I sometimes wondered what people were thinking as I passed them in the city where Hitler had risen to power just twenty years earlier. Perhaps, "How did this one get away?"

I finally met with the Cirkus Brumbach, and they were the real thing, a ramshackle touring troupe that had risked their lives to gain their freedom. I'd told Darryl that I'd make the movie if it was real history and not propaganda, and I had to keep my word. But that wasn't the only reason. I realized that I had to prove to myself that I wasn't afraid to say true things about communists, or about anyone else, regardless of how others might construe my motives.

149

The local crew members were less than second-rate, and the circus performers we hired to play themselves were no better. Plus, few of the people I relied on spoke English, and I did not know German. So, we had significant challenges. Nonetheless, I befriended some of the cast, including a circus dwarf with whom I regularly drank schnapps after work.

One of the American actresses, Terry Moore, quickly let me know she was Howard Hughes' mistress. She would receive long distance phone calls from Hughes at night in which they exchanged alligator mating calls. This was at a time when no one else was able to get any phone connection at all. As Scott Fitzgerald wrote, "The very rich are different from you and me." Out of curiosity I tried to seduce Terry – I had a history with Hughes' girlfriends. I even got as far as getting into bed with her, when her mother/chaperon slid in beside me. Nonetheless, Terry and I remained friendly throughout the years.

One day I arrived at the set only to find the crew and circus troupe gathered around a radio, listening intently. Radio Leipzig, the official East German station, was reading off a list of names – their names. The radio voice warned that if they did not quit immediately, they would face severe consequences. Many had relatives on the other side, so this was no empty threat. Nonetheless, after the broadcast concluded everyone returned to work. The war had hardened them. One man had snuck across the border beneath the hood of a car; he had the burn marks on his legs and chest to prove it. No one was going to push them around.

As we shot in harsh winter weather, they worked outside without complaint; and I came to admire their capacity for endurance. Then I decided to emulate it. At first the bitter cold made me miserable, but I made a point of sticking it out. Instead of retreating to the hut between shots to warm myself, I stayed outside with the crew, my dwarf pal by my side. I wanted to become as tough as they were. In time I was. And I'm convinced that my newfound physical toughness spread to other aspects of my being. I became more confident and relaxed because I knew I could endure anything.

The circus performers also helped erase any lingering doubts I had about outing my former Communist pals. When I expressed my concerns, they just laughed. Communism had been horrible, so bad they'd risked their lives and everything they owned to escape. How could I have any doubt about the need to stand up against it?

None of Art's crowd would have endured, much less thrived, in the kind of police state these circus performers had fled. But after the movie was released they overlooked all that and accused me of making propaganda to ingratiate myself with the Right. As though I needed to make a movie to defend myself!

151

"You can't condemn Hitler and give Stalin a free pass," I told myself and anyone who'd listen. No one was going to silence me from shining a light on despotism, whether it was on the Right or the Left. Later, when I saw how the capitalists and corporations were using folksy front men on TV to manipulate the masses, I shined a light on that too, in *A Face in the Crowd.*

So fuck you! That's what Terry Malloy tells the Mob and that's what I said in my mind to Art and his friends. Fuck you! Then, like I had promised Marilyn, my *Waterfront* pulverized Art's *Crucible.*

CHAPTER 33

Art

Of course, sixty years later, how many people have heard of, much less seen, *On the Waterfront*? And how many still read *The Crucible* in high school and attend performances on stage?

CHAPTER 34
Gadg

Who gives a fuck?

Molly was a good fuck. Even though I wasn't faithful to her -- everyone knows that -- she was still a good fuck. Molly came from an upper-class WASP family, and I was a dirt-poor Greek immigrant on scholarship when we met at Yale. Like Art and his *shiksas*, Mary, Marilyn and Inge, Molly and I were opposites drawn to each other by a powerful magnetic attraction.

I can't imagine what my life would have been without Molly. She was totally devoted to me, and in so many ways I was liberated and empowered by knowing she would always support me and advise me and keep me on track. All of which she did. And often she raised our four children by herself, at the sacrifice of pursuing her own art – a sacrifice I was never prepared to make.

Molly's devotion was a blessing to me; but at the same time I came to feel that by accepting her support and guidance I was surrendering my power to her. Over time I came to resent that, and my resentment grew into repressed fury. Of course, that was hardly fair to Molly, who acted only out of love and good intentions.

The differences in our backgrounds that had attracted us so strongly now fueled unfounded suspicions that she was condescending to me. "Oh, pity the sweet, earnest, compliant, hard-working little Greek boy (with the beautiful brown eyes)," I would imagine Molly saying to herself. In time I came to detest her pity, that was not even really pity but a projection of my own insecurities onto her. Of course, I had to strike back and take the kind of revenge men take on their wives. Molly deserved better.

My revenge -- the affairs with other women -- hurt her. I could have done something about that; I chose not to. In any case, I'm convinced Molly got what she needed from our marriage; otherwise, she wouldn't have stayed. Not Molly. I often wonder why people make such a fuss about infidelity. Sometimes it's the only thing that keeps a marriage together.

Molly was a committed leftist. That's how we met back in college. She'd get more worked up over social injustice than almost anyone I knew. But she backed me up when I left the Party in '36, and then she backed me up again in '52, when I named their names. My inclination had been to let the hearing speak for itself. Why should I be defensive? But Molly was a fighter. She even wrote the piece I published in the *Times* afterward, laying out in a single page why I thought it was important for me to speak out against communism and why I intended to continue making movies with the same social themes and point of view I had always had.

Molly had a good mind and a sharp eye. She was my best and toughest critic and an intellectual force in her own right. Her plays never met the success that my movies did though, and I know that sometimes pained her. Not much I could do about that. Molly's fundamental artistic flaw stemmed from an essential defect in her personality. She lived in an *either-or* universe; whereas mine was *both-and-neither*. Molly saw things as good or bad, black or white, in her life and in her plays. Her absolutist view gave her a moral rectitude that was both her strength and her weakness, although of course she never saw it that way. Molly had a clear sense of how things should be and what people should do, and on many occasions I benefitted greatly from it. More than once she set me back on a constructive path after I'd strayed.

But her absolutism also made Molly rigid and even old fashioned. There was no room in her moral universe for both sides in a dispute to be right. This was true for her friendships, her politics, her marriage, and her art. In her plays this meant there was only one point of view that was correct: the author's, and I have always found this to be a fatal flaw in theater. Eventually her rigidity alienated me. I came to regard her as stuffy and closed to change, which I believed was not only inevitable, whether we wanted it or not, but also desirable because change often mandated personal growth. But Molly didn't view life that way. She felt it was her mission in life to impose order on chaos. I, on the other hand, preferred the chaos, which I knew was essential to the creative process.

Molly did have one moment of artistic success for which I am deeply grateful. A poem she wrote eulogizing Jack Kennedy made a big splash shortly after the assassination. The *Herald Tribune* published it on the front page of its second section, and they were swamped with requests for reprints. Molly'd never received much recognition for her writing, and I know the enthusiasm for that poem meant a lot to her, all the more because it was so heartfelt. Molly was very logical and analytical, and I think her poem about Kennedy sprang from a deeper place within her than anything else she'd ever written. That's why people loved it. Molly had a great heart, all the way to its core.

Her poem began, *I think that what he gave us most was pride. / It felt good to have a president like that;/ bright, brave and funny, and good-looking.* She went on: *It felt good to have a president who read his mail, / who read the papers, / who read books and played touch football.* And *It was a pleasure and a cause for pride / to watch him take the quizzing of the press / with cameras grinding, / take it in stride, with zest.*

Times change, don't they? Molly died a couple of weeks later from a cerebral hemorrhage. I stayed with her in the hospital as her life eked away. Her face was beautiful. Relieved of life's tensions, it had relaxed, and the lines and wrinkles disappeared. She looked ten years younger. Her heart finally gave out on December 14, 1963, two days before her fifty-seventh birthday.

Barbara Loden and I had already had our son together when Molly died. By then, however, Barbara and I were seeing less and less of each other, and Molly and I were growing closer again. Funny how that worked.

I'd started seeing Barbara about seven years earlier. She had been a regular on Ernie Kovac's television show then. Barbara was on the set one day while I was finishing up *A Face in the Crowd*. I'm not sure why since she wasn't in the cast. I followed her into the Ladies Room after everyone else had gone home. She'd already made it clear what she wanted from me. We made out against one of the stalls. I was feeling her up pretty good, and she was feeling me up too. Later, it was pure, raw sex: dog on bitch. She was half my age: twenty-four to my almost forty-eight, and afterward I felt twenty years younger.

We kept at it throughout the shoot. It was all about sex. Back then neither of us wanted or expected anything more. I'd rent a hotel room and arrive before her. I'd be lying in the dark when she'd creep in, still wearing her work clothes from the house she was fixing up by herself. We'd go at it like wild beasts, and then I'd leave for an important meeting or a rehearsal or something. After I was gone she'd return to her work on the house. We both liked it that way. We rarely talked, but I enjoyed having her around.

Like Marilyn, Barbara came from a poor family, and she was making it on her own. She literally was a bitch, conceived out of wedlock in a field of daisies, born to be anti-respectable, and she had no use for the conventional middle-class boundaries that Molly worked so hard to uphold.

In *A Face in the Crowd* Marcia Jeffries, a proper middle-class country spinster, discovers a folksy drifter who is a natural entertainer, and she propels him to stardom while trying to civilize him, as Huck Finn might say. Barbara was from the country, and I drew on both her and Molly as I developed Marcia's character. Lonesome Rhodes becomes her creation, who she believes can become a force for good in the world. But Lonesome has his own ideas about that, and after Marcia shows him that he can sway radio and television audiences with his down-to-earth folksy ways, Lonesome recognizes that he can manipulate the public for his own gain and for that of his corporate benefactors and the cynical politicians they support. Marcia, who by then has fallen in love with Lonesome and become his mistress, realizes that she must destroy the dangerous monster she has created, and she does. Marcia's feistiness, her belief in herself, and her determination were

159

drawn from Barbara. But Molly was the would-be reformer who lost control of her creation, me.

CHAPTER 35

Marilyn

All of my marriages started to fall apart as soon as they began. I was barely sixteen when I married my neighbor, Jim Dougherty. But that wasn't my first sexual experience. I'd already been raped and molested in foster homes, even when I was still in elementary school. Of course, nobody would believe me when I complained. I was eight the first time a boarder assaulted me, almost nine. My foster mother slapped me across the face when I told her.

"I don't believe you!" she shouted. "Shame on you. Don't you dare say such things about that nice man. He's a paying customer!"

About a week later everyone went to a religious revival meeting; you know, the kind they used to hold under a big tent. When the preacher called for the sinners to come up and repent, I raced to the altar, fell on my knees and told how I'd been raped. But all the other sinners were confessing too, and they drowned me out. So once again no one, not even God, could hear me. After that I stuttered for a long time.

I lived with nine foster families altogether. The state kept passing me from one to another. I was a cash cow for those families. They collected a monthly payment for taking me in, and then on top of that, most of them used me like an indentured servant, the way Cinderella's stepmother and stepsisters treated her. I had to earn my keep by washing dishes, scrubbing floors, sweeping the sidewalks, and, of course, putting up with lurid advances from relatives and family friends.

When I was sixteen my last foster family decided to move from California. My real mother, who was locked up in a mental institution, wouldn't let my foster parents adopt me, and the law wouldn't let them take me with them out of state. So, it was either marry Jim or go back to the orphanage, and I'd had enough of *that* in between my foster homes. Besides, I *wasn't* an orphan. I didn't belong there. My parents were alive; they just weren't there for me.

Jim was twenty-one, and I was the girl next door. Like other girls on the block, I had a crush on him from afar, and after some conniving by my foster mom, we started dating soon after Pearl Harbor. Jim and I married six months later, in June, and I dropped out of high school to be with him in the San Fernando Valley. He was considered a good catch. Jim had played football for his high school team and been the student body president of his class, and now he had a steady job at Lockheed Aviation. I think my foster mother fixed us up so she wouldn't feel guilty about leaving me behind.

I don't know if it was that Jim didn't know how to make a girl come, or if he just didn't see any reason to try, but nothing he did felt good, except sometimes when he'd kiss my breasts. Jim did shift work, and he'd usually have a few beers afterward with his pals. By the time we'd go to bed it was all he could do to get an erection. When he finally did, he'd squeeze my tits and maybe kiss them for a few seconds; then he'd jump on top of me before I was ready, and he'd pump real hard for a minute or two. Then he'd come. Then he'd fall asleep. Can you believe it? Sometimes I even had to push him off of me. And I'd just lie there listening to him snore and thinking there had to be more to life than this.

Out of bed Jim and I barely spoke to each other. We weren't angry; we just had nothing to say. I was dying of boredom, even after I took a lover, a scrawny musician who *did* know how to make a girl come. Over and over again. Freddie called me a slut and treated me like shit, but he could sure get me going.

Jim was protected from the draft during the war because he worked in an essential industry, aviation. But toward the end he felt bad about staying home while his buddies were overseas; so, he joined the merchant marines. I got a job at the Radioplane Munitions factory while he was in the Pacific, and I moved in with his parents to save money.

That wasn't much fun, but the job got my modeling career started when an Army Air Corps photographer came to the factory to take pictures of us girls in order to help the troops

163

keep up their morale – and whatever else they needed help in keeping up. I had a sweater in my locker and the photographer, David Conover, told me to put it on. I made an impression. The Air Corps didn't use my picture, but Dave thought I looked swell, and I started modeling for him after that. My first job paid all of five bucks, but it wasn't long before I started getting steady work. So, I quit the factory during the Battle of the Bulge, and soon I was earning enough to move from my in-laws' house. Neither Jim nor his parents approved, but I was suffocating there.

I signed a contract with the Blue Book Modeling Agency about the time we dropped the bomb on Hiroshima. Those events might not seem to have much in common, but did you ever think about how often high explosives are used to describe sexy women? I've been called a *bombshell* and a *blond bomber*, and during the war guys would leer at my tits and holler, "Get a look at those bazookas." The Germans had a powerful cannon called Big Bertha, and someone once taped a photo of Rita Hayworth onto an atom bomb they exploded over Bikini Island, you know, the testing site they named the skimpy swimsuit after. So, what's up with all *that*?

Anyway, when Jim finally came home after the war I moved back with him, and we went back to having nothing in common, except that now I also missed my independence. I was into my modeling and enjoying it, but Jim couldn't stand it.

Joe DiMaggio was the same way. Somehow my self-expression threatened their manhood. Plus, Jim wanted children, but the very thought of having a baby with him made me shiver. I was terrified that something would happen to me, and Jim would disappear, and my little girl would become another Norma Jeane, stuck in an orphanage or a foster home, washing dishes and bathing in cold, dirty, leftover water on Saturday night. The mere possibility that my daughter might have to endure what I'd suffered through horrified me, but I was incapable of explaining that to Jim. And he was incapable of understanding, even if I'd tried. Later I desperately wanted children with Art, and I was devastated by the miscarriages; but I refused to have kids with Jim.

So, we divorced in September of '46. Now it hardly seems like we were ever married. I was free: just twenty and on my own again. I lived alone at first and then with roommates. One night at dinner, as a couple of my gay friends were arguing passionately about Leonardo and Botticelli and Freud and Jung, I suddenly realized how ignorant I was. The entire evening I had no idea what my pals were talking about. Not only that, but I finally admitted to myself that most of the time I knew very little at all about what other people were discussing. I didn't know anything about painting, music, books, history, geography, sports, or politics. "You're really

165

dumb," I thought to myself as my companions argued the pros and cons of penis envy.

So, I started taking classes. A woman was teaching art history at the University of Southern California, and I signed up for a course with her. At first I doubted she could teach me anything, since she was a woman. In my experiences at the orphanage, in my foster homes, with Jim's family, and at the factory, most of the women had not been very knowledgeable. Even my teachers in school. But my professor soon shined as one of the most exciting human beings I'd ever met. She brought the Renaissance to life, not just the art but also the newfound spirit of inquiry, trade, daring exploration, and inhumane exploitation that somehow coexisted with the most exquisite political intrigue and treachery. I drank in everything she said and came to adore Michelangelo, Raphael, and Tintoretto. Later I discovered Goya, with his grotesque twisted figures and scenes of carnage. The first time I saw one of his paintings I remember thinking, "We have the same dreams." I also branched out on my own and started reading Freud and his disciples. They blew my mind.

But I never had enough time to complete my education in the humanities. Between modeling jobs and PR stunts I was always running to classes in speech and singing, and then to lessons in acting, where I discovered my bliss. Right from the start acting infused something golden and beautiful into a life that was otherwise bleak. It reminded me of the bright colors I'd imagine as a little girl when I'd lapse into daydreams to escape the loneliness of my dreary existence.

For a while Shelley Winters and I shared an apartment. We were both just starting out, and I learned from her too. She taught me how to smile in that suggestive way, with my lips slightly parted to form a seductive O. Shelley shared my passion for sex and my desire to experience a variety of partners. "Men have the freedom to do what they want, and they're admired for it," she told me. And I agreed. "Why shouldn't women be free too?" I wanted to know.

So, one Sunday, we made a list of men we wanted to sleep with. Eventually, I made a pretty good dent in my list; I think Shelley did all right with hers too. No one on mine was under 50, and later on my shrinks had a thing or two to say about *that*, mostly in relation to my absent father.

My divorce from Jim brought about my death and transfiguration, as I put Norma Jeane to rest and reincarnated into Marilyn Monroe. Truly, I was starting a new life, and I felt like I had died and been reborn. Norma Jeane would never have studied the Renaissance or read Freud. Her life had been drab and constrained, shot in black and white in 16 millimeter film; but Marilyn Monroe was ready for the big screen and technicolor. Ben Lyon, the executive at 20th Century Fox who gave me my screen test and liked what he saw, chose *Marilyn*,

167

because I reminded him of another actress called that. *Monroe* was my mother's maiden name.

So that was my first marriage and how it ended and how its ending freed me. Looking back, I guess the collapse of all my marriages freed me in one way or another, although, except for Jim, my freedom came at a cost. I've already told you about how furious Joe DiMaggio got on our honeymoon when I gave those sexy USO performances for the soldiers in Korea. Of course, we did have good times together, and I know he loved me, which was no small thing. Sometimes we'd go out and fans would recognize him and come up and tell him how great he was, and I'd feel so proud to be his wife. But Joe's jealousy only grew worse, until he finally hit me after we shot that scene from *The Seven Year Itch*. And that was that.

Things were terrific between Art and me during our semi-secret torrid affair in New York, after we finally ran into each other at Paula Strasberg's soirée. It had to happen sooner or later, but neither of us planned it that way. We explored the city on foot and on bikes, picnicked in the park, attended parties, and just palled around with his friends. Art welcomed me into his community, and I loved being around people who talked seriously about poetry, novels, and ideas. It was much more stimulating than the blather that passed for conversation in Hollywood. Our forbidden sex in his pals' guest rooms was thrilling too. And, of course, Art's showdown with HUAC was exciting, if scary, and I was proud to publicly stand by my man. It felt good to be proud like that. I was part of something bigger than just me.

I'd started my own production company by then. I was tired of having the studios tell me what kinds of roles I could take and who would be my leading man. One way or another I was always the dumb blonde, and I wanted to do more, not just because I wanted to demonstrate to the world that I could, but because I craved the challenge. I needed to see how much I could stretch as an actor, how far I could go. I guess this is what we mean by *artistic freedom*. With the studios I had none.

Bus Stop was the first movie made by Marilyn Monroe Productions, and I went down to Las Vegas that winter to film it, while Art was making the arrangements for his divorce. Mary took him for a ride, but I guess she deserved what she got. Mary had gone through a lot. I never wanted to be a home wrecker, but somehow I always was. I guess that was just one of the roles life gave me, the way it's the role of the Trickster in the tarot deck to come in and shake everything up. Or the Cat in the Hat. Or Coyote or Elegguá. I felt sorry for Mary, but their marriage was on the rocks before I even entered the picture.

I hired George Axelrod to write the screenplay, which was based on a Broadway smash by William Inge. George had written *The Seven Year Itch*, the film that made me a star. That's why I chose him for *Bus Stop*. He went on to write

169

Breakfast at Tiffany's and *The Manchurian Candidate*, so he knew what he was doing. The plot doesn't hold up as well in the Harvey Weinstein era as it did in the Harry Cohn days, but it was one of my favorite roles. I play a poor saloon singer from the Ozarks who meets Bo, a young rodeo rider, on a bus headed toward California. The cowboy, who's never even kissed a woman before, becomes infatuated with me and wants to marry me and take me back to his ranch in Nowheresville, Montana, but he's as dumb as a mule, and besides, who wants to live in Nowheresville anyway? I had plans to go to Hollywood and make it big.

Plus Chérie, that's me, doesn't even know the guy. Why would she want to marry him? She takes a liking to Bo at first when he stands up for her and silences everyone in the saloon and forces the crowd to listen to her sing. But then he becomes possessive and self-absorbed. He ignores Chérie's refusal of his proposal – she has no say about this wedding at all, as far as Bo is concerned. Marrying Chérie is what he wants, and he's used to going all out for whatever he wants; so finally, he lassos her and carries her onto a bus headed for Montana. People watch but nobody comes to Chérie's aid. Sound familiar?

After that, Chérie only wants to escape. But finally the bus driver knocks some sense into Bo, with his fists, and Bo sees what an ass he's been. He apologizes to Chérie and actually starts listening to what she's saying. He shows her respect. It's like he's had a tragic recognition of his faults, the kind that Art was always talking about, except Bo has his realization in time. Once he starts taking Chérie seriously and treats her respectfully, she falls for him and willingly chooses to marry him and live with him in Nowheresville. But now it's *her* choice, not just his. The role of Chérie gave me a lot more to work with than Lorelei Lee and the other dumb blondes I used to play. She's more vulnerable, more real. Her story reminded me of why Art won me over the first time we met. He took me seriously and listened and respected me.

Things started to go bad with Art almost as soon as we arrived in England, just a week after our wedding. I was starring in *The Prince and the Showgirl* with Laurence Olivier. Guess which one I was. Larry also directed. This was the second movie Marilyn Monroe Productions made. My partner, Milton Greene, set up the whole deal. In retrospect maybe it wasn't such a good idea after all, although we got some good reviews and even won some awards.

While I was shooting *Showgirl*, Art was preparing the British debut of his new play, *A View from the Bridge*. Eddie is a goodhearted-but-jealous Sicilian immigrant who lusts for the young niece he and his wife have taken in after his brother died. Eddie eventually rats on his wife's cousin, a *submarine*, an illegal immigrant, who wants to marry the niece, and disaster

171

follows. Art told me he heard the story from a lawyer who worked with longshoremen and claimed that it was true. Maybe it was. I'd been reading some Greek tragedies Art had given me, and I could see how *View* created that same sense of watching a train wreck in slow motion. You just want to shake Eddie by his shoulders and tell him to look at what he's doing, just like you want to slap some sense into Othello. But, of course, you can't. Like with the Greeks, Eddie's self-serving betrayal dooms him, as well as the submarine and Eddie's own family. Art could get pretty heavy at times. A lot of times. Sometimes too heavy.

The play strikes at Gadg too. After all, it's a story about an informer who destroys everyone around him, and that's how Art had come to think about Gadg's testimony. I think *View* was Art's way of getting back at Gadg for taking *The Hook* and turning it into *On the Waterfront*, a huge hit in which Terry becomes a hero by informing, and not a tragic loser like Art had planned. Art originally wrote *View* as a one-act play that ran in New York the summer before, but Peter Brook, who was directing the British premier, wanted it to be longer, less mythic, and more realistic in order to appeal to an English audience. So, when Art wasn't "helping out" on the set of *Showgirl* -- *i.e.* keeping me in line and making sure I showed up for rehearsals on time and making excuses for me when I didn't -- he was adding a second act to *View*. I understand Art's anger at

HUAC; they were pure sleaze. But it had already been almost three years since Gadg named names when Art began working on that play. Gadg did what he had to. Couldn't Art have given him a rest?

After we married the press treated us like a fairytale couple. I think I was supposed to be the beautiful princess and Art, because they'd decided he was a nerdy intellectual who wore thick, black glasses, was the frog who turned into a prince when I kissed him. I didn't think that was at all fair to Art. I found him manly and attractive from the moment we met, and it was he who helped cultivate my mind and expand my horizons. I was the frog who made the wonderful transformation after we kissed, not him. Perhaps he would have been happier if he had been a frog too.

It was exciting to have the whole world hanging on everything we did and every word we said, and Art didn't seem to mind being cast as the lucky frog. He said I'd brought him back to life. After our plane landed in England the crowds almost shut down the airport. All of that adulation made me ecstatic.

We rented Parkside House, a stately manor house in Englefield Green about an hour's drive from London. It was all so British: there were maids and servants, lush, expansive lawns, a lovely rose garden for afternoon tea, and an iron gate that opened onto Windsor Park, one of the Queen's many properties scattered around what was still left of the empire. The master bathroom had an enormous bathtub I used to luxuriate in for hours at a time. When I was a little girl living in foster homes money was usually tight; so, they'd fill the tub once and everyone would bathe in the same water. Since I wasn't *really* a family member but was just supposed to be there temporarily until someone adopted me, I always went last. The water would be steamy and clean for the first two or three bathers, but it was always cold and cloudy by the time I climbed in, filled with other people's dirt and sweat and urine and God knows what else. So, I savored my time in that aristocratic bathtub, and if my soaks sometimes made me late on the set, well, they were worth it.

Olivier and I clashed right from the start. I thought he was pretentious, and he thought I was crass. He didn't think much of the method acting I'd been practicing at the Actors Studio, and he made no effort to hide his contempt. If it took me some time to really feel what the showgirl was experiencing, Larry would start pacing back and forth muttering to himself, but loud enough for me to hear, "She doesn't need to *feel* what her character's feeling. That's why it's called *acting*." I took my revenge by showing up late and forgetting my lines and watching him stew while we did take after take. I could have nailed my lines the first time if I'd wanted, but I liked to see the vein on his forehead bulge out like it might pop. Sometimes I hoped it would.

With all the shit I had to take from Larry, I expected total support from Art; I needed it. But I didn't always get it. That betrayal tore at the fabric of our love in a way that would not, perhaps could not, mend. And then one day I stumbled across his open notebook while I was looking for my pills, and that ripped the fabric wide open. It all came to a head one Sunday morning when I'd actually awakened feeling good. We'd finished breakfast and were sitting beside each other, nice and cozy, on a couch in the drawing room.

"I still can't believe it," I snuggled up beside him. "Norma Jeane can't believe it. Here I am in an English manor house with my husband, who is not only the greatest American playwright alive today, bar none. (Take *that*, Tennessee Williams and Eugene O'Neill!) Not only that, he's America's greatest political hero: the man who told HUAC where to get off. Honey, I'm so proud of you. And so is everyone else. At least everyone who counts." Then I kissed him on the cheek, and I think he blushed a little.

"No, not only is he the greatest playwright and greatest hero, he's the greatest lover I've ever had. Because you adore me for who I really am."

"I *do* adore you. And I admire you. I've always admired you."

175

"Why? Why would a great writer like you admire an uneducated girl like me?"

"I've told you a hundred times."

"But I love hearing you say it. Tell me again."

I snuggled even closer.

"I adore you not only for your legendary beauty and amazing sex appeal – of course for those too – but even more for your authenticity. You are the most authentic person I know. Bar none. Take *that*, Tennessee Williams and Eugene O'Neill!"

"Every time you tell me that it makes me all tingly inside. I still can't believe I'm your wife."

"I can't believe it's me on whom you've bestowed your love."

Art's words touched me. They were what I had longed to hear all of my life from someone who really meant them. And I knew he did. But then suddenly waves of insecurity shook me from my head to my toes. I shuddered, and a stark coldness enveloped my heart.

"You don't think our marriage is cursed, do you?"

"Cursed? Why would it be cursed? We're blessed. We're a fairytale couple. Just switch on any television channel."

"That woman photographer who died chasing us, driving like a maniac down that road. Her face still haunts me."

"Me too," Art whispered. I was surprised by that. Until then, Art hadn't seemed very affected by Mara's death. It was sometimes easy to confuse his stoicism with lack of feeling.

"I held her while she was dying," I whispered back. Then, in a louder voice, "Her blood soaked through my sweater. I felt it seep onto my chest. I told her I was sorry. I told her, 'I never wanted to hurt you. I only wanted to be alone with the man I love.'

"But Mara somehow managed to lift her head and hiss into my ear as I bent over her. I still remember her exact words, 'Selfish woman! What made you think you could have him all to yourself? My death is on your hands. You will never wash it off. I curse you and your ridiculous marriage.' Then her eyes shut, and her head fell back down, and she was dead."

"My poor Marilyn," Art stroked my head; his voice was tender. "How terrible that must have been for you. And you never said anything."

"I was afraid."

"Afraid?"

"Afraid you'd think we'd be doomed if we went ahead and got married. I was afraid you'd leave me and I'd be all alone again. I couldn't take that." I began to cry.

Art stroked my head some more and then my cheek. "You know I'd never leave you." His caresses were so gentle, and soon my sobbing stopped. "Not then, not now, not ever."

177

"The moment she... let go I felt like she was Mary, cursing me with all her hatred. She stared into my eyes, and her venom penetrated me. Then it spread inside me, all throughout my body. It felt like she was stealing my soul."

"Mara or Mary?"

"Both. They were the same. And then we still had to keep going and hold that wretched press conference."

"My poor Marilyn. I never knew." Art squeezed my hand. "How awful for you. How terrifying. I don't know how you held it together for those reporters. Especially with all those hateful questions they asked about the accident."

"There were so many of them, swarming like angry bees. You said there'd only be a few dozen, but there must have been over four hundred."

"They say ours was the most famous wedding in the history of world. At least since Helen of Troy ran off with Paris. That's mindboggling." Art kissed me softly and suddenly I felt good again.

"Norma Jeane is still stunned. It *is* a fairytale. Could you ever imagine that *Lee Strasberg*, the head of the Actors Studio, would give me away? *Me*! Norma Jeane couldn't. Not in a million, billion years.

"Well, Lee *has* become something of a father figure to you, don't you think?"

"No, silly," I gave Art a playful push. "That's what you're for. No, not you, your father. I adore him. I love your mother too. Don't get me wrong. They're both wonderful. But I adore your father."

"And he's smitten by you. I can tell. It meant a lot to him, to both of them, that you converted."

"I want to be family. I want to be *your* family. In every way possible. I want to have kids, lots of kids."

"We'll have to get started on that right away."

Art cupped his hands against my breasts and softly caressed them. At first I went along with him; it felt good. It always did. But then another wave of doubt passed through me and I pulled back, afraid.

"But what if they send you to jail, like they did to Trumbo and Lawson and the others? I couldn't raise our children alone. I don't want to. Not without you. I don't think I could survive without you for a year. Or even six months."

"It scares me too. Believe me, I don't look forward to prison. But that's what being a hero means. More to the point, it's what being a man of integrity means: being willing to pay the price of a clear conscience, regardless of the cost. That's what my writing has been all about. How could I author those plays and then cave in? How could I criticize Gadg and then cave in? I'd be a hypocrite in the world's eyes, in my own eyes, and worst of all, in yours."

179

"But I'm scared." I stood up, walked to a table across the room and shook a pill from its bottle. "Get me some water."

Art's expression and body language changed. Whereas before he'd been tender and solicitous, sympathetic and understanding, now he looked paternal and disapproving.

"Do you really think it's such a good idea to take another one of those? You already had one this morning, when you got up."

Now my demeanor changed too. My body stiffened and my tone became emphatic. "My shrink says it's OK. All of this talk about dead people and curses and you going to jail frightens me."

Art leaned over and poured a glass of water from a pitcher on the coffee table. Then he stood and brought it to me.

"Here."

I took it and swallowed the pill.

"Thanks."

"You're welcome. But pay attention to how much of that stuff you're consuming. You don't want to become addicted. I think they affect your mood. Haven't you noticed the swings?"

"Don't be silly. I can handle my alcohol, and I can handle my barbiturates." I walked back to the couch and Art followed. We sat together, however not as close as we'd been before.

"But sometimes I get so afraid you'll leave me. Like Mommy and Daddy and Johnny and Joe and all the rest of them."

"I'll never leave you. You know that."

"What if they send you to jail?"

Art put on a tough-guy voice, "They've never built a lock-up yet strong enough to keep me from *you*, Baby."

Sometimes his hardened-criminal persona could make me laugh, but not that day. So he continued in his normal voice, "If they do, it will just be for a while. And I'll come right back to you. Besides, it would be bad politics for them to lock me up, and that's all they really care about, politics."

"How would it be bad politics?"

"They'd look pretty bad before the rest of the world if they threw me in prison so soon after the most highly publicized wedding in human history. That's why the State Department changed its tune after all and gave me the visa to come here with you."

"If they do lock you up, I'll visit you every weekend. I'll bring homemade matzo-ball soup. Your mother can teach me how to cook it."

"You can sneak a hacksaw blade into one of the matzo balls."

181

That made me giggle. "Yes. That's it! I'll mastermind a jail break. Then we'll run away some place where no one can ever find us."

"And you could do it too. I have no doubt. But I don't think it will come to that."

Now I felt anxious. I don't know why, but I just had to move. So I started pacing around the room. Art remained on the sofa looking concerned at first, but he was used to being around actors, and sudden mood changes weren't anything he hadn't seen a million times before. At any rate, he didn't say anything.

"I can't wait until we wrap up *Showgirl*. Then I'll be free to spend all my time with you. Besides, I've had it with these Brits. Larry Olivier is a real pain in the ass. He acts like working with me is slumming. Sir Laurence is enough high and mighty Englishman for me."

"No one likes being condescended to." Art was trying to be sympathetic, but I felt he was holding something back.

"He patronizes me. He treats me like I'm a twit. A slutty, simple-minded twit. You should punch him in the nose."

"Perhaps if you would stick to the shooting schedule and arrive on time more often, he'd be better disposed towards you."

I always wondered how far Art would go to stand up for my honor. Apparently getting into fisticuffs with Larry Olivier

182

was a step too many. OK, fighting wasn't his way. I could get that. But now he was turning on *me*.

"You're taking his side now. You've abandoned me already! I should have known it."

"Of course, I haven't abandoned you. I love you. I'll never abandon you." Art was trying to reassure me with his words, but I sensed the irritation in his voice. As if he had one foot out the door.

"You already have." I raised my voice. "You're siding with *him*!"

"I'm not siding with anyone but you." He said it so sincerely I almost believed him. Then he changed his tune again.

"But *I'm* the one who takes the phone calls when you don't show up on the set. I'm the one who has to come up with explanations. It places me in an uncomfortable position."

"So don't take the calls. What's the big deal?"

"How can I do that, and just leave them hanging?"

"It's easy. Don't pick up the phone. "

"That's not an option. It could be Peter about the play. It could be my mother. Or Jane."

"No, you mustn't dare miss a call from your daughter."

"What's that mean?"

"Never mind. Suit yourself then. Answer the damn phone. But don't complain to me about it."

I plopped down into one of the overstuffed chairs that framed the couch. Art moved to be closer to me, but I just folded my arms across my chest and crossed my legs to boot. Then I looked away.

"What if it's your shrink? Wouldn't you want to talk to him?"

I faced Art again. He couldn't stand to argue with me, and his frustration showed on his face. "Well good." I thought. "He deserves it."

"My shrink can wait. What's the big deal?" I uncrossed my legs and re-crossed them again in the opposite order.

"I don't see why you needed to fly him out here to be on the set with you. He hasn't helped much that I can see. Or Lee and Paula either, for that matter. It's like they're all struggling for your soul. And they're doing it on your dime."

I uncrossed my arms and legs, sat up straight, and leaned toward him.

"Along with you."

"Who has a better claim to it than I?"

"Me. I do. It's my soul. And my dime. I let you push out Milton from my production company. He was my best friend when I first came to New York, and I let you put your friends and relatives on the board instead. I stabbed Milton in the back for you. Isn't that enough. Now you want my soul too?"

"Milton was taking your career in all the wrong directions. I like him too, but I have a better feel for your abilities than he does. Listen, he's the one who paired you with Olivier, and look how wretched that's made you. We had to make that move."

I made a frumpy sound to show my doubt, but I grudgingly admitted to myself that Art was right. Milton Greene had had to go.

"I don't want to take your soul," Art went on. "I only want to bask in its full glory." Art was so good with words; I let him squeeze my hand. "I just wish your psychiatrist would ease off on the barbiturates. They make you erratic."

With that I burst into tears. "I knew you'd see the monster sooner or later. I knew I couldn't hide it from you forever. You hate me, don't you?"

"Of course, I don't hate you. I love you."

Art was almost pleading, but that didn't console me, not at all.

"I'm not the sweet, perfect, loving Marilyn you courted. I'm the mean, angry, bitchy Marilyn too. And you hate me for that, don't you? Don't you!"

I leapt up and threw the water glass across the room. Thick rugs covered the floor, so it didn't shatter; but Art was stunned. He stood and tried to put his arms around me, but I pushed him away.

"I love you, Marilyn. All of you. You know I do. The sweet-tempered Marilyn *and* the bitchy one too. You're human, after all. We all have our shadow sides. God knows, you put up with mine."

He was trying to make me feel better, but I knew better. I had proof, and finally I let it out. My big secret.

"I read your notebook."

"What?" Art looked shocked and then distressed.

"I read what you wrote about me and about Jane. You said you used to think I was some kind of angel, but now you see that you were wrong. You said Mary had let you down, but I've done something even worse. You said, and I'm quoting you here, you said, 'Olivier is beginning to think Marilyn is a troublesome bitch, and frankly, I have no answer for him.'"

"Where did you find my notebook?" His voice grew louder and his tone was sharp. No more Mister Nice Guy, Art was accusing me now.

"On your desk. I was looking for my pills and I saw the notebook there. It was open to that page. I was curious, so I looked."

"Why would your pills be on my desk. Or even in my study?"

"I don't know. I couldn't find them. Maybe I had left them in your study when I came by to tell you I love you. Anyway, that's not the point. The point is what you wrote.

"That was an accident. I never leave my notebook out."

"Freud says there are no accidents. Remember?"

"Honestly -"

"And what's even worse, on the next page you wrote, 'The only one I will ever love is my daughter.' How do you think that makes me feel?" I started sobbing. "I guess the honeymoon is over, Norma Jeane. It was nice while it lasted."

"Those were notes for my play. The one I've been working on forever." Art's voice was no longer harsh, but it wasn't tender either. It was insistent. He tried to place his arm around me again, but I shoved him away again. This time harder than before.

"They sure didn't look like notes to me."

"You can't think that what I write in those notebooks represents what I actually think or feel. If you do, that would totally stifle me." Art was almost pleading now. "I wouldn't be free to let my imagination soar. It would cripple me as an artist."

"And reading that I'm a bitch and that your daughter is the only person you will ever love won't cripple me as your wife? As your lover?"

I turned my back to him and went to the table where that bottle of pills sat. The top was still open, and I poured a couple into my hand. But then I felt Art's hand gripping my wrist hard.

"Don't!" And he squeezed even harder.

187

We glared into each other's eyes for a long moment, and then I let the pills drop onto the table. I didn't really need them anyway. Art let me go, and I slapped him across the face. Hard. Then I stood there defiantly, with my hands on my hips. Joe DiMaggio flashed across my mind, and I thought, "OK, this is it, the beginning of the end," as I prepared for Art to strike back. But instead he just rubbed his cheek with his hand and grimaced and shook his head sadly.

"I'm so sorry that you ever found that notebook. I love you. I adore you. Even when you descend into these dark places, I love you still. You know I do."

"So I'm not a bitch?" My voice was tentative.

"Of course you're not. Olivier's a prick."

"That's the first honest thing you've said."

"Come on, Marilyn." He was pleading again. "You know that's not true."

"That notebook really hurt me."

"I'm sorry for that. But you must understand my notebooks are among my most valuable tools. If I hold back, I'll be finished as a playwright. You can't hold me accountable for anything I write there. They're like psychotherapy for me, a place where I'm free to express any thought that passes through my mind, however silly or absurd or utterly wrong or detestable. That's why I never show them to anyone. You have a psychiatrist. You know about free association and exploration of the unconscious and all that. You understand, don't you?"

"I guess so," I admitted reluctantly as I returned to my chair and plopped back down. Suddenly the energy drained from me, along with my need to fight. Art followed me but he didn't sit. He just stood there, a very tall and imposing figure looking down at me.

"So do you forgive me?"

But I wasn't ready to give in altogether. "Do you know what? Gadg was right to testify. Gadg did what he had to do. He was right to name names, and you should let all that go now."

"What do you mean, let it go? For God's sake, I may be sent to prison for refusing to do what he did."

"Gadg was true to himself."

"And I'm not true to myself?"

"No. You sell yourself out in order to be true to your ideals."

"I don't know how to separate myself from my ideals. They're who I am."

"That's the difference between you and Gadg. He can separate himself out when he needs to. You're willing to go to jail and leave me all alone and unprotected, just to stand up for some abstract principle."

"But Marilyn -" The frustration returned to Art's voice.

189

"Gadg would never do that. If he loved someone, he wouldn't let himself be taken from her. Not for any reason. Not when she needs him to be there."

"Gadg loves himself. And yes, you're right, he will do whatever it takes to protect his beloved."

"So, what's wrong with that? Maybe if you loved yourself more and your precious code of conduct less, you'd be a lot happier. And I'd feel more secure. You're willing to sacrifice my happiness along with your own. That's not fair!"

Art stood there, dumbfounded.

"I have no answer for that. I'll be the one making license plates; you'll continue to be a star, pampered in every way. Anyway, if people don't stand for anything beyond their own self-interest, then civilization ceases to exist. It's like Rabbi Hillel said, 'If I am only for myself, who am I?'"

"But first he said, 'If I am not for myself, who will be for me?'"

Now Art looked amazed.

"Don't be so shocked. They made me study Hillel before I converted. So now I'm asking you, Mr. Playwright, when they take you to jail, who will be for you? Your Lefty pals? I don't think so. They don't exactly have a great track record for that."

"I thought you were for me. I thought you were going to free me from prison with a hacksaw blade stuck inside a matzo ball. But now I'm not so sure."

"And I thought you loved me and you'd always be there for me. But now I'm not so sure. After that notebook, I can't trust you any longer."

"If not now, when?"

We stared silently at each other for a long moment.

"I don't know. Maybe never."

As I stormed out of the room Art just stood there watching me leave.   Finally he shouted at my back, "Goddammit, Marilyn, I love you! I will always love you! I will never leave you. But you're ripping my heart out. These tantrums are shredding my soul!"

CHAPTER 36

Art

That autumn it seemed like the world was coming unglued. In October, while Hungary was in open revolt against its Communist regime and their Soviet masters, Israel, France, and Britain invaded Egypt. Israel was preempting an almost-certain invasion by the Egyptians, while France and Britain were trying to reclaim control over the strategic and very profitable Suez Canal, which Egypt's President Nasser had nationalized while Marilyn and I were in England. Eisenhower was furious that his allies hadn't consulted him in advance, and he made the invaders withdraw. So, in the end Nasser was the big winner because he'd stuck it to the European colonialists and gotten away with it. This made him a big hero in the Arab world, where he tried to form a pan-Arab alliance that Egypt would naturally lead. As my parents said at the time, this wasn't good for the Jews, even though Israel did successfully forestall the attack Nasser had been planning.

On top of all that, Khrushchev threatened to rain missiles down on France and England in retaliation for striking at his Arab ally, but Eisenhower wouldn't stand for that either, and he made it clear to Khrushchev that the U.S. would hit him back with H-bombs, which, of course, would lead to global, thermonuclear war. Khrushchev backed down, and we all breathed a sigh of relief. Marilyn actually met Khrushchev a few years later when he visited Hollywood.

The Suez crisis not only brought the world to the brink of Armageddon, it distracted attention from what was going on in Hungary, which was a big deal. I'd been disgusted by Stalin ever since we learned about his purge trails in the '30s, but Stalin died abruptly in '53, just as he was about to foment another pogrom against the Jews – remember his manufactured Doctors' Plot? Once Stalin was gone, Nikita Khrushchev muscled out his competition and seized control. At first I thought Khrushchev offered a ray of hope. He denounced Stalin's personality cult, introduced some encouraging economic changes and expanded personal freedoms, and he talked about peaceful co-existence with the capitalist West. So maybe endless tyranny and nuclear war were not inevitable after all. But my hopes were dashed when he sent tanks roaring into Budapest to crush the Hungarians who, like Gadg in his testimony, had had enough of living in a police state. Except for them, it was for real.

Ike's Secretary of State, John Foster Dulles, had made a big deal of denouncing Truman's policy of not contesting Soviet dominance where it already existed but refusing to let it spread further. Truman called it containment. Dulles wanted a more robust "liberation policy" that would drive Soviet tyranny from Eastern Europe, where Communists ruled from behind what

Churchill had called an iron curtain. But when the Hungarians, who were laying their lives and everything else on the line, begged America to save them, Ike acknowledged that Hungary was in Russia's sphere of influence after all, and he did nothing more than offer comforting words.

They were all hypocrites. Truman too, for that matter, calling the Korean War a *police action* so he wouldn't have to ask Congress for a declaration of war, which he never would have received. And shouldn't have, in my opinion. Why the hell did we need to interfere in a country halfway across the world where we knew nothing of its history, politics, or customs, just because communism was involved? Always that boogey man, *communism*. If Kim Il Sung had just been a power-crazed, homicidal maniac grabbing land and power, we'd have written off the conflict between North and South Korea as a civil war that we had no stake in. But because it was a *communist* invasion, we sent 36,000 GI's to their death. I never saw the logic to that. And, of course, don't get me started on Vietnam.

Anyway, just two days after the Soviet tanks rumbled into Budapest and squelched the revolution Eisenhower trounced Stevenson for a second time, which meant four more years of Republican rule. I almost resorted to some of Marilyn's pills as the election results trickled in over the radio, but I anesthetized myself with whiskey instead. At least the Democrats had control of Congress.

194

Sure enough, autumn 1956 was a tough time for the world, for the country, and for Marilyn and me. Earlier in the summer I wrote a short story, "The Misfits," in response to my sense that life was spinning out of control and there was little we could do about it. It's about three drifters in Nevada who have lost their bearings and an equally lost woman whose compassion for animals changes them. The woman was clearly indebted to Marilyn, and I wrote the story to show how heartfelt compassion, like what Marilyn felt for all living things, could be the answer to the craziness around us, if only it was more widely shared. Later I adapted that story into a screenplay that Marilyn could star in. It was my gift to her.

Bus Stop came out at the end of August, soon after we returned from England, and that, at least, cheered her up. Bosley Crowther at the *New York Times* loved her performance. He said that Marilyn had finally proven herself as an actress and that she and the picture were "swell." He loved that Marilyn had really become "the beat-up B-girl of Mr. Inge's play, even down to the Ozark accent and the look of pellagra about her skin" and, more important, that she had succeeded in lighting "the small flame of dignity that sputters pathetically in this chippie and to make a rather moving sort of her." Marilyn was ecstatic after she read the review. She called all of her friends, first of all Lee and Paula Strasberg. I wasn't always on

195

the same page with the Strasbergs, but I had to admit that her studies in method acting paid off in *Bus Stop.*

And if Marilyn had her big success with *Bus Stop*, I had mine with *A View from the Bridge.* We almost didn't get the London production made at all, because the Lord Chamberlain objected to the hints of homosexuality some of the characters exhibited, and he refused to authorize the license required by the Office of the Censor. So, we employed the same strategy Tennessee used earlier for *Cat on a Hot Tin* Roof and circumvented the censor altogether by putting on the play in a private club that added a modest membership fee to the cost of the ticket. Marilyn and I were still the fairytale couple, and her star power, and to a lesser extent mine, made the premier that October the cultural event of the season. In the first two weeks that little club in the West End gained twelve thousand new subscribers.

Opening night was incredible. Marilyn wore a sexy scarlet gown that offered up ample cleavage, and when we arrived with Olivier and Vivien Leigh, we were mobbed by a crowd that became hysterical in the same way that crowds went crazy a decade later over the Beatles. I'd never had a debut like this before. On top of that, the reviews were terrific. It was my first great dramatic success since *Death of a Salesman* seven years before, and it gave me a shot in the arm that I sorely needed.

196

I lucked out a little on the timing as well. Until then, most British theater centered around middle-class or professional-class or upper-class characters and situations, but the Angry Young Men changed all that shortly before *View* premiered. A few months earlier John Osborne had shocked London's theater world with *Look Back in Anger*, which took the lid off the repressed fury seething within working-class youth. *View* also presents the problems of repressed workers, and so it was able to ride of the wave of enthusiasm for this new trend in British drama.

On the other hand, *Waiting for Godot* had debuted on Broadway that spring, about a month before I testified, and by the end of the year the Theater of the Absurd became the new rage in America. I was disgusted. The ultimate goal of any serious play is to explore and convey the intimate dynamics of human relationships. But *Godot* and the other absurdist dramas had no use for greatness; they reveled in trivial self-absorption. In those plays the world won't end in either a bang or a whimper, as T.S. Eliot would have it, but as two hollow men on a slag heap trying unsuccessfully to make out what the other one is saying.

It's the Theater of Despair, and who needs it? It's nihilism. What's the sense in pointing out the fundamental meaninglessness of the human condition unless you can somehow offer something uplifting to address it, to overcome it

197

or at least ameliorate the absurd nature of our existence? If you can't do that, then you are just fomenting frustration and inviting your audience to wallow in self-pity. Gadg had a few things to say about the odiousness of self-pity, and he was right on target there. Look, Oedipus at least – indeed, most importantly – finally recognizes how his anger, pride and presumption undermined him, and that insight redeems his fall from fortune, and it precludes self-pity. But what redemption is there for Vladimir and Estragon as they wait for a Giver of Purpose and Meaning who will never come? However, in 1956, theater audiences, racked by Cold War fears of nuclear holocaust, found more solace in absurdity than realism, and I found myself being crowded off the stage.

CHAPTER 37

Gadg

While Art and Marilyn were playing out their fairytale in England, I was immersed in my next movie, *Baby Doll*. Even if I hadn't made it in the sexually repressed '50s, I still would have only suggested the sexual interplay between the middle-aged immigrant Silva Vacarro, played by Eli Wallach, and barely-a-woman Baby Doll Meighan, played by my newest discovery, Carroll Baker, who was by then already twenty-five, five years older than her character. Carroll projected enough latent sexuality that I had no need to be explicit. In fact, I think the movie was more erotic without showing any sex on camera at all. Apparently, Francis Cardinal Spellman thought so too, because after *Baby Doll* came out, he ascended his pulpit during a mass at St. Patrick's Cathedral for the first time since 1949 and denounced my movie for its moral turpitude. But more of that later.

Tennessee Williams had been unenthusiastic about writing the screenplay until I showed him Carroll at work at the Actors Studio. He was bowled over the minute he saw her onstage and immediately agreed to join me in rural Mississippi to make the movie. But Tennessee didn't feel comfortable there, and he left after a few days. We managed to work things out though. He sent me his corrections in the mail.

Shooting on location in Benoit, Mississippi, population 341, put me in touch with part of America I'd rarely seen before. At first the locals were suspicious of us out-of-towners, but soon enough their curiosity got the better of them, and they proved both helpful and friendly. My family joined me for the shoot, and the community embraced them, providing ponies for my children to ride and inviting us for meals and good times. Years later I still received pecans from their trees at Christmas. Some of the residents worked on the set, and I even gave a few of them small parts in the movie. The man who plays the deputy sheriff was a cotton grower with a great sense of humor and a fearlessness that I found engaging. This was my first real taste of Southern hospitality, and for an immigrant like me it made a big impression. We received more open-heartedness, more genuine hospitality in Benoit than in any other location I've worked at.

Of course, there was a dark side to rural Mississippi in the mid '50s too. Some of the locals invited me to go deer hunting with them. The experience was not just barbaric, it was primal, and that was scary. Their hunting dogs would chase down the does and fawns and bucks and rip them apart, and the hunters would hang the dead deer on a long rack with blood still oozing from their mouths. Altogether thirty animals were slaughtered in the most gruesome ways, and I never ate venison again.

Even more scary were the treacherous relations between whites and blacks. This was just two years after the Supreme Court integrated the public schools, declaring that "Separate but equal is not equal." That ruling set off the civil rights movement, but it also ignited a furious and deadly backlash in the South. Just ask Emmett Till, a black boy visiting from integrated Chicago who was murdered the year before in Money, about fifty miles from Benoit. Emmett's crime was that he'd been *talking fresh* to a white woman, something he'd taken for granted he could do back home, or at least not be butchered for it. However, a few nights later the woman's husband and his brother-in-law stormed into the house where Emmett was staying and ripped him from his grandaunt's arms, throwing the old lady onto the floor as she tried to protect him. They beat and mutilated Emmett and gauged out his eye before shooting him in the head and dumping his body in the Tallahatchie River.

The men were soon arrested, quickly put on trial, and in less than an hour an all-white jury acquitted them. Afterward, when the killers knew they couldn't be tried again for the same crime, they boasted how they'd murdered the boy. All of this struck close to home one evening during the shoot when a black man who'd somehow overstepped *his place* came up to me desperately seeking refuge. We stashed him away in a

201

trailer for two nights before someone with a car could smuggle him out.

I made friends with several of the local blacks as well as with the whites, and I cast some of them in the movie too. Mostly I just showed them looking on amused by the ridiculous antics of the whites who dominate the action. I thought it would be nice to give them the last laugh.

The plot is simple but satisfying. While Baby Doll was still a minor, her dying grandmother married her off to an older man who owned a cotton mill in order to guarantee the girl's future. But Archie Lee, the lecherous mill owner, is going mad with sexual frustration because he promised he wouldn't screw Baby Doll until she turned twenty, which is two days after my story picks up. Baby Doll, who still sleeps in a crib, wants nothing to do with Archie Lee and manages to put him off. Then she is seduced, or almost seduced, by Silva, who is taking his revenge on Archie Lee for burning down his competing mill. It doesn't really matter whether Silva actually had relations with Baby Doll. What drives Archie Lee mad is that he thinks someone he regards as an inferior immigrant did. Ultimately Archie Lee is destroyed by his greed, his racism, and his improper lust.

There's something almost Chaucerian about this story of a May–December marriage, something evocative of the "Miller's Tale" in which an old man married to a young girl is played for a cuckold and a fool. I thought *Baby Doll* was a nice little film. It wasn't a masterpiece or deeply profound, but I thought it worked, and it got some nice reviews. Carroll got an Oscar nomination for her work. So did Tennessee.

Baby Doll would have simply had its moment and come and gone like a thousand other movies, if Cardinal Spellman had not intervened. He'd gone to Korea to say a mass for the GI's over there, and "What did I find when I got home? *Baby Doll.*" The pairing of Carroll's innocence and her sexuality was too much for the old fool, and he forbade Catholics to see it "under pain of sin." Can you believe that? And he meant business too. He sent priests into theater lobbies with notebooks so they could take the names of any parishioners they spotted going in or coming out. It turned out that Spellman, that old bag of sanctified wind, never even saw the film.

"Must you have a disease to know what it is?" was his defense. I gave up on religion because of crap like that.

CHAPTER 38

Marilyn

After Art and I returned from England we rented a farmhouse in Amagansett on Long Island. The house was on a one-hundred acre parcel of land that included a working potato farm. Willem de Kooning, the artist, was our neighbor. He was cordial but we each mostly kept to ourselves. If England brought out the worst in our marriage, living by the ocean brought out the best. Art and I would drive down to the beach and walk hand-in-hand along the dunes. Sometimes I'd sit in the sun on the sand in my bathing suit and watch Art, shirtless, cast his fishing line into the crashing surf. Even though we were apart – me on land and him up to his knees in seawater – we felt so together. In England Art was often distant, stern, and preoccupied, but here, with a fresh sea breeze in our faces and the sun on our bodies, he was tender and relaxed. I was more at ease too, less consumed by anxiety and self-doubt and more receptive to his love.

Art wrote a short story about me while we were there. He called it, "Please Don't Kill Anything." He said he was trying to express my "fierce tenderness" toward everything that was alive. It touched my heart. My character in *The Misfits* is like that too, only that movie came a few years later, and I wasn't very moved by it. Funny how time changed everything. But

"Please Don't Kill Anything" made me feel the depth of Art's love.

The story is about a man and a woman who are watching a couple of fishermen on the beach. The woman is deeply distraught because instead of throwing back the fish they can't eat, the fishermen toss them onto the beach, where they flop back and forth gasping for air. Unable to watch them suffer, the woman picks up a fish and throws it into the sea. Her companion joins her, but it is clear to us and to her that he finds the dying fish repugnant and is just humoring her. As they rescue the sea robins, he explains to her in a dispassionate, scientific way how death and suffering are all part of the cycle of life. When they are done, the woman turns to him and apologizes for overreacting to the creatures' suffering. But instead of responding in a superior or patronizing way, which is what she expects, the man surprises her with his gratitude. She enabled him to save lives; fish are now swimming in the ocean because of him, and he feels a great joy in his heart because of it. And the woman replies, "Oh how I love you."

Isn't that a beautiful and tender story? I think it was Art at his best. He was always fascinated with moments of sudden insight – James Joyce called them epiphanies. I bet you didn't know I'd read James Joyce, but I did. And Tolstoy and Dostoyevsky too. Anyway, Art mostly wrote about tragic recognitions of people going to their doom, but "Please Don't

Kill Anything" turns on an insight that brings joy and love and deep connection between a man and a woman. To me it has the softness of a Monet painting and the tenderness of a Renoir.

When we weren't squirreled away in Amagansett, we were in a new apartment we'd rented in New York on 57th Street. It had a large living room filled with shelves that were stuffed with books – I loved that – and a baby grand piano opposite the fireplace. Most importantly, it had a room for Art to write in. While he was sequestered with his typewriter, I'd go off to explore the city with Norm Rothstein or take off to hang out with Paula and Lee Strasberg.

Art spent a lot of time at his writing that winter, but he wasn't happy with what he produced. For one thing, he was preoccupied with his upcoming trial for contempt of Congress. He called the proceeding, "The Case of Miller Versus American Civilization," and he believed that the whole thing was a sham, about a crime that was not a crime, and one that he did not commit. The trial was in May, and it lasted a week. Art's lawyer pointed out that the information HUAC wanted, the names of writers who'd attended certain meetings, was irrelevant to the purpose of the hearing, which was about supposed abuse of U.S. passports. But the judge didn't see it that way. For a while Art thought he might go to jail, but in the end he got a suspended sentence and a five-hundred dollar fine. But between early May1957, when Art was convicted, and mid-July, when he received the sentence, the Sword of Damocles was hanging over his head. Some of the Hollywood Ten had served a whole year for the same thing Art did, and he certainly wasn't looking forward to that. Imagine trying to write a story or a play when any day you might be torn from your home and thrown into a prison cell.

That period was tough for me too. As connected as I'd felt to Art when we were on the beach or in the farmhouse at Amagansett, I felt increasingly alone and insecure in the city. I can't fully account for that. Some of it surely had to do with my concern over Art's trial and then his conviction, plus I felt cut off from him when he'd immerse himself in his writing that was going nowhere. He didn't seem pleased with himself, and that seemed to leave him not-pleased with me. *The Prince and the Showgirl* came out in June, and it got some good reviews, and I was even nominated for a BAFTA award for best foreign actress and a Laurel award for my comedy, and I won the David di Donatello golden plate in Italy. But my experience with Olivier and the blow-ups in England with Art left a bitter taste in my mouth, and I didn't take much pleasure from my success.

In fact, I was taking increasingly less pleasure in life, and a familiar dark cloud was once again descending. I was drinking and taking more and more barbiturates, but nothing made me happy. Sometimes, the slightest little thing, even a

207

wounded seagull, would reduce me to tears. Art checked me into Doctors Hospital in Manhattan for a while because I was so depressed, although we told the press that it was to see why I was having trouble getting pregnant. Now that's something everyone woman wants to share with the world, don't you think? Let's just start a global conversation about my ovaries. My stay in the hospital didn't do much good. Not long after I got out Art caught me trying to jump from a window, and he saved me.

However, I did become pregnant early in the summer, and my depression evaporated. At least at first. I'd always wanted to have children, and now it was finally going to happen. It was my dream come true. But even my pregnancy was a source of anxiety. I'd had abortions in my time, and I didn't know if I could carry a child to term. It turns out that I couldn't. In August I felt a pain in my abdomen that was so severe it knocked me out. The fetus was ectopic – attached outside of my uterus – and the pregnancy was terminated.

I was devastated. Art and my friends tried to console me, but, really, what could they say? When I was released from the hospital, I went back to Long Island with Art and rested while he worked on a new screenplay he was writing for me, so I could really show off my acting talent. It was based on a story he'd written in England, "The Misfits." Art hoped it would lift my spirits, but I was still suffering from anxiety and panic attacks and medicating myself with pills. Art always kept track of how many I consumed, because he knew me, and sure enough, one day, when he was taking a break, he noticed that a lot were missing. He called the paramedics right away, and they rescued me. When I came to, I was so happy to be alive that all I could do at first was kiss Art's hands.

CHAPTER 39

Art

1957 was hard on us. I was convicted for contempt of Congress; Marilyn was hospitalized for depression, and after her release she tried to jump out of a window. I pulled her back just in time. Then she became pregnant and was ecstatic. But our elation turned to sudden sorrow when the fetus had to be terminated. Later, I saved Marilyn from another suicide attempt, this time with barbiturates. And that just took us to the end of summer.

My writing on the play I'd been working on forever was going nowhere. It had gone nowhere the previous summer in England, what with all the distractions from producing *A View from the Bridge* and Marilyn's tantrums on her set and in our house. Now those distractions were gone; but new concerns had taken their place, and my writing was still flat. Besides, I wasn't even sure that American audiences remained interested in the kind of drama I'd always believed in.

Moreover, day by day the outside world was becoming more fraught with danger and doom than ever before, as the threat of nuclear annihilation loomed ever greater. The atom bomb had been bad enough, but in 1952, about half a year after Gadg testified, America exploded the world's first, far-more-potent hydrogen bomb.

Naturally, the Soviets remained hard at work, and they exploded their first hydrogen bomb in '53. These H-bombs were hundreds of times more potent than the one that destroyed Hiroshima. They offered "a bigger bang for the buck," as Ike said to justify making our nuclear arsenal the cornerstone of America's military might. This had been largely a financial decision. Since we couldn't afford to match the Soviet tanks and soldiers on the ground in Europe, Ike promised "massive retaliation" (read nuclear strikes) in response to Soviet aggression, and this kept Khrushchev in check for a while. Our missiles in Europe and Turkey could reach deep into the Soviet Union, while theirs had to cross an ocean to hit us, and that distance was just too great.

But then in 1957, just weeks after Marilyn and I lost the baby and, inauspiciously, on the same day the Ford Motor Company unveiled the Edsel, which was an affront to car lovers everywhere, the Russians fired the world's first intercontinental ballistic missile. With a range of five thousand miles it could devastate the U.S. heartland, and Khrushchev was suddenly walking with newfound swagger. In November he challenged America to a rocket-range shooting match, which frankly scared the hell out of me, and after we tested our own ICBM in December, our policy of massive retaliation morphed into one of mutually assured destruction. Somehow, I never found MAD very comforting, especially after Ike had a stroke that fall, and no one seemed to know who was in charge. I literally lost sleep knowing that Tricky Dick Nixon, the old red-baiter who'd gotten his start on HUAC, might have his finger on the button.

As if the Nixon and ICBMs weren't bad enough, in October the Soviets launched Sputnik, the first satellite to leave the earth's atmosphere and orbit our planet. I remember walking along the dunes with Marilyn one dark, moonless night, listening to the waves crash against the shore, smelling the briny ocean, and feeling the cold, salty wind against our faces as we watched a miniscule speck of light inch across the sky. Tiny as it was, there was something spooky about Sputnik that evoked a sense of awe. Humanity had just taken its first baby step into outer space. And even though I knew Sputnik was harmless, it was eerie to think that a piece of Russian machinery was peering down on me, on us. Out there, exposed on the beach, there was no place to hide. Marilyn's response was even more visceral. "It gives me the creeps," she complained as she pulled her jacket tighter and shivered. "I feel violated."

We both were also distraught over the intensifying brutality against civil rights activists in the South. In earlier times we would only read about the atrocities or hear about them second-hand. But now television screens everywhere were beginning to show peaceful protestors being beaten, firehosed, and attacked by dogs; and parts of the nation, anyway, were outraged.

Marilyn had always been sympathetic to the plight of black Americans, and from time to time she'd step in to help. For instance, after she'd become a big star Marilyn learned that the owner of one of the swanky Hollywood clubs wouldn't book Ella Fitzgerald, who was then just starting out, because Ella was black. So, Marilyn phoned the owner and said that if he'd let Ella sing there, she, Marilyn, would sit at a front row table every night, and the place would be packed with fans, photographers, and reporters. He'd get lots of free publicity. The owner agreed; the press went wild, and Ella never had to play in a small jazz club again.

Many of the Southern states mightily resisted integration throughout the '50s and '60s. Some cities even shut down their public schools rather than desegregate them. At the beginning of the year four black churches were firebombed in Montgomery, Alabama, and in September a public school in Nashville was attacked. These acts of terrorism angered us and troubled us both deeply. And that's exactly what they were: acts of terrorism designed to intimidate black Americans from claiming their basic rights as citizens. But far from protecting black children and pursuing the terrorists, local authorities ignored or thwarted the law at every opportunity and left the children to fend for themselves. Peaceful acts of

213

resistance typically were met with unrestrained and unpunished violence, and Marilyn and our friends and I anguished over how all this might turn out.

"What good is the Supreme Court ruling if no one's going to enforce it?" Marilyn demanded.

Things finally came to a head at the beginning of the school year in Little Rock. In my opinion it was Eisenhower's finest hour. Orval Faubus, the governor of Arkansas, defied orders from a federal court and instructed the state's National Guard to block nine black students trying to enter Central High. Ike met personally with Faubus and insisted that the students be allowed to enroll, but Faubus kept dragging his feet. Finally, three weeks after classes had begun those nine students evaded a huge crowd rallying outside and snuck into the school through a side entrance. When the protestors found out they went berserk, shouting, "The niggers are in our school; the niggers are in our school." They threatened to break inside and lynch the black kids. A vice-principal even suggested they might have to surrender one of kids to the mob in order to distract it, so the others could escape.

The students all finally made it out alive, but the next day, in defiance of another order by Eisenhower, an even larger crowd gathered to block their entrance. So, Ike federalized the National Guard and ordered them to protect the kids now, instead of bar them, and he sent in a thousand reinforcements from the 101st Airborne Division, a unit that had distinguished itself during the Normandy D-Day invasion. The next day paratroopers faced the crowd with their bayonets fixed, and the students enrolled in the school. The soldiers left after two months, but the federalized guardsmen remained throughout the school year protecting those young men and women.

What a piece of history to witness! What an era to live through. It was terrifying and fascinating at the same time. Think about the courage those teenagers had. They knew they could have been lynched and mutilated and their killers let off scot-free. Look at what happened to Emmett Till just two years before. But they never backed down.

As we watched the showdown unfold on our black-and-white sets, we had no idea what the final outcome might be. Those kids could have been massacred, and then what? Or the crowd could have rioted and the soldiers fired on them. The dead white protestors would then have surely become martyrs, and hundreds of blacks might have been slaughtered in their name, an anti-black pogrom. Or here's another scenario. Those guardsmen, all from Arkansas, could have mutinied against Eisenhower and fought openly with the Army paratroopers. Another civil war could have broken out. What I mean is that things didn't have to play out as they did; the situation could easily have devolved into a catastrophe we couldn't even imagine, and it was frightening to try.

Nonetheless, although we paid close attention to what was going on down South and throughout the world, we had no choice but to proceed with our lives. We figured the best way to preserve our sanity and avoid despair was to keep practicing our crafts until everything blew up one way or another, KABOOM! And that's what we did.

I was working on my *Third Play*, that was the working title of the drama I'd been writing since 1952. I wanted to make a humorous tragedy that would reveal the disaster that America had become. But I wanted to do it in a very funny way, because I believed that the laughter, itself, offered our greatest hope. If only we could see our self-destructive faults and still be able to laugh at ourselves as we rectified them, we would be OK. By 1958, I'd accumulated about three thousand pages that I needed to chop down by about ninety-five percent. I hoped to have it ready for production that fall, but it didn't happen. I never could get that play to cohere.

My screenplay adaptation of "The Misfits" fared better. I thought of it as three cowboys and a girl from Nevada -- each of them terribly isolated in their own way -- trying to find or create connection in their lives. Marilyn would star in it, and privately I regarded it as her spiritual biography. She wasn't crazy about the early drafts, and she insisted on many rewrites of her lines. Marilyn often became shrill and demanding, and that wasn't much fun for me. It made me feel like just one more of her

216

flunkies instead of her life partner. But I tried to accommodate her because I wanted her to love what I was writing for her. At least Marilyn was pleased when John Huston agreed to direct. She'd liked him early in her career when they made *The Asphalt Jungle.*

At the end of summer, while *The Misfits* continued to take shape, Marilyn went out to Hollywood to shoot Billy Wilder's new comedy, *Some Like It Hot.* I'd always admired Wilder's writing as well as his directing, and I joined Marilyn out there for a while. But between her bad behavior and her endless complaints about the movie, I found it difficult to write; so I returned to New York.

In *Bus Stop* Marilyn had gotten to play a character with some depth and dimension. But in *Some Like It Hot* she reverted back to the dumb blonde roles she'd been trying to shake. So, her mood was foul and she was convinced the film was going to be a disaster. I was always having to reassure her over the phone that everything would turn out great. And it did. She had a special gift for comedy, and she nailed her part. Despite the enormous difficulties she caused on the set – Tony Curtis notoriously said that kissing her was like kissing Hitler – the movie was a great hit when it came out the next year. Wilder and Jack Lemmon each won Oscars, and Marilyn received a Golden Globe Award for best actress. Still, her success and that of the film did little to make her happy.

CHAPTER 40

Gadg

I started filming *A Face in the Crowd* right after *Baby* Doll, and it came out in May of '57. Andy Griffith made his debut in this movie, so did Lee Remick; so, I guess you can say that I discovered them. Chalk up two more for me. I'd seen Andy acting onstage in *No Time for Sergeants*, and I could tell right away that he had the folksy charm Lonesome Rhodes required. I thought they both did outstanding work, but the film didn't make a big splash. Still, it had some good reviews and was one of my personal favorites.

The idea for the movie started when Budd Schulberg and I were talking one day about Arthur Godfrey, a prominent television pitchman who'd come out of nowhere in the early days of television and amassed a vast audience with his down-home mannerisms, colloquial figures of speech, and a ukulele, all of which he used to sell soap and politics. Television wasn't even a decade old by then, but in Godfrey we could see how readily capitalists could employ the new medium to control the masses.

That reminded Budd of a conversation he'd had with Will Rogers, Jr., when Junior was running for Congress years earlier, entirely on the strength of his father's name. Will Senior was already dead by then, but he'd made himself a household icon with his homespun philosophizing, his *I never met a man I didn't like* optimism, and his cowboy's talent for twirling a rope.

"My dad was so full of shit," is what Junior told Budd over a few too many drinks. "He pretended to be just one of the guys, but the only ones he ever got close to, the only ones he ever invited over to the house, were always the richest men in L.A.: the bankers, the powerbrokers, you know, the bigwigs with money and clout. Will Rogers was a goddamn reactionary, for Christ's sake."

"Don't say that too loud," Budd warned him, "because you can't win without his legend."

After Junior sobered up he took Budd's advice, kept the legend alive, and won his seat in Congress. Budd later based a short story on what Junior told him. It's about a good-natured hillbilly with the common touch who realizes he has the power to shape his followers' politics, and I kept thinking about that story as Budd and I discussed the Arthur Godfrey phenomenon.

"What if Will Rogers had lived in the age of television?"

"Yeah, imagine that." I could see Budd trying to picture Will Senior plugging some brand of chewing tobacco while doing rope tricks on a small screen.

"So why don't we?"

"Why don't we, what?"

219

"Why don't we imagine some shrewd, cynical hick with the common touch and down-home ways turning into a huge TV star?"

"We should make him lecherous too."

"And secretly full of himself."

"He'll need a prop and a catchy name."

"How about Fred Freedom."

"Come on, Gadg, you can do better than that."

"Liberty Lane?"

"Not Liberty Lane. That's too heavy handed. But I like street concept. It projects freedom of movement and unknown possibilities ahead. But there should be a darker side too."

"A dark side will scare some people away. But if his name hints at some underlying melancholy, they might feel sorry for him."

"Women will want to comfort him."

"That's right. And men won't be threatened."

Budd paused a moment and thought. "I've got it! Lonesome Rhodes. His prop can be a harmonica."

"'Lonesome Rhodes' is perfect. But no harmonicas. They're too shrill and too small; they suggest impotence. What about a guitar?"

And we were on our way. Ultimately, our Lonesome Rhodes would become an overnight sensation who is corrupted by his newfound power and finally brought down by the woman who loves him in order to save the country and his soul. Or something like that. In addition to the political aspects of Lonesome's rise and fall I wanted to explore the theme of a woman as a man's conscience.

The movie didn't get much recognition, which was too bad. It worked. It had humor and drama. It wasn't heavy-handed, but it was prescient. Lonesome anticipated Ronald Reagan, only Ronnie didn't have a lasso or a guitar or a tragic fall from fortune. Fortunately for all of us, he went out more with a whimper than a bang.

The movie's greatest recognition came, surprisingly, from the Communists, who loved it. But that didn't stop them from twisting their knives a little deeper into Budd and me. "When two stool-pigeon witnesses before the Un-American Activities Committee conspire to produce one of the finest progressive films we have seen in years," began their review, "something more than oversimplification of motives is needed to explain it." Those pricks couldn't believe that Budd and I could have held onto our progressive values even after we turned our backs on them and their police-state tactics. They patted themselves on the back, claiming that we must have retained something from our time as Party members, and they even suggested that we'd made a progressive movie to heal our guilty consciences. Bullshit!

No one took their review seriously. No one even read it except, of course, the fanatical right-wingers at *Counterattack*. They cited the review and the film, itself, as proof that Budd and I had never really meant it when we renounced the Party. In short, we should be blacklisted and never allowed to work in Hollywood again.

This was already half a decade after I testified before HUAC, but I still couldn't shake it from the radical Right or the extreme Left. Whenever I gave a talk or made a public appearance some Party ideologue was always in the crowd ready to heckle me or accuse me of being a stool pigeon.

In fact, the Red Scare kept popping back up in different ways all throughout 1957. That summer Charlie Chapin released *A King in New York*, a brilliant spoof on HUAC. He made it in Britain, where he had been living since 1952, after the State Department barred him from reentering the country. They said it was because of Charlie's bad morals – he had a thing for underage women – but the right-wingers never minded that when it suited them not to. The real reason was they didn't like his liberal politics. Charlie was never a Party member – he told HUAC that he'd never joined any political organization in his life. But he also was never a U.S. citizen – he'd never bothered to officially immigrate. So, when he went to London to see the premier of *Limelight*, they denied him permission to return. He never again stepped foot in the United States for

222

over twenty years. What a loss for Hollywood. What a loss for America.

A King in New York is about a usurped monarch who flees to the city and is reduced to earning a living making TV commercials, giving Chaplin an opportunity to ridicule consumerism and mindless advertising. After he befriends a lively boy whose parents are Communists, the king finds himself summoned to appear before HUAC. The farce of the hearing becomes a literal farce when the king accidently turns a fire hose on the committee members and inadvertently gives them the dousing the audience knows they deserve. That's the high point of the film, but the ending isn't so happy. The committee summons and intimidates the boy, who protects his parents by informing on some of their friends. Afterward, the once-high-spirited child is beaten down and withdrawn. I liked the movie a lot when I finally got to see it. But that wasn't until 1976, when they finally showed it in America.

In June, the Supreme Court overturned several of its worst anti-Communist rulings from the late '40s and early '50s. In particular, the justices maintained that people can only be prosecuted for what they do, not for what they believe. More to the point, simply belonging to an organization whose ideology calls for the eventual overthrow of the U.S. government -- *i.e.* the Communist Party -- is not, by itself, grounds for arresting people or denying them their First Amendment protections of

223

free speech, however radical. There has to be a *clear and present danger.*

Some other outrageous rulings from the darkest days of the Red Scare were also reversed, but that was the big one. *Counterattack* went berserk, denouncing the Court and ranting on and on about "Red Monday," and J. Edgar Hoover, the fascist head of the FBI, called the ruling the greatest victory the Communist Party had ever won. Ike didn't say much publicly, but he let the chief justice know that he was mad as hell. Naturally, the Lefties were delighted and some felt vindicated, especially the Foley Square Eleven -- Party leaders who'd done prison time for violating the Smith Act, which criminalized advocating the violent overthrow of our government. The government's argument had been a huge stretch, but the Eleven were convicted anyway. The prosecution maintained that since Marx and Lenin called for the eventual overthrow of the capitalist democracies, all Communists must necessarily advocate it too. Thus mere membership in the Party, much less leadership of it, was sufficient proof of a Smith Act violation. The Eleven had already served their terms by the time the Supreme Court came to its senses and imposed the clear-and-present-danger requirement.

I.F. Stone wrote that Red Monday would go down in history as the day the Supreme Court crippled the witch hunt. Maybe, maybe not. The ruling that really brought the witch hunt to its knees came in 1962, and it wasn't about politics at all. It was about money. Surprised?

In a case of mistaken identity one of the organizations whose self-appointed mission was to expose Commies and fellow travelers listed John Henry Faulk, a Texas humorist and radio personality, as having Communist ties. Faulk was blacklisted as a result of the error, and he sued the agency for libel. It took seven years, but eventually a jury awarded Faulk three-and-a-half million dollars. Later, of course, that amount was chopped down by a lot, and I don't know if Faulk ever collected a cent. I'm sure those sanctimonious sleaze balls, who never took responsibility for anything, did all they could to stiff him.

Until the Faulk judgment, publishing blacklists could bring in big bucks with little risk, if you played it right. Not only would these creeps sell their lists to movie studios, local television stations, national networks, and other places that were terrified of boycotts and bad publicity if it came out that they'd hired Reds or Red sympathizers, they also sold "clearance" services for restoring the good names of writers, actors, and directors on their lists and getting them back to work.

That often entailed arranging some act of public contrition and repudiation. Julie Garfield, for instance, had been desperate to be cleared. His was in his prime of his

225

career, but the blacklist derailed him. The poor bastard couldn't even sell out if he wanted to, because he had never been in the Party or even been a fellow traveler. So he didn't have any names to name. But naming names was the acid test for demonstrating your loyalty, and if you didn't do it, everyone concluded you were secretly on the side of the Commies, and on the list you went. So, Julie was screwed. What was he supposed to do? Make up names?

Finally, he hired a clearance man to rehabilitate him, and the clearance guy arranged for him to publish an article in *Look* magazine, "I Was a Sucker for a Left Hook." The title played off Julie's well-known passion for boxing. But Julie never found out if his act of penance was enough to do the trick, because he dropped dead from a heart attack about a month after I testified. You know, his funeral was the biggest one New York had seen since Rudy Valentino's way back when. Thousands of people filled the streets. They loved him; he was such a sweet guy. He was only thirty-nine. Julie had a family history of heart disease, and he was going through a divorce, but all the shit those heartless sons-of-bitches put him through sure didn't help. A lot of us thought the stress killed him. Not long after he died, HUAC concluded that there was no convincing evidence that he had ever been a Red, and it closed the investigation. A lot of good that did Julie in his grave.

My point is that the listing agencies got the poor bastards coming and going -- sort of a capitalist version of Stalin's more brutal reeducation and rehabilitation practices. But once the blacklisters found out they could be held financially accountable for their recklessness, they quickly leapt back into pond scum from which they'd risen.

Humphrey Bogart died in January and Joe McCarthy died about a month before *A Face in the Crowd* came out. Bogie was felled by throat cancer – no surprise there, the way he smoked. And Tail-Gunner Joe croaked from hepatitis caused by alcoholism – no surprise there either.

Few people remember that when the Hollywood Ten were summoned before HUAC in '47, Bogie and Bacall and a bunch of other Hollywood big names joined the Committee for the First Amendment and traveled to Washington in a strong show of liberal support. That is until they found out that these guys really were Communists. Can you believe it? They didn't know. Lawson was a Party theorist, for Christ's sake, as Red as they come. Bogie, Bacall, and their pals tucked their tails between their legs and went crying back to Hollywood, complaining that the Ten had duped them. A lot of those liberal suckers found themselves blacklisted for all their good intentions. But Bogie published an article explaining how he'd been misled, and since he was a cash cow for the studio, his public act of contrition was deemed acceptable, and he kept his job.

I was sorry when Bogie died, I really was. But, as someone once said, the trouble was Bogie was that he thought he was Bogart. He was trying to take a heroic and principled stand like Rick does at the end of *Casablanca*, but he didn't know what the fuck he was talking about. Anyway, I confess to some residual resentment of Bogie too. Nobody derided *him* for turning against the Reds he once supported.

CHAPTER 41

Marilyn

I lost another baby! I'd gotten pregnant when Art was visiting while we shot *Some Like It Hot*, unless it was when Tony Curtis and I rekindled our old flame while Art was busy working on *The Misfits* in New York. Actually, that never happened. True, Tony and I had had a fling a decade earlier; I'd had a lot of flings back then. But he was furious with me on the set, and that carried over off the set too. He didn't want to fuck me then. I was such a perfectionist when I acted, and I made him do take after take with me until I was satisfied I'd nailed it. Once I took three days just to shoot a short sequence that most actors could do in an hour. Tony couldn't stand all the repetition and the endless waiting around. Plus, I cried every time I screwed up, and my tears would ruin my make-up; so, he'd have to cool his heels even longer while they applied it again. Billy Wilder, the director, couldn't stand the delays either, but I had to get it right. Plus, I'd been taking a lot of pills and showing up late pretty often and forgetting my lines. None of that really bothered me. I was the big star, after all, the money in the bank; so being late was one of my perks. Call it a fringe benefit. But it meant more waiting for everyone else and a bigger hole in the budget.

I was being a bitch because Sugar Kane was still just another dumb blonde. I thought Billy was going to do something more for me, although I guess the movie's particular humor requires Sugar to be mostly one-dimensional. Tony, Billy, and even Jack Lemmon, who was the epitome of patience and good will, were barely speaking to me by the time the filming ended, much less screwing me. So I don't know why Tony thought he needed to brag in his autobiography that he'd been doing me, and that the baby I'd conceived was his. And as long as he was making up shit, why not embellish even more. He claimed that he found out I was pregnant while we were confessing our affair to Art, who told Tony to finish the film and then stay the hell out of our lives. As a matter of fact, that *is* how Art probably would have responded; but the whole thing was bullshit, a complete fabrication.

I tried so, so hard to be careful once I found out I was going to have a baby. I stopped drinking and cut out all the pills except my sleeping pills. I absolutely needed my Amytal. I even took an ambulance to the airport when we finished the shoot and flew back home to New York. But then I did a stupid thing. I forgot that I was never to take Amytal on an empty stomach. And I drank some sherry. Could that have been what killed my baby? Could that have been why I miscarried after only three months? I tortured myself over that possibility for a long, long time.

New Year wasn't much fun for me, and the winter of '59 felt cold and dark and bleak. I was still recovering physically and mentally from the miscarriage and was frequently bloated and back to popping pills, which never cheered me or relaxed me as much as I wanted them to.

Fortunately, there were some bright spots. I enjoyed fixing up our apartment and inviting Art's parents over for dinner or just to visit. It gave me such pleasure to be around them and dote on them. Especially Izzy, his father. We really hit it off. Somehow Izzy understood me better than almost anyone I ever knew, even Art. They were the parents I never had.

I got to talk books one day with Carson McCullers and Isak Dinesen. And Carl Sandburg, the poet, often stopped by to discuss literature and have fun play acting and doing imitations. I'd met Carl in California, and he was a good friend; we shared some great laughs together.

But Art, for all of his proclamations of deep, abiding love, was growing more distant and detached. And judgmental. While my star was still rising, his seemed to be setting, and that was hard on him. On me too. I think there's a movie about that. Oh yes, *A Star is Born*. I had always looked to Art, an older and successful man, to be my literary and cultural mentor, but now sometimes it seemed as though our roles had reversed, and he had started calling on me to be his muse. I never signed up for that. I didn't want to inspire his creativity or

231

have my life serve as fodder for his stories. I wanted to be his wife.

CHAPTER 42

Art

Not long after Billy Wilder broke the set on *Some Like It Hot*, Khrushchev initiated a second crisis in Berlin in November 1958. It persisted on and off for three years as the most dangerous period in the Cold War, until it was superseded in 1962 by the Cuban Missile Crisis. The first Berlin Crisis came in 1948-49, when Stalin closed off access to West Berlin, and Truman averted a head-on confrontation by air-lifting coal and food to the cold and hungry West Berliners, who were surrounded by communist East Germany on every side.

But now it didn't seem like the solution would be so easy, not that making those dangerous flights over Soviet-controlled territory had ever been easy. Everyone believed the Soviets had missile superiority over us – the infamous "missile gap" that Kennedy harped on when he was going after Eisenhower and Nixon. It turned out not to be true – something we learned later, after we developed reconnaissance satellites. But what mattered was that everyone believed it, including the Russians. So Khrushchev issued an ultimatum: evacuate West Berlin within six months, or else. Naturally, Ike refused to back down, and we began a three-year period when all-out nuclear war appeared to be not only possible but likely.

233

In other words, the extinction or near-extinction of the human race seemed to be at hand. Armageddon. No wonder church attendance was never higher, and fire-and-brimstone preachers and television evangelists like Billy Graham, who shouted from his pulpit that communism was masterminded by Satan, amassed vast flocks of followers. Between fall 1958 and fall 1961, if the threat of total annihilation wasn't making headlines, it loomed constantly over our heads, ready to destroy human civilization at a moment's notice. How much of Marilyn's anxiety, and my own, stemmed from that? How big a role did it play in her miscarriage or the dissolution of our marriage? I've often wondered.

Surprisingly, Marilyn played her own small role during the Berlin Crisis. As crises go, this one was bipolar. One day Khrushchev would threaten all-out war; the next he'd support a UN resolution calling for peaceful exploration of outer space. One day he'd be lecturing Nixon in their "kitchen debate" on the virtues of communism and the inevitable decline of the West; the next he'd announce a friendly visit to the United States. One day we'd be checking the supply cabinets in our bomb shelters, if we had one -- a whole new industry sprang up in months -- then the next day things would cool off and life could return to "normal." By the way, did you know that *snafu* really stands for *Situation Normal: All Fucked Up*? Increasingly *snafu* was the new normal for my marriage to Marilyn.

In September, Marilyn was in Hollywood filming *Let's Make Love*, a musical she was making with Yves Montand, when Khrushchev dropped-in to Hollywood as part of his unprecedented tour of America. The visit produced a great thaw in the Cold War and raised our hopes, however briefly, for an end to the ongoing nuclear brinkmanship. Without even trying, Marilyn used her sex appeal to stir the passion in Khrushchev's blood and turn up the flame that was melting the ice between our nations.

What happened was this. The film industry held a fancy banquet for Khrushchev at Fox's prestigious commissary, Café de Paris. All the stars came out to see Nikita, who, far from seeming like the ruthless tyrant that he was, projected a warm and friendly persona during his U.S. visit. Ike and Nikita both came across as the kindly grandfathers we always wanted. They could have done laxative commercials together.

Khrushchev was often photographed dressed casually and laughing heartily. The invasion of Hungary and his promise to the West that, "We will bury you," were already three years in the past – ancient history to Americans. And everyone, especially all the big-name liberals, wanted to believe in the robust, good-natured dictator who'd come to visit, the one with a hearty laugh and a passion for sharp repartee.

He gave as good as he got; no one pushed him around, that's for sure. But Nikita didn't seem unreasonable; he came across as a man with good intentions. Apparently, he'd discarded Marx and Lenin's insistence on the inevitable triumph of communism over capitalism and professed instead a desire for peaceful coexistence, a willingness to live and let live. I confess I wanted to believe in him too and was disappointed when I was not invited to his reception. But, although I was a celebrity of some renown in my own right, as well as Marilyn's husband, my tangle with HUAC kept me off the guest list. Apparently, I was too un-American, too much in league with the Reds, to greet the leader of world communism.

Marilyn went. She was seated at the main table along with other A-list stars. There were, of course, the requisite speeches. Gadg's pal Spyros Skouras described how he'd arrived in America as an impoverished immigrant, and now, because of the American system, he was the president of 20th Century Fox. Everyone applauded and even Khrushchev praised Skouras for what he'd achieved. Then he topped him. "I worked in a factory for a German. Then I worked in a French-owned mine. Today, I am the premier of the great Soviet state," and the audience laughed.

Khrushchev went on in a mostly good-natured way, making observations from his trip about the American system – he found Can-Can decadent. Then he would point out how the Soviet way was better. Would you expect any different? Isn't that what Nixon tried to do to him in the Kitchen Debate? But,

236

according to everyone I spoke to who was there, he seemed genuinely enraged when, for some unexplained reason, his planned trip to Disneyland was abruptly cancelled.

"Just now, I was told that I could not go to Disneyland. Why not? Do you have rocket-launching pads there?" The audience laughed, but as he continued his anger became apparent.

"Is there an epidemic of cholera there?" Khrushchev demanded. "Have gangsters taken hold of the place? For me, such a situation is inconceivable. I cannot find words to explain this to my people." His face turned red, and he started punching the air as he spoke. That's how he could get. His daughter later described how he would curse his opponents, interrupt them and bang his fists on the table, pound his feet, and even whistle and hoot when something set him off. A year after this Hollywood tirade Khrushchev famously took off his shoe and banged it on his desk to protest a speaker at the United Nations.

Imagine if World War III had started because the head of worldwide communism could not get into Disneyland. Maybe Beckett and the absurdists were on to something after all. With apologies to T.S. Eliot, who should apologize for enabling Ezra Pound, "This is the way the world ends. This is the way the world ends. Not with a bang but a" *tantrum*.

Finally, whoever was running the show got around to introducing Khrushchev to the celebrities. When it was Marilyn's turn, he smiled at her, gazed into her eyes and then down her dress. He shook her hand so firmly she said it hurt for days.

"It was like he was claiming me, seizing his property. He didn't let me go. He looked at me the way a man looks at a woman – that's how he looked at me."

When Khrushchev finally released his grip, they talked through an interpreter. Marilyn spoke of her passion for Dostoyevsky and how she'd always wanted to play Grushenka in an adaptation of *The Brothers Karamazov*. Reporters used to laugh when she said that, which is why she wanted to shake her dumb-blonde persona so badly. Whenever she tried to talk about literature or art or ideas, people imagined Lorelei Lee or Sugar Kane, and they didn't take her seriously. That's why she so valued her friends who did. That's why she returned home elated after her afternoon discussing poetry with Carson McCullers and Isak Dinesen.

Khrushchev seemed to take her thoughts about Grushenka seriously, or so she said. But I wonder what are the chances that an ex-pipe-fitter like Nikita Khrushchev ever even read Dostoyevsky, much less gave a thought to Grushenka. I doubt he spent any time with the classics, even the Russian classics. He never finished high school, and later he was busy running a revolution, then fighting off Nazis, starving out Ukrainian farm owners, and ingratiating himself with Stalin. So, Khrushchev was probably faking it so *she* wouldn't think *he* was stupid and uncultured. How's that for a reversal? The man who was then perhaps the most powerful person in the world felt the need to impress *her* with his erudition. Khrushchev asked Marilyn to visit Russia sometime, and she told him she'd love to.

"He liked my tits," she confided to me. "I could tell by the way he kept looking down at them." Then she giggled. "I confess my dress gave him something to look at. But finally I had to let him know I was a married woman, so I told him, 'My husband, Arthur Miller, sends you his greetings.'"

Khrushchev finally moved on to the next celebrity, but he was charmed. Marilyn, not so much. She conceded to me later that she liked the way he'd thrown Skouras' life-story back in his face, and she admired his plainness. I think she identified with his rags-to-riches biography and the way he'd always been an outsider. She might even have appreciated his tantrum, something else they had in common. But then she told me Khrushchev was fat and ugly with warts on his face.

"And he growled. He squeezed my hand so long and hard that I thought he would break it. I guess it was better, though, than if I'd had to kiss him, even on the cheek." Marilyn made a face and shuddered at the very thought.

239

Nikita Khrushchev had greater rocket thrust and a bigger payload than any man alive, even more than Ike and his bigger-bang-for-the-buck. But apparently Khrushchev was one rival I didn't have to worry about. Ike turned her off too, and Jack Kennedy had not yet arrived on the scene.

Yves Montand was another matter.

CHAPTER 43

Gadg

1959 was the year I got in touch with my anger. I'd always prided myself on my open-mindedness, my ability to see both sides of an argument, my willingness to take my critics seriously and consider the possibility that they might be right. I'd long parted from the Church, but I saw Christian virtue in my humility and my willingness to turn the other cheek -- or submit to Party discipline -- although, of course, I finally reached my limit with the latter.

My new shrink, Dr. Harold Kelman, helped me see that all this fair-mindedness, this willingness to see things from others' point-of-view, might have been awfully evolved and civilized of me, but for the fact that I had been unconsciously using it to suppress my rage, a hidden fury that I felt comfortable releasing only in front of Molly, who'd been complaining about it ever more frequently.

Dr. Kelman referred to it as my *lump* – a repressed, amorphous mass of resentment, anger, and spite. I'd been telling myself for years that I could take it, that I was impervious to all the hatred directed at me since I cooperated with HUAC, that sticks and stones could break my bones, but names could never harm me. My sessions with Dr. Kelman showed me I was wrong.

"Have you had an ulcer or gall stones or heartburn or other problems with your digestion?" he wondered. "Those ailments are often your unconscious self's way of letting you know that you don't have the *gall* to stand up for yourself anymore, and that it cannot *stomach* your self-deceit any longer."

I touched a place on my left side where I'd been feeling a persistent, dull ache for a year or more. It had become an ongoing presence. Most of the time I could block it from my mind, except for when I couldn't.

"It could be related," he acknowledged. "But my greater fear is that over time your emotional lump could become a physical one."

"A tumor? Cancer?"

He nodded.

"Nothing showed up during my last physical. I haven't had any symptoms."

"So far so good. Let's keep it that way." Then he bent forward and looked me directly in the eyes. "You've told me how your old friends have been kicking the hell out of you for years, and that you've responded with silence. You never protested; you never got angry; you never even defended your position, which, by the way, I think was the correct one. Why should you sacrifice everything to protect people who despise you and who are in league with our enemy?"

"I've got a grip on my temper."

"No!" The word erupted from his mouth and slapped me across my face. "You only think you do." He looked hard at me. "That grip will become a real lump some day and kill you, unless you do something about it. Why are you so ready to forgive your murderers?"

"I don't forgive them."

"How would anyone know? You don't say a word. You swallow your rage. You know, every time you suppress an impulse to lash out, you betray yourself." Then he spoke deliberately, with slow emphasis: "Self-betrayal is the worst kind."

I pursed my lips and nodded my head slightly to acknowledge what he was saying. I didn't like hearing it, but I couldn't deny it.

"That's why you've been feeling empty and detached from yourself and your wife and lovers. That's why you're here."

And I cried. I sobbed.

Dr. Kelman sat silently while I fought back my tears. When I was capable of listening, he spoke again. "That's the first emotion you've shown since you've come here, even though we've been talking about your life and your death. Think about that."

Finally, I found my voice. "Why do you call it a lump?"

My question was genuine. I truly wanted to know. But it was also a manipulation, a way from diverting our discussion from what I'd found so painful: my self-betrayal."

Dr. Kelman either missed the diversion, which I doubt, or he simply chose to ignore it. "Deep down inside, where you once were vibrant and alive, is an inert lump that refuses to be awakened. It can't feel pain or anger, but the price for that is you can't feel joy or love. It's as if something has died of neglect. You're ashamed to let me see you cry, even though it's the first sign of real life you've shown since you entered the room. Think about that. And ask yourself when this lump first started to form? Was it with HUAC or before?"

I pondered his question silently for several moments. Then I spoke. "My family lived in Turkey under the Ottoman Empire, when Greeks in Turkey had no rights and were treated like shit. Worse than shit. Then we came to America when I was a boy, and we were still powerless: impoverished immigrants struggling to survive in a strange, new land. Suppressing our anger, our outrage and resentment was a survival skill. If my father had told the Turks what he really thought, or even let it show in a fleeting expression across his face, he'd have been dead, and I'd never have been born."

Dr. Kelman nodded. "I'm sure there's something to that, but go deeper, to some hidden fear that is even more threatening than an Ottoman with a sword or a policeman with a billy club."

Again, I sat silently for quite a while. Then, finally, "My father."

Dr. Kelman nodded but said nothing.

"He was so severe. He never approved of me. He thought I was worthless, that I'd never amount to shit. And he'd tell that to anyone who'd listen."

"Pardon the cliché," Dr. Kelman shifted in his chair, "but how did that make you feel?"

"I felt hurt and humiliated. I wanted to smash him in the face. Or kick him in the balls."

Still Dr. Kelman said nothing.

"Of course, he'd have broken my skull if I did. He was so strong, and I was so weak by comparison. I was powerless, so I had to smile and take it."

"That's a good start, Elia. But maybe a little too pat. We can pick it up from there at our next session. Meanwhile, think some more about you and your father. Also, ask yourself if there's another fear trapped at even deeper level that you don't consciously perceive. The way Nietzsche would put it, I think, is to ask, if you weren't worrying about your father, what *would* you be worrying about."

"I'm not sure I get it."

"Our neuroses can be like those bombs with multiple triggers that the Germans rigged during the war. A sapper might get the first one, or even the first two, and think he'd defused the bomb, but sometimes there'd be yet another one deeper inside the mechanism that he missed."

"*Kaboom*," I whispered.

"Yes. *Kaboom*."

All his talk of hidden triggers made me anxious. I twisted in the chair and changed the subject. "I won't be back for a while. It seems like a coincidence, although I know Freud says there are no coincidences, but I'm traveling to Turkey to do research for a film I want to make. I'm going to trace my ancestry and get some sense of what life was like for my father and my uncle and why they were so driven to come to America. This session gives me a lot to think about over there."

"Yes, you mentioned you are going away. You hadn't said why. Think about that too. It's a shame you must leave now. You've had a big breakthrough today, and it would be very useful to follow up on it soon. You know, strike while the iron is hot."

I winced at the expression but said nothing.

"OK. You are going. Have a good trip and see me when you get back."

My trip to Turkey resurrected *America, America,* a project I'd been thinking about for some time. Its genesis had come four years earlier, when I first went to Istanbul to explore my roots and get a feel for life as a Greek living under Turkish rule. This was to be research for a screenplay I hoped to write about my uncle Avraam, later known as Joe, who, in the 1890s, had made the treacherous trip from a remote and barren region in Anatolia to Constantinople (now called Istanbul), where he finally managed to sneak aboard a ship bound for New York City. The closest American analogy would be to a black teenager traveling alone across the American South during the worst days of Jim Crow, carrying all of his family's hopes and aspirations, and its fortune, on his back. After Uncle Avraam got settled in America, he brought over my father and his family. I was four years-old. Then, eventually, his sister came and his stepbrothers and stepmother, whom I remembered so warmly. She used to take me into her bed and tell me about life in the old country and how we had escaped and started a new life in America. I never forgot her stories.

Molly accompanied me on that first trip. She liked the idea of my making a movie about Uncle Avraam but questioned my intention to write it myself. Molly, of course, was a writer, and I think that secretly she felt threatened by my desire to become one too. My career already far outshined hers, but at least we'd never been in direct competition. What if I eclipsed her with the written word too?

Of course, she didn't say it that way. "Stick with what you already know, at what you're good at – directing. Why the hell do you need to be a writer too?" was how she put it.

But who else knew my uncle's story as well as I? Who knew the culture from which he sprang, the sounds of the men arguing over raki, or the women gossiping in the kitchen as they baked eggplant and stuffed grape leaves? Or the rhythms of my countrymen's language, their aspirations and their fears? No, I insisted, I must write the screenplay myself.

We sailed across the Atlantic Ocean and through the Straights of Gibraltar into the Mediterranean Sea and on to Athens. We spent a few days in Greece and visited the sites; then we flew to Istanbul, where we were greeted by relatives I barely remembered, if I remembered them at all. They were delighted to see me. To them, I was the Greek who had left to go to America and made it big, but never forgot where he came from or the people he'd left behind. After all, we all shared the same complexion, the same eyes and nose and manner and memories. They loved it that I still spoke the language. And after all the hostility I still faced in Hollywood, their joy at seeing me lifted my spirits enormously.

I spent two weeks with my cousin Stellio. We were almost exactly the same age, and I realized his life would essentially have been my own, if my father, still a young man with few belongings, had not gathered his family and followed his brother to America. I came privately to think of Stellio as my discarded self.

The first thing I noticed about Stellio was his furtiveness, his efforts to keep from being noticed. Right away he told me not to draw attention to myself, even though I was a celebrity. I should be discreet and make as few public statements as possible. When we walked through the city he would slither against the buildings, keeping as far from the street as possible. He reminded me of small animals that, being easy prey for their predators, dart from their holes, take what they food they can quickly gather, and then scurry back inside.

Stellio took me through the parts of Istanbul where Armenian and Greek merchants like my uncle had sold their wares in better times. Once the buildings had been decorated and painted and well maintained, but now everything was squalid. Horses and donkeys competed with handcarts and automobiles for room on the narrow, curving, cobblestone roads. The horses were beaten routinely, and the donkeys prodded with sharp sticks that pierced their skin and left open wounds for flies to feast on. Men stood on corners hawking fruit, baked goods, nuts and candies for sale. Others offered cool water by the glass, while cripples and indigents begged for food and money.

On the waterfront I observed hamals, human beasts of burden, carrying on their backs heavy loads that went into the cargo holds of the ships docked at piers along the Bosporus. The hamals were treated little better than the horses and donkeys, and when I looked closely in their eyes – the window to their soul – I often saw that the spark had gone out. They were spiritless, totally beaten down, the end products of deep despair.

Finally, the sounds of the street distracted me. The voices of the beggars and hawkers, of the merchants loafing outside their stores, and the urchins chasing each other among the stalls formed a kind of poetry in my mind, and I knew right away that I must make my movie here, in the same setting my father and uncle had fled so many years before. I knew also that a hamal would be the hero.

After a few days Stellio drove us to Ankara, the capital of Turkey, a country whose western foot stands firmly in Europe but whose eastern leg is planted in Asia. Ankara is in Anatolia, the Asian side. We passed women working in the fields on their hands and knees, while the men sat around in town, inside coffee shops where they bickered and played backgammon. As we drove, Stellio told us about what amounted to a pogrom that had taken place some years earlier in the Greek and Armenian section of Istanbul, where Stellio lived with his family and ran a small store that provided cotton goods to merchants in rural Anatolia. Alone with us in the car Stellio could speak freely and with feeling.

"I'm convinced the government was behind it. One night, hundreds of criminals from the interior, drunk on raki, poured into the Greek quarter and ransacked it. They took anything that caught their eye and defiled the rest." Stellio paused a moment. "That included girls and women, and sometimes even young boys."

Molly and I were shocked. "How could such a thing occur?" she demanded. "Did they destroy your store?"

"No. They didn't touch it. I had a Turkish friend, another merchant in the cotton district. These outrages happened every so often. They were supposed to appear spontaneous, but in fact they were planned, and my friend happened to learn when this one was going to be unleashed upon our market. The day before he came by my store and placed a tiny crescent over my door where no one would notice it, unless they were looking for it. He told me to keep my family inside with the windows barricaded until the rioting subsided."

"Like the Jewish Passover," Molly pointed out. "The protective mark over the door," but Stellio just shrugged to show he didn't know what she was talking about.

"For three days we stayed in the back room listening to the sounds of drunken men cursing, windows crashing, glass breaking, girls shrieking, women screaming, and children

251

crying. When it finally seemed safe, we ventured outside. Every Greek store had been destroyed but mine. The few cotton products that hadn't been looted littered the streets and were ruined beyond repair by mud, sewage, and donkey dung. Years of hard work undone in three days. For nothing. It broke my heart. That night I took my friend to dinner."

"That's horrible!" Molly was indignant as only Molly could be. "What did the authorities do?"

"The authorities," Stellio laughed bitterly. "The authorities were behind the whole thing. They were the ones who rounded up the criminals, pointed them our way, liquored them up with cheap raki -- a full bottle apiece -- and told them to take whatever they wanted, so long as it was Greek or Armenian. Intermittent rape and pillaging were the Turks' way of reminding us outsiders who was in charge, of keeping us in our place. I was just lucky to have a connected friend."

"Keeping us in our place," I muttered, thinking about what was going on in the American South.

In Ankara I watched Stellio kneel and kiss the hand of the local Turkish strongman, much like Brando's suppliants when he was playing the Godfather. As an American, this show of submission wasn't expected of me, but for Stellio it was required. Stellio had arranged the meeting so I could hear from the strongman's own lips the Turkish line on how Greeks in his country fared. Secret police filled the corridor leading to his

252

room. They were big, powerful men who never smiled, and instinctively I became fearful and circumspect, afraid to ask or say anything that might upset my host. In short, I became Stellio. Only Molly was not intimidated, and she asked the only meaningful questions from our group.

After Ankara, Stellio and I went on to Kayseri, the city where my uncle and father grew up. Molly, who'd developed a bad cold and an abhorrence of Turkey's treatment Greeks and Armenians, flew back to New York. Kayseri was half a century behind Istanbul. Few automobiles maneuvered down the narrow, partially paved streets. Instead donkeys, hamals, and horse-drawn carts carried goods to their destinations. Unlike in Istanbul, which was already becoming Westernized, Kayseri women wore burkas that concealed all but their eyes, and no woman went out in public unaccompanied by a man who walked several feet in front of her. It's probably just as well that Molly missed that. I don't think she'd have been able to contain her outrage.

Stellio took me to the office of Osman Kavundju, the Turkish governor of the province. A very small man with one leg shorter than the other, Osman, as he soon had me call him, was the opposite of the godfather I'd met in Ankara. He projected warmth and seemed genuinely happy to meet me and show off the progress the region was making under his administration. We quickly became friends.

Osman insisted on taking me around for the next few days, proudly showing me new factories for sugar, textiles, and rugs that were springing up throughout the province, providing jobs for the local residents, bolstering the economy, and lifting the standard of living. On the second day he brought me to what had once been the Greek part of the city, where my father had grown up. The well-kept homes had deteriorated; now entire impoverished families shared a single room. No Greeks had resided in Kayseri since 1922, when, as Osman put it, they "moved out of the city" following the victory over Germany that left Turkey in complete control of Anatolia.

"Moved out, or were moved?" I asked. It sounded to me like what would later be called ethnic cleansing. Osman simply shrugged. History was what it was. Nothing could be done about it.

Stellio and I drove back to Istanbul a day or two later, and I prepared to return home to America. But first I spent two days following hamals around the docks, secretly taking notes on what they did, what they ate, what languages they spoke, where they were from, and anything else that might give me some clue about their interior life. When I needed a break I'd meet Stellio at a restaurant, and he would talk to me about my father, who'd been greatly admired for his cleverness and his ability to navigate among the many dangers that threatened ethnic Greeks. My father, after all, had been smart enough to

254

get out and take his family with him before World War I erupted, and the Ottoman Empire collapsed, and Turkey fell into murderous chaos.

"You owe him a great debt," Stellio insisted. "You should kiss his feet the next time you see him." This was a far cry from the way I typically regarded my father, who could be a real S.O.B., but I began to see that Stellio had a point.

The night before I left, Stellio and his wife threw a banquet in my honor. Many of my cousins came and the wine flowed freely. I was happy among my relatives, who were interesting and well educated, kind and discreet. More discreet than I. After I'd emptied several glasses, I started saying how impressed I was by what was happening in Kayseri and how well Osman had treated us. I spoke of the new factories and other signs of progress and of my hope that perhaps a new era was beginning, one where the enmity of the past could be put behind us, and bonds of trust and good will between Greeks and Turks could be forged.

My words were not well received. Stellio's wife, Vili, took special offense. She spoke to me, but she glared at her husband as the words poured from her mouth, as though somehow he was responsible for what I'd said.

"It's easy for you, Elia, to go where you want and say what you think and be so brave, and then come here and tell us

255

how we must understand the Turk, when we're the ones who've lived here all our lives under his foot."

Her words stung like a slap across the face.

Next, she addressed her husband directly. "Yes, it's easy for him to talk big and play the hero. But Stellio, you don't have an American passport in your pocket, do you?"

Then she turned to me again. "Did Stellio here tell you how they broke into his store the first time and threw everything into the filth outside, and how, except for a friend, they would have done it again?"

"Yes, he told me how a Turkish friend had put a tiny crescent over your door, and that spared you. Don't you think that proves my point that there are good Turks as well as bad ones, and we mustn't think of them as our enemies forever?"

"*Had* a friend," Vili laughed bitterly. He *bought* himself a friend. I guess that makes him clever." Stellio tried to interrupt her, but Vili was all worked up and would have none of it. "Did he tell you how many of his own best customers he freely sent over to this Turk, his competitor, asking nothing in return? How he always had me bake something extra for the Turk, no matter what I was making? How we would shorten our vacations and give our remaining days at the island cottage to him and his families? Yes, that's *families*. The pig had two wives."

"My investment paid off, didn't it?" Stellio shouted back. "We survived when everyone else was destroyed."

256

"At what price? At what price? Is this any kind of example for your sons? Does it teach them how to be strong; or does it show them that Greeks must kiss the Turk's ass in order to survive?"

With that Vili stormed from the room, slamming the door behind her. The party broke up soon after, and Stellio came over to me to apologize.

"She's had some scary moments on the streets. To tell you the truth, although I wish she'd been more tactful, I agree with what she said. We have no rights here in Turkey, only favors that our masters bestow upon us from time to time, favors they can retract at a moment's notice."

I told him I understood, and shortly afterward we said goodnight. On my walk back to the hotel I asked myself if Stellio was tough enough to uproot his family from everyone and everything they knew and escape this life that so clearly was emasculating him. I had my doubts. But in thinking about Stellio I also began to think about my father and about how tough he was. For the first time I started to understand him and, for the first time, I respected him and what he'd done.

That was my first trip to Turkey, back in 1955. Now, four years later, I was about to return, wondering whether I was tough enough to escape the life that was snuffing out my spirit.

I wanted to visit Germeer, the town where my mother's family had lived. It was on a mountaintop, and I was especially interested in the part that resided on the face of a steep cliff that looked down upon a valley below. So, I flew to Turkey and took a train to Ankara, where Osman greeted me at the station. He now lived in the capital, as he'd been made a member of parliament, and, diminutive and crippled as he was, he walked a swagger I hadn't seen before.

We went straight from the train station to the airport, where an Army plane was waiting to fly us to Kayseri, an hour away. From there we went straight to Germeer, where the locals had prepared a banquet in my honor. There was much joy and dancing and singing, but only among the men. The women, clad from head-to-toe in their black burkas, remained in the kitchen or otherwise out of sight. The food was tasty, the wine flowed freely, and I confess I had a good time. But I missed the company of women, and I was ready to sleep. So I excused myself before the last of the fires was extinguished.

That night I dreamt of my father. Uncharacteristically, he was smiling at me, but it was the smile of the man trying to curry favor, to get along, to reassure that he was harmless and non-threatening. I heard him say, "So now you know what it's like here. How do you like it?" And then his face turned into my own, and I was saying, "Don't be mad at me; I can take it," all the while choking on my own fury as I shoved it deep inside of me where it couldn't erupt, where, instead, it was forming a lump.

My dream scared me awake, and it stayed with me. I remembered how my father would frequently rage throughout the house, often directing his temper at me; but he never showed his anger outside our home or to an American. It crossed my mind that I had been the same way with Molly. I felt safe to lash out at her when no one else was around. Why? Because she never threatened me.

Now that I was in Germeer I was gaining some sense of how life must have been for Greeks in Anatolia seventy-five years earlier, and I wondered if I would have ever had the luxury of displaying anger outside my home. Or would I, like my father, have learned early on that my survival required me to push my resentment and my rage deep within. And then I wondered if my father had had a lump like mine.

Soon after daylight I got a ride to the cliff and found a goat path that led to the top. As I ascended, I passed caves where my ancestors once had lived and where, later on, they hid for safety when bands of Turkish marauders would terrorize them, believing that they would be rewarded in heaven for killing as many non-believers as they could. Now a few old and impoverished dwellers occupied some of the caves, although, of course, they were not Greek. The Greeks had been long displaced.

When I finally reached the summit I was surrounded in silence, and I stood on the precipice looking out onto the vast plain below. I recalled Dr. Kelman's words once again, and for the first time I felt anger toward my so-called friends who had hurt me. And I recognized that my struggle to maintain my dignity and self-respect after HUAC was actually a battle for my soul. What a slap in the face that was! I suddenly realized I could be become just like a hamal if I lost that battle, a spiritless zombie, the walking dead.

I felt the anger I'd suppressed when former friends and confidants would turn their backs on me as I passed them on the street, and when I learned how they'd try to convince actors not to work with me. When Marlon Brando told me he was acting in *Waterfront* only because he wanted to stay in New York, where he could see his analyst, I should have spat in his face. Now, in my mind's eye, I did. For Christ sake, he owed his career to me. And then there was Lilian Hellman, who'd been out to skin my hide. Still, I'd pretended to like her, to tell people I thought she was OK, when I knew she was a liar and hypocrite and a self-righteous phony. Most of all she was my enemy, and I'd betrayed myself by acting as though she wasn't. I hated her for that more than anything.

Dr. Kelman had told me that I'd trained myself not to feel, and I knew from a lifetime in theater that an artist who works only from intellect instead of his deepest feelings can

260

never be more than just a technician. Then I realized that I'd never made a movie or put on a play that expressed *me*, who I was. I'd always put myself at the service of writers who were, at some level, in one way or another expressing themselves. I'd done good work in that capacity, and I was proud of what I'd achieved. But none of it was *me*; it was Art, or Tennessee, or Bill Inge, or Budd Schulberg, or someone else. Those movies and plays might have been compelling, cathartic, and profound – certainly nothing to be ashamed of, and I'm glad I could bring them to life. But, apart from *Waterfront*, they were never me.

"Stop being anonymous!" I shouted out to the vista below. "Anonymity doesn't protect you from anything. Not a damned thing. It never has." Then I spoke more softly to myself. "Admit your pain, your rejection, your pettiness and shame, your resentment and frustration, your fury. And anything else you feel. Be honest and uncalculating. Otherwise, you will die." Hearing myself speak those words aloud made them concrete and real to me, and I felt good as I made my way back down that goat path.

On my way back to America I stopped in England to visit John Steinbeck, who was also in a bad way. He was going through a crisis similar to my own, sickened by his own failures in authenticity and, at times, almost suicidal. Nonetheless, John reaffirmed my new resolve. He told me my problem was that I had become a nice guy, that I was so needy for approval

261

I'd lost myself. I'd become so accustomed to sacrificing my own desires that I know longer even knew what I wanted.

"And stop being *Gadg*! That goddamn nickname isn't you. You're not – at least you weren't – a handy, adaptable little gadget. You made yourself that way to get along, to be accepted, to become invisible. For God's sake, what a neutered nickname – useful to everyone else but not to yourself. Give it up! Be selfish. Get mean. Find out what your place in the world is and claim it for your own and never let anyone take it from you."

I'm sure that John was speaking to himself as much as to me, and when he finished he seemed more spirited and engaged than at any time since I'd arrived. His words resonated inside of me, and I returned home a different man from the one who'd left just weeks before.

CHAPTER 44

Marilyn

It was Art's idea to get Yves Montand to replace Gregory Peck in *Let's Make Love.* Peck left in a huff because Art revised the script to play up my part at the expense of his. Can't say as I blame him. I'd probably have done the same.

I met Yves and his wife, Simone Signoret, in September, when Yves was knocking 'em dead on Broadway in his one-man show. We caught his song-and-dance routine one night and invited them back to our apartment afterward. Yves and Art hit it off great, and I found Simone fascinating. I'd seen *Room at the Top* a few months earlier and admired her performance. Apparently, I wasn't the only one since she won an Oscar for it. Yves and I hit it off too, and somewhere out of the conviviality of the evening the possibility that Yves might replace Peck arose. Art suggested it to the producers, and the rest became history.

Rehearsals began right after new year, so the studio gave Art and me a bungalow right next to Yves and Simone at the Beverly Hills Hotel on Sunset Boulevard. At first, we were all one big, happy family. After rehearsal they'd come by for drinks and whatever I felt like whipping up for dinner: spaghetti, lamb stew, nothing fancy. Sometimes Art and Simone would go off to discuss politics – all of us were leftists, although I never really thought of myself that way. Mostly, except for my outrage at HUAC and the blacklisters and the injustices inflicted upon blacks, I didn't consider myself political at all. Politics had never been part of my life until I met Art and Gadg, and mostly I stayed away from them, that is until the 1960 election. But Yves had been raised by Communists, and Simone was a lefty too, so she and Art exchanged opinions about the state of the world, while Yves and I went over our next scene together.

Sometimes I helped Yves with his English, which was heavily accented. The studio initially feared that might be a problem, but then they figured that his drop-dead good looks more than compensated. And since this was a musical, it didn't hurt that he could sing and dance too. After all, people weren't paying cold cash to hear the dialogue. That was a good thing too; the dialogue stank. The producers knew that women would come to swoon over Yves, and men would shell out good money to drool over me, no matter how lousy the script was. But Yves understood that a better command of English would help his career, and he sincerely wanted to improve.

So, we spent a lot of time together helping each other out, and we came to appreciate each other as friends. Yves was compassionate and gentlemanly. He didn't treat me just as a sex symbol, unlike everyone else in Hollywood. That meant a lot. So did the way he approached women with kindness and consideration. Not just me, all the women on the

264

set. I don't know why that should have been so remarkable, but in Hollywood it was.

Meanwhile things went from bad to worse between Art and me. He hadn't written the screenplay, just consulted on it, and even he agreed the script was a disaster. My character was another one-dimensional blonde, static and boring. Chérie in *Bus Stop* was the only character I'd played with any depth to her, and now I felt like I was going backward in my career. Maybe I took it out on him. I was back to popping pills and showing up late on the set, forgetting my lines, you know the routine. And like he did in England, Art took it upon himself to be my personal manager. Somehow, he felt it was his responsibility to get me going in the morning and make excuses for me and keep track of which pills I was using and how many of them I was taking at one time. I never asked him to.

But he did, and he resented it. He complained how looking after me took him away from his writing. Boo hoo. His writing hadn't gone anywhere since we'd been married, even when he had all the time in the world squirreled away by himself in his writing rooms. It wasn't my fault; it happens to authors. Maybe he'd just run out of things to say. Did he ever think of that? No, his resentment cut through the air and pierced my heart, and I resented him for that too.

Finally, at the end of January, Art went off to Ireland to work some more on *The Misfits*. John Huston was lending him

265

his house in Galway, and Art's delight at getting away from me and *Let's Make Love* was exceeded only by my pleasure at seeing him go. It was about that time that Simone also left too. She was starring in a movie back in France.

With our spouses gone, Yves and I spent more time together, working on our scenes and trying to improve our craft. His character was also badly written, and he confided to me how frightened he was of messing up his lines or acting badly. The script didn't give either of us much to work with.

I found Yves' openness endearing. No other leading man had ever spoken to me of his fears like that. More often they were arrogant and condescending, like Olivier. Yves might have been the first man to treat me as an equal, at least on an emotional level. Art didn't. He saw himself as my more-knowledgeable, more experienced mentor, my superior. Joe had too. So had Gadg and Johnny Hyde, and even poor Jim Dougherty. But Yves' anxieties mirrored my own, and that common bond drew us together like a magnet.

And one day, not long after Art and Simone had departed, Yves came by with some chicken soup for me because I'd come down with a cold. I had learned about this Jewish penicillin from my mother-in-law, Gussie, and it worked. Yves set the soup down on a table and then sat on the bed beside me, holding my hand to comfort me. He was gentle like that. When he stood to go, he bent over to kiss my forehead,

266

but somehow his sweet gesture became a wild, passionate kiss – a *French* kiss, as I liked to call it. And we were lovers.

Norma Jeane never worried about her privacy. No one paid enough attention to her to violate it, at least not until she developed tits. But Marilyn Monroe rarely had any privacy at all. Naturally the bottom-feeders that feast upon the droppings of the rich and famous soon discovered what was going on, and they plastered our affair all over the scandal sheets and gossip columns. I felt sorry for Simone, not so much for Art. Perhaps that was cruel of me, but that was how I felt.

The shooting on the film was going nowhere because the script was so bad that Yves and I couldn't make sense of our roles. Whatever our differences, Art was a first-rate writer; so, in March I had him fly back from Ireland to revise the screenplay. His additions helped some, but even Art agreed it was like trying to bail water from a sinking ship. Still, the studio paid him twenty-five thousand dollars for his efforts, which was more than he'd made on a play in quite some time. And we were able to resume filming.

Between the stress of the shoot, my romance with Yves, my disintegrating marriage to Art, plus the alcohol and pills, I wasn't really aware that the Screen Writers Guild had gone on strike about the time Art left for Galway. So, I didn't think about it at first when Art came back to make those revisions. But then it hit me. Art was crossing the picket line. He was a sellout.

The great man I'd loved and admired for his unshakable commitment to principle was a fink. The remaining crust of respect I had for him disintegrated, and all hope for our marriage perished with it.

CHAPTER 45

Art

It pained me to think that Marilyn believed I was a strike-breaker, a scab, a fink. That assault on my reputation hurt me more than her sordid affair with my pal, Yves, or the headlines I couldn't help read in one paper or another almost every day. Marilyn got the idea from Sidney Skolsky, who put out the word in his gossip column that I had made those revisions secretly, at night. But that was all bullshit. I wrote those pages before the strike began. I don't know why the producers were slow to incorporate them. Maybe they had enough on their plate dealing with Marilyn's tantrums. Or maybe they didn't want Yves to have to learn to pronounce any new words. In any case, I didn't come back from Galway to work on *Let's Make Love*. I returned to scout locations in Nevada with Huston for *The Misfits*. If Skolsky's charge truly turned Marilyn inextricably against me, then it's a shame. A goddamn, fucking shame.

CHAPTER 46

Marilyn

If you believe that cock and bull story about coming back to scout locations in Nevada, then I have a bridge to sell you. I was there. I saw it. I heard the typewriter keys slamming against the cold white paper in the middle of the night.

CHAPTER 47

Art

This from a woman who was so strung out on barbiturates and booze that she didn't know what day it was, much less what I was working on in the privacy of my writing room.

CHAPTER 48

Gadg

I was in town doing the final post-production on *Wild River*, and like everyone else, I read about how Marilyn was carrying on with Yves Montand. Except for some *pro forma* greetings at receptions and award ceremonies, Art and I hadn't communicated in eight years, but still, I couldn't help feeling sorry for him. Whatever our differences had been, he didn't deserve that sort of coldhearted public humiliation, and I wondered if he could take the punishment. So, I gave him a call one day and invited him to lunch. It was springtime, so we ate outside at a Beverly Hills café. Naturally, there was some awkwardness at first.

"Gadg, it was awfully nice of you to invite me to lunch this way. After...everything."

"You know, after...everything, I never stopped caring about you. We've been through too much together. True, I wanted to kill you a few times. You and your liberal pals. I wanted to kick you in the ass so hard that you wouldn't be able to walk for a week. Or your nuts. You wouldn't be able to fuck for a week. I mean that. But even so, I never wished you ill."

"Thank you for that. I guess I can say the same."

There was a brief silence. Where could we go from there? Then Art opened another line of communication, our professional achievements.

"You've been on quite a roll these past few years: *East of Eden, Baby Doll, A Face in the Crowd*. Not to mention the plays. *J.B.* won a Pulitzer. Congratulations on that, the second one you've directed. I wish I'd been so productive."

"Yeah, you and Archie MacLeish. To tell you the truth, I never loved *J.B.* It never spoke to me like *Salesman*. I did all I could to bring out the best in it, and I guess that paid off. But the outstanding merits of that play still elude me."

"That's an even greater testament to your genius. You made it work anyway." Art paused a moment to think. "No one does drama with a social conscience like you, Gadg."

"Don't forget *Waterfront*. I got an Academy Award for it." I was curious how Art would react to that.

"Of course, *Waterfront*." The words stuck in his throat, and Art took a sip of water, which he seemed to slosh around inside his mouth before swallowing. But he didn't take the bait.

"And the plays you collaborated on with Tennessee. Very impressive."

"Tennessee was the only friend who stood by me."

I guess I just needed to get that off my chest. There was another silence as Art again drank from his water glass and I fiddled with my fork. At last a waiter showed up and we

273

ordered drinks, Manhattans for a couple of old New Yorkers. The waiter left, and we wondered what to say, where to go from here. I decided to return to what we still had in common, our passion for art that has substance.

"I've got another movie coming out in a few weeks, *Wild River*."

"Yes, I've read about it. Marilyn and I were talking about it just the other day. But the snippets I read in *Variety* never gave me a clear sense of what it's about."

"It's in post-production now. In the thirties an idealistic bureaucrat from the TVA comes to rural Tennessee to buy up land to be flooded for the hydroelectric dams that will generate electricity for the entire Tennessee River Valley. The young bureaucrat is a true believer. Roosevelt wants to bring all of America into the twentieth century, kicking and screaming if he must, and Chuck -- that's his name, Chuck -- is proud be doing his part to help. For him it's all about the promise of progress, and he's not the kind of person who would ever let emotional sentiment override science and rational thought. I based him on a version of my younger self, back when I was in the Party."

Art nodded to show he understood. "Somehow progress seemed so much more promising back then." He sounded both wistful and bitter.

"Of course, the people whose families have been farming that land for generations don't quite see it that way, and

Chuck encounters especially stiff resistance from an eighty year-old woman who has never known any other life. Relocating will kill her; she feels it in her bones. But that argument carries no weight with an apparatchik like Chuck."

"Hmmm." Art was already imagining the dramatic possibilities.

"However, the plot takes a twist when Chuck falls in love with the old lady's granddaughter."

"Good," Art nodded. "The love angle will increase the tension and keep the story from devolving into a morality play. I assume you found a way to integrate it into the conflict over the land."

"Of course. Plus. I use it to humanize Chuck more completely. He's no longer so unfeeling, and the struggle between his duty and his heart ultimately drives the plot."

"I like that. Who's the love interest?"

"Actually, I first I thought of asking Marilyn, but then I settled on Lee Remick. She was great in *A Face in the Crowd*, and she did fine work here too. I like working with her."

Art was listening closely, like he always did when we talked about our craft. He ignored the reference to Marilyn. I wasn't sure what that implied, but he was into the story.

"I wouldn't have thought of writing about the TVA, but from what you've told me, it seems to work. Who do you want us to root for, the old lady or Chuck?"

"Good question.   Like I said, Chuck reminds me of myself when I was in my early twenties: cocky and sure of myself, a great believer that reason and technology could solve all our social problems, that progress and progressivism would shine light where it was dark. You know, the Party line."

"And the line of the Renaissance and the Enlightenment," Art quickly added.

"Well, the TVA project literally brought light to darkness. It introduced electric lighting to the rural South, and the rural South into the twentieth century. That's no small achievement, and it was absolutely necessary. It had to be done. But it also destroyed these folks' way of life, and sometimes the folks themselves.   Pursuing the greatest good for the greatest number of people may have been logically sound, but it dumped these dirt farmers onto the trash heap of history with the same indifference as a smoker tossing away a used-up match."

"True enough, and that's a good dichotomy you're setting up. But you haven't answered my question. Who wins out in the end, and how do we feel about it? On which side of the trash heap of history do we ultimately stand?"

"You know, I first came up with the idea years ago. F.D.R. was my hero, and I wanted to show the kind of resistance he had to overcome from ignorant and stubborn rural reactionaries who were slowing down the march of progress. Originally, I was going to have Chuck be Jewish, so I could make their bigotry another obstacle. But I don't think that's necessary anymore. It'd be overkill and distract from the core conflict. So I dropped it. Plus, that was twenty-five years ago. I see things differently now."

"The South isn't still bigoted? Where have you been?"

"No. Of course it is, and that plays a prominent role in *Wild River.* The coloreds do all the work, while the whites sit around and reap the benefits."

"Sounds like capitalism." Again, Art sounded bitter.

"A little, but this was worse. Chuck gets the crap beat out of him when he gives Negros he hires to clear the land the same hourly rate as he pays the whites. The white employers are outraged. They're afraid they'll have to raise their wages too in order to keep the coloreds, who they depend on, working for them."

"Still sounds like capitalism. Don't forget the Pinkertons."

I shrugged. "*Baby Doll* also calls out Southern prejudice. The local police stonewall the Italian immigrant in order to protect the good old boy who burned down the *wop's* cotton gin. They even warn Silva against accusing Archie Lee. "Naming names that sound suspicious can be risky business."

Art raised an eyebrow at that, but I continued. "It's an oversimplification though to think these country folk are *just*

277

bigoted. When we were filming down in Mississippi I saw both extremes, and that really opened my eyes. I became aware of my own stereotypes and prejudices. I saw coloreds being treated like shit, but not generally, not as a rule among the people we were working with. Certainly, Negroes were second-class citizens down there; that's why I gave them the last laugh. And, of course, we did have to rescue one poor fellow from some hopped-up rednecks who wanted to cut off his balls. And they would have too."

"Sounds bigoted to me."

"But I also met people who were warm and kindhearted and generous. They'd lend a helping hand without ever being asked and then invite you over for supper afterward. Some even treated the coloreds with consideration and respect. On top of that, a number of them struck me as being truly authentic. They were who they were, and they were never ashamed of it. I've come to appreciate that."

"Up to a point," Art interrupted. "Some folks hide behind their claim to authenticity in order to justify complacency and insensitivity, even prejudice. *I'm just being myself* becomes an excuse not to evolve or a justification for selfishness and narcissism. Nobody else matters but them. They must be true to themselves, no matter how it makes others suffer."

I suspected Art was thinking of Marilyn and the way she'd been treating him.

"I used to think like you do," I continued, "and to some extent I still do. But sometimes you have to put your foot down. You can't let your concern for others eviscerate who you are. There's a balance we all must find."

Then I looked Art directly in the eye. "Think about it. How often have you neglected your writing and your career to prop up Marilyn?"

"I can't let her fall apart in front of me and do nothing."

"So you sacrifice yourself and your art, and she falls apart in front of the whole world instead. And emasculates you in the process."

"That's Marilyn. What can I do?"

"So Marilyn gets to be authentic, but you don't? If that's the price you must pay for loving her, it's pretty steep, don't you think? Is it really worth it?"

"We're back to Hillel. 'If I am not for myself, who will be for me. If I am only for myself, who am I?' Some of those old Jews knew a thing or two."

"Fair enough," I conceded. "There is a golden mean, and some of the rural Southerners I met have found it. That's something I've been thinking about a lot lately. Anyway, my experiences in Mississippi, and even my travels in Turkey – I'll you about them sometime – have changed how I look at things. Now I have more sympathy for that old lady and her neighbors."

Art nodded again. "Well, science and rational thought certainly have a dark side we never considered back then. We should have."

"It was a failure of imagination. We only pictured the positive uses of social engineering and advanced technology; we never conceived the possibility of H-bombs that can wipe out the planet."

"Or what happens to people when you uproot them by the thousands for the so-called greater good?" Art brought the conversation back to *Wild River.*

"And who gets to decide what the greater good is, anyway? Back then we never envisioned the emotional devastation our rational solutions could cause. Or if we did, we never considered it very important. But I just returned from Turkey. I visited the homeland my parents and grandparents were kicked out of not so long ago, and I've been asking myself what that did to their psyche, to their sense of who they were and how they must behave, to their spirit? I'm sure that rubbed off on the movie. I'm glad it did."

"The negation of the spirit," Art muttered, and then he sighed.

I reached across the table and squeezed his hand. "If one is to believe the press, you've been in a bad way. Is your life really the shambles they say it is?"

"Yes, I suppose it is." Art squeezed back softly and then let go. He seemed suddenly beaten down and spoke barely louder than a whisper. "It's not just that Marilyn's carrying on openly with Yves Montand. We used to be pals, Yves and I."

"It's hard when your friends betray you."

"I thought he was credible as Proctor in *The Crucible*. In the French production."

"Didn't see it."

"He was innocent of witchcraft but guilty of lechery."

The waiter came, set our Manhattans down on the table, smiled, and left. I lifted my drink. "Cheers."

Art tapped my glass with his and answered wryly, "Cheers."

"You know," he sighed, "*I* recommended Yves to Cukor to replace Peck. Peck left because my revisions built up Marilyn's part at the expense of his. I did that for her. That's what I've sunk to. This affair is Peck's revenge on me. Now Marilyn's not even pretending she and Yves aren't fucking. Can you imagine how it feels to be cuckolded so publicly? The world's most famous marriage has degenerated into the world's most famous adultery."

"Right up there with Helen of Troy."

"You can't begin to guess how humiliating it is to see my horns plastered all over the headlines. Not to mention the betrayal. She was always saying that I'd be the one to betray her."

"It's Marilyn. What did you expect?"

"I know her views on fidelity have always been different from mine; but still, I thought she'd be faithful. Out of love, not from obligation or any sense of moral duty. I still love her, but I don't think she loves me anymore." Art sighed. Then he drank.

"But still you feel obligated to her. Always the romantic." I took a sip from my own glass. "Always the idealist."

"On top of that, Marilyn blames me for everything. She drinks too much. She can't sleep, so she pops pills every night. She's hooked on barbiturates. Has been for a long time now. She's already overdosed a couple times and had to be rushed to the hospital. She almost died."

"It was everywhere on television."

"Plus, the miscarriages really got her down. She wanted a baby so much. At least she thought she did."

I took another sip of my Manhattan. "To be frank, I never saw Marilyn as the mothering type. She's always needed a mother too much to be one. A good one, anyway."

"Now on the set she acts like the junkie she is. She was a disaster to work with on *Some Like It Hot*. Curtis said kissing her was like kissing Hitler."

"That's harsh. I think it was her best work so far."

"But it was like pulling teeth to get her to behave. Now on *Let's Make Love* -- what a title -- she's always late to rehearsal. She forgets her lines; she's rude to the other actors. Then she pretends to be sick and takes off for a three-day tryst with Montand.

"What's worse is that I'm the one who has to make the excuses for her. If I don't back her up one hundred percent, she accuses me of abandoning her, betraying her. Not standing up for her when she needs me. And when I try to restrain her outrageous behavior, or if I refuse to obey her every command, she calls me Old Grouchy Grumps. Can you believe it? Grouchy Grumps."

"So why do you put up with it? Dump her. I would."

"It might come down to that. Trust me, it might. But you know, in spite of everything, I love her. And she needs me. For all of her success, she's still that scared, vulnerable little girl who thinks she's worthless, who needs protection."

"So that makes you Art the Rescuer. The knight in shining armor who earns her adoration by saving her from herself. Do you really want to get stuck in that role? Does she want to be stuck in hers?"

"Good questions." Art sighed and shook his head. "Her adoration has disintegrated into disdain and disgust. I don't know what I've done to deserve it, except pander to her, I

283

suppose. I thought I was showing my love. But somehow, she sees it as weakness."

"Isn't it? Besides, I think deep down Marilyn believes that anyone who loves her must have something wrong with him. She resents you for not recognizing her worthlessness and punishing her for it. It's what you have in common."

"You think so?"

I shrugged, and the waiter appeared with our salads. Mine had black olives and feta cheese covered in olive oil. Art ordered iceberg lettuce, cucumbers, and tomatoes smothered in Thousand Island dressing.

He looked up just before he took his first bite. "I used to order French dressing, but now I can't stomach it." He ate a cucumber and then speared a tomato with his fork. "She's written me off. There's nothing I can do about it. She's degraded everything. She treats me with contempt. She treats the movie with contempt. She treats herself with contempt."

"How much of this did you bring on yourself?"

"I don't know." Art seemed so sad. "I don't know."

It was time to change the subject. "You know, I've been seeing someone who reminds me of Marilyn, Barbara Loden. I met her while shooting *A Face in the Crowd*. She's an actress, although she wasn't in my movie."

"I liked that film. Schulberg did a good job with the screenplay. It's got a lot of meat to it. "

"Barbara has Marilyn's authenticity and her gutsiness. She's always up front about what she wants and how she feels, in bed and out of it. She never pretends to be anything that she isn't. Just like Marilyn. Neither of them ever apologized for anything, least of all their lust. I got Barbara a small part in *Wild* River so she could be with me on the shoot."

Art raised an eyebrow again. "Molly just accepts Barbara, like the others?"

"Molly doesn't know. It's better that way."

He played some more with his salad. "You know," it wasn't always this way between us. Marilyn was so proud of me after my testimony. The studio put the screws to her to pressure me. They told her she'd never work again in Hollywood; but she refused to give in."

"Good for her. Molly was a real bulwark during my HUAC days. When the chips were down, she was right there. Unlike some friends I can think of."

I'm not even sure why I made that last remark. It certainly wasn't likely to help Art through his problems or reconcile our grudges. I guess those words just wanted to come out, and since my return from Turkey I was trying not to hold back my real feelings any longer. It was part of the lump-clearing practice I'd been working on. I knew I ran the risk of alienating people, even old friends and lovers, especially old

285

friends and lovers; but, convinced that continued self-betrayal was tantamount to suicide, I was determined to be authentic.

It was Art's fortune or misfortune to be among the first recipients of my long-repressed thoughts and impulses, and I watched closely to see how he'd react. But to my surprise he just let my jibe pass by without even seeming to notice. I guess he was preoccupied with Marilyn.

"She and I married right after I testified. You might have read about it."

"It was hard not to. Even though I tried. I was surprised they let you leave the country".

"Rauh's a good lawyer. The best."

"And now you're the great hero of the Left. The man who stood up to HUAC and got away with it."

"It cost me a pretty penny, but I did what I had to do."

"So did I."

"I never said you didn't. You know, the Committee even asked me about that. In their eyes condemning you is apparently reason enough to deny a person the right to travel."

"At least they got something right."

"I told them I've never criticized your testimony. Which is true."

"No, you just wrote two plays that anyone reading between the lines could see were directed at me."

"And you retaliated with *Waterfront*. You took *my* original idea and turned it into everything I was against. Not just an apology for informing, a celebration."

"That was mostly Schulberg's doing. But I confess I helped. It felt good."

"You could have broken that insidious blacklist. You know that don't you?"

"No, I don't. If I had known that for a fact, I would have. I hated the blacklist as much as anyone. But I wasn't going to ruin my career fighting a lost cause. That's the problem with your kind of liberal. You love lost causes. You romanticize them."

"It *wasn't* a lost cause."

Fortunately, the waiter interrupted with our meals. Art ordered another Manhattan, but I was still working on my first; so I passed on a second round. We ate in silence for a while. Finally Art tried to reach some middle ground.

"I guess that's all water under the bridge. Besides, it was the Committee that screwed everyone. They put you and me and everyone else in an untenable situation. No sense in holding grudges."

"Is that why you had Monty give me the manuscript of *The Misfits* last winter? I was quite surprised when I saw it. Very unexpected. I didn't know what to make of it."

"I thought you'd be good for it. And for Marilyn too."

287

"I liked her in *Bus Stop.* I liked your screenplay too. But my schedule. I've started preliminary work on a new movie, *America, America*, and it's been consuming me."

I finished off my Manhattan before I continued. "You know, being ostracized these past eight years has changed me. For the better, I think."

Art raised his eyebrows.

"It's forced me to delve within and take inventory of my life. I'm a stronger person now. There's nothing to be gained by seeking approval anymore, and that's surprisingly liberating. Now I'm more true to myself."

"You think so?"

"I firmly believe that the only genuinely good and original films I've directed were all made after April 10, 1952."

"I wouldn't say that. *Streetcar* was masterful."

"My earlier films were adept, but the ones I made after I testified were personal."

"I can see that."

"You know, life was brutal for Greeks living in eastern Turkey before the first world war. My film is based on my uncle who struggled to make his way from the boondocks of Anatolia to Istanbul, so he could somehow scrounge passage on an ocean liner to New York."

"Fascinating. What are you calling it?"

288

"I'm calling it *America, America.* I want to catch that fierce spirit so many immigrants possess, to show what it takes to arrive in a strange land with nothing but guts and the determination to do whatever they must, not just to survive but to thrive. To come out on top."

"That could have been my grandfather emigrating from Poland. Or my father. He came all by himself when he was only six years old. Someone put a sign around his neck with the name of the ship he was to board. Then he was on his own until my uncles met him at the dock in New York City. Izzy made himself a rich man, until he lost it all."

"Exactly. I want this to be a tribute to my father and what it took for him to uproot his family from Istanbul and start a new life in this totally foreign world, America. Different customs, different values, different rules. You know, I never really appreciated him before I started this movie. To tell you the truth, I always thought he was a real bastard."

"Sounds like quite a project. Who's doing the screenplay?"

For a second I wondered if Art was hinting that he wanted to collaborate on it with me, but then I didn't think so.

"I'm writing it myself. No one knows the characters and the culture like I do. When I was in Turkey and walking through the same cobblestone streets and town squares my uncle passed through, I wondered a lot about what life was like for

289

him. Of course, no Greeks live there anymore. They were social-engineered out of town back in the twenties, the ones who survived."

Art's grimace twisted his face. "All that cruelty. It's so unnecessary, but sometimes it seems we humans just seek it out."

"My visit opened my eyes. When I met my cousin on an earlier trip, I came face-to-face with the person I probably would have become if my family had stayed. For the first time in my life I felt grateful to my father. And I decided that life's too short. From now on I only want to make movies that allow me somehow to explore something of myself. I'm tired of using my gift only for others and not myself. No offense intended."

"None taken."

"Anyway, I don't know if I could direct Marilyn at this stage of our lives. But let me ask you something, just to clear the air. How much of your break with me was over HUAC? And how much was because I was still schtooping Marilyn back then, the great love of your life, even if you were married?"

"I don't even know anymore. Both things bothered me. A lot. But how could I complain under the circumstances? About either?"

"I figured that's what you were talking about in your testimony."

"So, you listened after all. Of course that's what I was talking about. It's a shame, though, that they came between us. HUAC and Marilyn."

"We may have another chance."

"Oh?"

"Bob Whitehead has asked me to be the artistic director for the new Lincoln Center Theater. It's what we've always wanted for this country, a first-rate repertory theater for productions with real depth and character exploration. Not the fluff that Broadway's in love with nowadays."

"Or that ridiculous Theater of the Absurd that's the rage Off Broadway. The whole point of theater is to plumb the human soul, but they don't even try."

"Some of them, maybe."

"Oh, come on!" Art's tone was so sharp he startled the young couple beside us. "The only thing worse than rubbish is pretentious rubbish with a French accent. That includes Yves Montand too."

Thinking perhaps I could take advantage of his outrage, I brought up the other reason I'd asked him to lunch. "Here's your chance to fight back. A new play written by Arthur Miller and directed by Elia Kazan would make for one hell of an inauguration. What do you think?"

CHAPTER 49

Art

Spring of 1960 felt like the beginning of the end to me. I doubted our marriage could survive Marilyn's front-page affair with Montand, although I was still determined to make *The Misfits* for her. And I doubted the world could survive the nuclear brinkmanship the East and West were playing. The day Gadg and I got together for lunch, the Russians shot down an American U-2 spy plane over Soviet airspace and hopes that a superpower summit might defuse the tensions over Berlin were dashed. Ike was still president, and Nixon looked like a good bet to win in November. Moreover, Fidel Castro, who'd seized power in Cuba the year before, was already showing his true communist colors and cozying up to Khrushchev just ninety miles south of Key West and about two hundred from Miami. And Charles De Gaulle, who'd already removed France from NATO's military command, became even more of a loose cannon when France detonated its own nuclear device. That's what the world needed, another wild card with an atom bomb.

My writing career had stalled, and I was losing my self-respect, but my reunion with Gadg gave me a boost. We'd both still nursed wounds from the ruptures in our friendship and our professional collaboration, and we both had the scars to prove it. But making peace with Gadg lifted a huge weight from me that I hadn't even known was there. I felt freer and more relaxed than I had in a long time. Maybe *The Misfits* could somehow rekindle the spark that Marilyn and I had lost, after all, and maybe working on a new play with Gadg would get my creative juices flowing again.

But *The Misfits* was a disaster. We started rehearsals in July and then filmed on location in the Nevada desert into the fall. By the end of the shoot our marriage had shriveled in the heat, and Marilyn and I were barely even talking. I wanted the script to be perfect, so I was always revising one passage or another, but this angered Marilyn, who resented having to learn new lines all the time, especially while she was spaced out on pills. In spite of everything, though, she insisted that her performances be perfect; so, she never took the revisions lightly, even though my changes created a lot of extra work for her. I understood her frustration, but that's how movies are made. The process is fluid and the story often evolves as we shoot.

I wanted to create a character Marilyn could relate to, so she could really go deep into her psyche. I wanted Roslyn, who'd come to Reno for a divorce, to be broken and fragile but also sensitive and loving and desperate for connection, which is how Marilyn was. And, to her credit, Marilyn truly lived the part. Huston told me that when she was playing Roslyn, Marilyn

293

never pretended to feel an emotion; it was always the real thing. She would go far down within herself and find it and bring it up into her consciousness. That was method acting at its best.

But Marilyn didn't want to act the role of Norma Jeane, or of Marilyn Monroe either, and she resented all of the elements from her own life that I'd incorporated into Roslyn's. She said she wanted to play someone altogether different from her, so she could *act*. "Why don't you write me a role for someone mean and spiteful like Grushenka? Or for a woman who's intelligent and can express her beliefs cogently and articulately, instead of always resorting to tears and screaming fits?" If I'd written the script more for her, as I'd originally set out to do, and less for me, as I ended up doing, I would have listened to her, and maybe we'd have stayed married, at least until the next crisis came along.

However, I didn't listen to her, and the shit hit the fan. Maybe that was just as well, after all. Perhaps it stopped us from carrying on our charade longer than was good for either of us. Sometimes you've just got to amputate in order to survive, and her tantrums were the scalpel.

Who was severing whom? We severed each other. I must give her credit though. Marilyn was more forceful in doing what had to be done; in Gadg's terms, she was more authentic. I was passive and inauthentic, just as I'd been with Mary. I

294

catered to her, comforted her when I could, and was careful not to upset her, when all the while I was seething inside. I should have stood up to her and let the chips fall where they may. But I was afraid.

"Afraid of what?" you ask. Afraid I'd lose someone who was very dear to me, a woman I loved and had built my life around, my soulmate. Yes, I'm convinced we were soulmates; our attraction had been so strong, so complete and instantaneous, our lives so intertwined.

And I was afraid that without me, Marilyn would self-destruct. She continually complained about her lines, demanded changes in the script, and she berated me, my writing and the movie in front of anyone listening. And still I took it, because I loved her and because I couldn't watch her crash and burn. Until I could.

CHAPTER 50

Marilyn

He was famous for creating characters with depth and contradictions and complicated inner lives. Why couldn't he do that for me? All my life I'd played Marilyn Monroe, Marilyn Monroe, Marilyn Monroe. I so wanted to do something different, to *be* something different. That's what attracted me to Art in the first place. When we got married, I fantasized about escaping from Marilyn Monroe through his writing. Maybe he could have created a forceful woman for me to act, someone creative, confident and crafty.

Maybe if I'd played a woman like that I could have discovered those qualities hidden deep inside of me and developed them and nurtured them. Art could have helped me become that woman. Instead he must have wanted me to stay frail and vulnerable so he could remain my protector. But I no longer wanted a protector; I desired a partner. Still, Art doubled-down on the wounded bird who was too sensitive to survive on her own. If this was his love offering, I wanted nothing to do with it. I wanted nothing more to do with Marilyn Monroe either, that superficial, emotionally-stunted, intellectually-empty twit.

CHAPTER 51

Art

I don't need to tell you how she made everyone bake in the desert heat, while she overslept and showed up two hours later in the hottest part of the day. How she was so spaced out from lack of sleep and too much medication that she'd forget her lines and slur her speech. How they suspended filming so Marilyn could be hospitalized and weaned off her pills. For all of that, though, she put everything into her acting whenever she was able to perform, and she did a hell of a job.

I don't need to tell you that because those stories are legendary: what she put me through, what she put all of us through. I couldn't remember the last time I'd been really happy. Not since our wedding. Maybe that paparazza, Mara Scherbatoff, really did curse our marriage with her dying words.

However, for all Marilyn made us suffer, the charge that she was somehow responsible for Clark Gable's fatal heart attack never seemed fair. It's true that her frequent tardiness often required him to act at midday instead of in the relative cool of the morning, and I'm sure this was tough on Gable; it was tough on everyone. But don't forget that Gable did his own stunts, and it was Huston, not Marilyn, who made him perform repeated takes under the broiling sun. And let's not overlook the fact that Clark smoked three packs a day for most of his life.

Nonetheless, Marilyn fretted over the possibility that she might have contributed to his sudden death a few days after the filming ended, and that disturbed her greatly. You see, Gable had always treated her kindly on the set. Plus, as a child she'd worshipped him. She'd kept a picture of him in her bedroom, pretending he was her father, instead of the real one she never knew. So, Gable's death hit her hard. But I never believed she had anything to do with it.

Instead of Marilyn's self-destruction, let me tell you about Inge, Ingebord Morath, who was to become my third wife. We met on the set of *The Misfits*, and we both sensed an attraction right away. If I'd been Gadg and she'd been Barbara Loden, I'd have followed her into the Ladies Room after work and fucked her brains out in one of the stalls. But I didn't cheat on Mary after I felt that first bolt of lightning from Marilyn, and I wasn't about to cheat on Marilyn now. Nonetheless, the writing on the wall was clear: our marriage was doomed. Marilyn and I weren't speaking; we weren't living in the same hotel room; we took different limousines to the shoot each day, and at the end she wouldn't even let me see her off the set. She literally kicked me out of the room, and I had to send messages to her through Paula Strasberg, who, against my better judgment, had become Marilyn's highly-paid personal adviser and confidant.

So, while the prospect of working with Gadg again at Lincoln Center sparked new optimism for my career, the twinkle

298

in Inge's eyes gave me hope for the future. With apologies to Gerard Manley Hopkins, my heart in hiding stirred for a nerd.

To put it crudely, Inge and Marilyn hailed from opposite sides of the tracks, and Inge was everything Marilyn was not: tall, dark, and Austrian. She came from a prominent military family and was well educated, highly cultured, and accomplished in many ways. Inge was a photojournalist who was shooting still pictures of the movie; so she was around the set a lot. It's ironic – or maybe it isn't, maybe by then it just didn't matter – but Marilyn really liked Inge's work. Inge had somehow captured a tenderness that Marilyn had not shown me in a long, long time.

Inge had befriended John Huston the previous year, when he was on location in Mexico filming *The Unforgiven* and she was shooting stills for *Life* and *Paris-Match*. They were sitting together at a Reno bar when I came in and found them laughing their heads off. Inge was aristocratic-looking with a charming accent, but it was her confidence and high spirits that made me take notice. John introduced me, and, as I seated myself, I asked them what was so funny.

"Inge was reminding me how she saved Audie Murphy's life while I was too preoccupied blasting ducks from the sky to notice he was drowning. To my credit though, I did bag a number of mallards, and Inge and Audie feasted heartily on them that evening. It was her reward."

"You saved Audie Murphy?" I was impressed. Murphy had been America's most decorated soldier in all of World War II. Now he was an actor, and the slender woman across from me had rescued him. "How?"

"On one of the off days when they weren't filming and I was secretly looking forward to finally sleeping in, John here insisted that I get up before the crack of dawn and photograph him and his compadres shooting fowl over a lake outside Durango. How exciting for me."

"Inge's pretending she was bored," John interrupted, "but I was a crack shot and she was mightily impressed. Don't let her fool you."

"I was so impressed I couldn't contain myself; so, I took off alone to explore the shore. I didn't get far before I noticed a rowboat about half a mile out, where two guys were thrashing around and making a big commotion.

"'Do you think they're OK?' I shouted over to John, but a flock was flying overhead and he barely paid attention."

"Murphy was always clowning around," John defended himself. "I figured this was just another of his antics."

"But I didn't. There was something desperate and frenetic about their gestures. So, while John ignored us I ran to the water's edge and stripped down to my panties and bra. Then I jumped into the water – believe me, it was freezing – and I swam all that distance to the boat. When I got there I found Audie flailing in the water, exhausted, looking like he might go under any second. His companion in the boat couldn't swim, so he couldn't jump in to help, and he hadn't been able to grab Audie's arms to haul him back inside. I swam over to Audie and told him to grab onto my bra."

"Front or back?" John jumped in.

"Front." Inge's voice dripped with sarcasm. "I did the breaststroke. What do you think?

John broke out laughing, but Inge clarified for my benefit, just in case I was obtuse. "The back, of course. I swam the crawl and towed him to shore. When we finally got there, John was still shooting away, you bastard."

"I had confidence in you. I knew you were up to the task. Besides, that water was cold!"

"Don't I know it."

"I like Audie and all," John went on. "He's a fine fellow. But I can't stand cold water."

"What did Audie say after you saved him?" I wondered.

Inge held out her arm. "He gave me one of his most prized possessions, the wristwatch he wore through all those battles during the war. I'm wearing it now." She turned her wrist so I could see.

Later I learned that Inge's brothers had fought in the German army and that her uncle had even been a general. Not in the SS, thank God, but still, they'd all done Hitler's bidding.

At least they didn't have blood from the concentration camps on their hands, just the blood of Allied soldiers. It took me some time to come to terms with that, but, of course, I wanted to.

I never thought I'd marry an Aryan, much less one connected to the German high command. But I took some solace from the fact that Inge had refused to comply when her teachers insisted she join a Nazi student organization. As punishment, they made her work at a munitions factory in Berlin's Tempelhof airport. She stood on an assembly line alongside Ukrainian women who were essentially slaves. You know, the Nazi's use of slave labor has been so overshadowed by the other horrors of the Holocaust that it's been largely overlooked, but it was there. Just ask Bayer and Volkswagen and Audi. The list goes on, in case you ever wondered about the connection between fascism and big business. The Allies were bombing that airport nearly every day, and Inge was lucky to come out of the war alive. Nonetheless, she never backed down or sought to save her skin by joining a group that she abhorred, and I've always admired her for that.

Like I said, Inge made a big first impression on me, but the set of The Misfits was neither the time nor the place to act on it. However, days after the filming ended, about the time John Kennedy was elected president and Gable dropped dead from his cardiac arrest, Marilyn and I announced our divorce. Not long after that I returned to New York, where Inge was also

302

living. A mutual friend gave me her phone number, and we married about a year later.

CHAPTER 52

Gadg

While Art was banging Inge in New York, I was banging Barbara on the set of *Splendor in the Grass*, also in New York. And when I wasn't filming or screwing, I was writing the screenplay for *America, America*, my own movie about my own family and my newfound appreciation of people who do whatever takes to survive extreme adversity and still prevail. Finally, I was making a movie for myself. Spring 1961 was one of the happiest times in my life.

My relationship with bourgeois morality had always been tentative, and now that I'd committed to clearing that lump by living authentically and reclaiming my life, my spirit and my inner soul, I found myself more and more impatient with bourgeois hypocrisy, especially as it pertained to sex. So, I led a double life. Mornings on the set were for my libido: screwing Barbara in her dressing room and then unleashing my artistic creativity through my directing. Evenings were for my superego: returning to the ordered and restrained middle-class life that Molly had engineered. Daytime was exhilarating; nighttime was restful and restorative. I had achieved a balance.

Why didn't I just leave Molly and take up with Barbara, if it was Barbara who was rekindling my thirst for life? Because, apart from the diminished sexual attraction between us, I still loved Molly and valued the structure she brought to my life, as well as her sound advice about my writing and my career. If I had not grown up with people who believed in Puritan values, if I were living in a difference place and time, I would never have questioned my double life. Even so, I refused to feel bad about it; I had no sense of guilt.

I wasn't the only one conducting a torrid and illicit love affair off the set. So too were the co-stars, Natalie Wood and Warren Beatty. I had mixed feelings about theirs. On the one hand, the passion Warren and Natalie felt for each other off camera showed through in their acting, and that was terrific for the movie. Natalie's desire for Warren was so convincing, she received an Oscar nomination. On the other hand, I felt bad for her husband, Robert Wagner, a friend of mine who was often around the set and must have known what was going on; everyone knew what was going on. Bob was a kind and decent guy, and he and Natalie had been known as Hollywood's perfect couple, much as Art and Marilyn had been the world's fairytale couple. The revelation that the perfect marriage was less than ideal made Bob's public humiliation even greater. He had fallen from a pedestal. In fact, Bob's cuckolding reminded me a lot of Art's when Marilyn was carrying on with Yves Montand. Unlike Art and Marilyn, however, Bob and Natalie later reunited.

Warren was yet another of my discoveries. He was just twenty-two when I cast him for the role of Bud, a high school football star who is torn by his lust for his girlfriend, Wilma, and his desire to be "good" – which meant chaste – and his need to fulfill his parents' expectations of him. Warren hadn't appeared in any movies then, just some TV shows and a Broadway production of Bill Inge's *A Loss of Roses*. That's where I first saw him act.

I liked Warren right from the start. He reminded me of a younger version of myself: awkward but hungry, willing to do whatever it took to succeed, and very, very ambitious. Now that I think of it, those were also the qualities my uncle had when he came to America. Maybe that's why I took to Warren so readily. He also projected enormous sex appeal and self-confidence. I always believed it was his self-confidence that made him so attractive to women.

Warren had a lot of *chutzpah* too, more than any Jew I had ever met, which impressed me because Jews were outsiders too. Ivy League schools even had quotas in those days for how many Jews they would admit, and advertisements for apartment rentals still said things like, "No dogs, no coloreds, and no Jews allowed." So, Warren knocked me for a loop one day when, out of nowhere, he came up to me and said, "Tell me, why did you name all those names?"

"What did you say?" I couldn't believe this kid could have the balls to ask me that. Of course, later on, his balls became the stuff of legends.

"When you testified before Congress, why did you give them all those names?"

When I regained my balance I grabbed him by the arm, sat him down in a dressing room, and explained carefully, and in great detail, why I joined and why I left the Communist Party. I described the whole business of blacklisting and red-baiting and exactly what I'd done and why. He'd been only twelve or thirteen when I appeared before HUAC and really knew almost nothing about it. My explanation made sense to him, and I think it meant a lot that I took so much time with him and that his opinion mattered to me. After that we got along great.

I didn't know Natalie as well. When I cast her, her career was in crisis, and the studio executives thought she might be washed up; so they let me use her at a reduced price. Natalie was anxious for the opportunity to prove them wrong, and her Oscar nomination reignited her career. Plus, Natalie, like many of us, sensed that Warren was going places, and she was happy to hitch her wagon to his star. On top of all that, I take it that the sex between them was very good.

One scene sticks out in my memory. Natalie was terrified of water, especially dark water where she couldn't see anything around her. So, when we shot the scene where

Wilma tries to kill herself by plunging into a lake and flails in panic, Natalie wasn't just acting. She made it through OK -- fortunately we needed only one take -- but she was visibly shaken. Naturally, all of this flashed into my mind when, years later, Natalie drowned after she somehow fell from her yacht into the murky ocean late one night at the anchorage. Bob Wagner, with whom she had by then reconciled, and Christopher Walken, with whom she was starring in *Brainstorm*, were with her. I don't know any more than anyone else about what really happened out there, whether she slid on a slippery deck, whether she fell while trying to hop into the dinghy to escape a fierce quarrel between the men, or whether something more sinister was at play, as some have speculated. But I do know that the name of her boat was *Splendor*.

I wrote most of the screenplay myself. I adapted it from a small novel Bill Inge had authored. Bill made some changes to my dialogue and to the narrative flow. Those helped significantly, but I was still responsible for most of the writing. Nonetheless, we credited Bill for the screenplay, and he won an Oscar for his efforts. That was OK with me. I learned a few things about storytelling from one of the world's best, and I gained the confidence from writing *Splendor* to proceed full throttle with *America, America*, the project I cared about most.

Splendor in the Grass mirrored my own growing dissatisfaction with middle-class puritanism, and the plot shows how Bud's family values destroy the deep and meaningful love he feels for Wilma. Personally, Bud's parents, Ace and Mrs. Stamper, disgusted me. I regarded them as murderers who kill their son's romantic love in the name of Eisenhower virtues. They think they are doing what is best for their child, and there is a sense of self-righteousness about them. After all, they are upholding their culture's values and passing them on to the next generation. But Ace is rigid and never shows a moment of self-doubt. Neither does his wife. They never examine their motives or wonder if Bud might be better off following his own impulses and pursuing his own dreams instead of conforming to the life they've mapped out for him.

Barbara Loden played Bud's sister, a floozy who loses the respect of her parents. But they never try to understand her or question whether it is really in their daughter's best interest to marry the first person she screws, even if the experience is brutal or boring or worse. Warren's take on Mrs. Stamper: "She withheld approval as only a WASP woman can."

Moreover, the Stampers' rules are business rules centered around what is most practical and what will earn the most money, not what will produce their children's greatest fulfillment and joy. Beneath their respectability, the Stampers represent all that's spirit-squelching about the bourgeoise, and I detested them. Would I have felt the same way before I began my lump-clearing practice? Probably.

CHAPTER 53

Marilyn

I started off the new year by getting divorced. That felt both liberating and disappointing. I'd loved Art so much and admired him so much, but our marriage had degenerated into just so much crap. I'm sorry, but there's no better way to say it. I was happy to be free again, just as I was after Joe and I split. But at the same time the divorce felt like another defeat. Why couldn't I sustain a loving relationship? Was it that I always chose men who, deep down, didn't know how to love me? Or was it because I was fundamentally unlovable?

Whatever the explanation, the love Art and I had shared before we married had dissolved months, if not years, before. Maybe everything started to fall apart on our wedding day when that dying photographer cursed us. In any case, on January 20, 1961, my lawyer and I flew down to El Paso and then drove across the border into Mexico, where a judge granted my petition to terminate our union without delay. "Incompatibility of character" was the justification. On the advice of my attorney I chose January 20, because that was the day of Jack Kennedy's inauguration, and we thought with everyone so focused on that, the paparazzi wouldn't be paying attention to me. I certainly didn't relish the publicity.

My first impression of Jack was that he was too young and inexperienced to be president. He was just forty-three. I'd never followed politics closely before, but Nixon had no soul, and I felt it was crucial that the Democrats win. So, I read up on several possible candidates: Adlai Stevenson, Hubert Humphrey, even Supreme Court Justice William O. Douglas. But Stevenson was already a two-time loser who only knew how to talk to college professors, not real people; and no one knew much at all about Humphrey. I thought Douglas would be the ideal candidate, perhaps with Jack as his VP. But Judge Douglas was divorced, and Americans would never forgive him for that. Back then divorce carried such a stigma. People saw it as a deep personal failure. Indeed, that's how I felt about my own.

So, I wasn't hopeful about the field of Democrats seeking the nomination. I even wrote a little ditty about it.

Nix on Nixon

Over the hump with Humphrey

Stymied with Symington

Back to Boston by Xmas – Kennedy

But Jack won me over as the campaign heated up over the summer. I liked the "New Frontier" speech he gave when he accepted his nomination; it seemed so fresh and full of hope and vigor, and his election in early November was just about

311

the only good news during what had been a terribly bleak period for me.

That winter was even bleaker. The divorce was getting me down; *The Misfits* was a flop; a TV dramatization of Somerset Maugham's *Rain* I'd planned to do with Lee Strasberg got canceled; I had no new projects lined up for the future, and I fell into a deep depression. So, in early February my New York shrink, Marianne Kris, drove me to New York Hospital, where I voluntarily signed my own admission papers to the Payne Whitney Clinic for psychiatric disorders. Maybe the doctors there could figure out what was wrong with me and reignite the spark that seemed absent for so long.

Boy, was I wrong! Instead of making things better, that clinic made everything far worse. To my horror, the doctors stuck me in a padded cell with people who were genuinely nuts, and I feared I'd go crazy there too. I begged to be released, crying and shouting and banging on the steel door until my hands were almost bleeding. But the doctors ignored me or threatened to place me in a straitjacket if I didn't behave. I couldn't even use the toilet, because they'd locked the door; so I broke a window to get in. Then the doctors cited that as evidence that I was self-destructive. Even as a child I hated being locked inside any place, and here I was being treated like a lunatic in an insane asylum. It was my worst nightmare come true.

312

I could go on and on about how awful that hospital was, but what's the point? Finally, after four days of terror they let me make a phone call. The first few friends I tried to reach weren't home; so at last I called Joe DiMaggio, who was down in Florida with the Yankees for their spring training. He flew to New York that night, and the next day Joe told Dr. Kris that if they didn't discharge me right away, he would take the hospital apart "brick by brick." That had an impact, and they set me free. Dr. Kris felt horrible when she learned what they'd done to me, but when I got home I fired her right away. Still, I was in bad shape, much worse than when I'd entered that looney bin; so, I agreed to check-in to the Columbia University–Presbyterian Hospital, but only if Joe would stay there too and see me every day. He agreed without a moment's hesitation. He was so kind and loving. I remained there for almost a month.

Three days after I got out, Art's mother died, and I went to the funeral. Art and I didn't have much to say to one another; his new girl, Inge, was with him. But his father Izzy and I never lost our affection for each other, and I called him every day when he was later hospitalized for an operation.

Joe had already flown back to St. Petersburg to be with the Yankees, and I joined him there at the end of March. We found a secluded resort in Redington Beach and spent several lovely days just swimming and shelling and sleeping. Winter

313

had finally ended, and as spring ushered in new blooms on the citrus trees and the scent of orange blossoms filled the air, I felt myself coming back to life again too.

Satisfied that I was now OK, Joe resumed his busy business schedule traveling around the world promoting products and services, and in late April I returned to Los Angeles, where Frank Sinatra and I hooked up from time to time throughout the rest of the year. We'd met in New York back in '55, before Art and I found each other again, and now he was smitten by me. I liked Frank. He was good to me, generous and caring, and we had good times; but I never really loved him.

Joe, on the other hand, was working his way back into my heart, although our schedules diverged so much we couldn't spend much time together. He did stay with me in New York for a week at the beginning of July, when once again I was hospitalized, this time to have my gallbladder removed. After I recovered and Joe went off to be with his family in San Francisco and then on to Europe on business, I drove with a friend to Connecticut in order to retrieve the last of my possessions in the house Art and I had bought there. It was strange and sad to smell the scent of another woman that lingered in the rooms. I only wished Art well, and I'd hoped he might drop by, just to say hi and maybe give me a little smile, but he didn't.

However, Jack Kennedy smiled at me. I first met him in October at a dinner party Peter Lawford was hosting at his beach house in Santa Monica. Peter, of course, was married to Jack's sister, Pat. I could see that Jack had an eye for me, but it was a wandering eye that also rested on the bosoms of Kim Novak, Janet Leigh, and Angie Dickinson. I liked him right off. He was bright, cheerful, and witty. He made me laugh, and that was so refreshing. Still, nothing happened between us that night, and I went home alone.

I met him again in February at another dinner, this time in New York. Again, nothing happened between us. But, as they say, the third time is the charm. The following month we were both house guests at Bing Crosby's place in Palm Springs, and that evening, after everyone had gone to bed, President Kennedy welcomed me into his bedroom. It was exciting; I'd never fucked anyone so powerful before. It was good for him too; I could tell by the grin on his face. But that was our only time, which was too bad. I liked Jack, and I could tell he liked me. A lot. In different circumstances maybe there could have been something real between us. But he was a floosy, and I was too; so at least we understood each other about that. Plus, I had a movie to make, *Something's Got to Give*, or at least I thought I did until they fired me; and Jack had to run the country and lead the fight against worldwide communism.

The only other time I ever saw him was at his birthday party at Madison Square Garden, when I put on my slinkiest sequined dress and serenaded him breathlessly with "Happy birthday, Mr. President. Happy birthday to you." You've probably seen the video clips. Ike never had anyone sing to him like that, that's for sure. Jackie wasn't happy about my performance, but it delighted Jack. He got a lot of laughs when he told the crowd that he could now retire after having had "Happy Birthday" sung to him "in such a sweet and wholesome way." Still, we were surrounded by thousands of people and never had a moment together alone, not even at the party afterward. Izzy was my date for the evening, and the old man who'd come to America as a penniless child from Poland was thrilled to shake hands with the president of the United States.

So that was my history with Jack Kennedy. It was far beyond anything Norma Jeane could ever dream of, even more unimaginable than my fairytale marriage to Art and the most famous wedding in the history of the world. But it was never the long-term love affair the tabloids said it was. I wish it had been. As for Bobby, it's true that we became good friends. I especially admired what he was doing for civil rights, and I adored his sense of humor. He certainly played no part in my death, despite the sinister and salacious lies in the scandal sheets. That was all made up just to sell papers in the check-out lines of grocery stores. But Bobby and his brother were as different as night and day when it came to marital fidelity. Bobby was totally devoted to his wife, Ethel, and he and I were never more than pals.

Besides, I loved Joe, and Joe loved me. We saw each other whenever we could, which was never as often as we wanted, and in July I finally agreed to marry him. We set August 8 as our wedding date, and I was so happy. Unfortunately, I died on August 5, and, instead of getting married, I was buried on August 8 instead. Poor Joe.

CHAPTER 54

Art

1962 was the year of the almost-Apocalypse, except for Marilyn there was no *almost* about it. A year earlier, about the time Marilyn first met Kennedy, American and Soviet tanks had faced down each other at Checkpoint Charlie, after Khrushchev built the Berlin Wall and threatened nuclear war unless we pulled our troops from the city. That crisis was somehow averted, but the following October the next face-off featured nuclear-armed missiles instead of tanks. As Dean Rusk, our secretary of state, described the Cuban Missile Crisis, "We were eyeball to eyeball, and the other guy blinked." Those were scary times. Scary in so many ways.

CHAPTER 55

Marilyn

OK, so this is what happened. It wasn't suicide! I was about to marry the man I loved; new roles were coming my way, good roles, challenging roles; I was about to liberate myself from my longtime shrink. Why, then, would I kill myself?

That morning Dr. Greenson, the so-called Psychiatrist to the Stars, came to my home and we talked for several hours. I told him I wanted to discontinue my treatment, and he tried hard to make me change my mind. It was emotional for both of us. Plus, I was firing the housekeeper Dr. Greenson had fixed me up with, and he discouraged that too. But Joe was suspicious of Dr. Greenson; he found him too controlling, and he thought Dr. Greenson didn't really want to see me "cured" because that would mean he'd lose his most famous patient. And the housekeeper always made me nervous, like I was being constantly spied upon or monitored. So that Saturday was to be my last day with both of them. I guess it was, after all.

In spite of Dr. Greenson's insistence that I retain both him and the housekeeper, I held firm. But the drama of our talk upset me greatly. After he finally left that afternoon, I took more barbiturates, Nembutal tablets that my internist, Dr. Engleberg, had prescribed on Friday. Dr. Engleberg was supposed to coordinate my medication with Dr. Greenson, but he had just left his wife, and I guess he forget to mention the Nembutal.

When Dr. Greenson returned early that evening I was still upset, so he prescribed a sedative for me, choral hydrate. Normally Dr. Engleberg would have given me a shot in the arm, but he wasn't available, and the next most-potent way to administer choral hydrate is through an enema. I'd taken enemas before for "cleansings" that were a fad back then in Hollywood; so, the prospect of having choral hydrate forced up my rectum didn't faze me. The problem was that the choral hydrate suppressed the enzymes in my body necessary for metabolizing the Nembutal, and that's basically what killed me.

Dr. Greenson told the housekeeper to administer the enema, even though she wasn't a nurse and had no professional training in such matters, and then he left a little after 7 PM. I was coherent for about half an hour. I even took a call from Joe's son and was delighted to learn he was breaking up with his girlfriend, whom I'd never cared for. But when Peter Lawford called me fifteen minutes later, my speech was already slurred and my life was slipping away. I knew I was losing it, but I by then I couldn't even ask for help. All I could do was think about the men I'd loved and lost throughout the years, and all the pain and disappointment and bitterness returned as I lay immobile on my bed.

CHAPTER 56

Art

The day she died I was on the opposite side of the continent writing the play I was working on with Gadg for the inauguration of the Lincoln Center Repertory Theatre. It was a thinly veiled dramatization of my time with Marilyn. I knew how she resented the way I sometimes used her life as fodder for my art, but it was a story I needed to tell.

I asked Gadg to come by that evening to go over a scene I'd just reworked. He arrived after dinner and stayed until a little after eleven o'clock, or 8:00 PM on the west coast, about the time they think Marilyn expired. I was sitting at my typewriter and staring into space when he entered my writing studio.

"Inge let me in."

"Thanks for coming out at night like this. Here, have a seat."

Gadg sat on the couch beside me, and I poured him a whiskey on the rocks and one for myself. Gadg raised his glass in a quick salute.

"I can use this drink. Molly and I had a tiff before I came over. She thinks I'm using you as a cover for a secret tryst with some new lover. As a matter of fact, there is no secret lover

321

and I'm not having a tryst with anyone. I'm here with you, as you can see."

"I thought Molly wasn't the jealous type."

"Normally she isn't. But she's human." Gadg took a sip of the whiskey. "She's become a little insecure as she's gotten older. Aging is not a pleasant prospect for anyone."

"No, it's not. Still, an insecure spouse is no fun. I know."

"Yes, I guess you do."

"Inge's been a refreshing change in that regard." I thought about that observation for a moment; then I got down to business. "I was working on the play all day, and I want to get your feedback on the draft I gave you before I go any further. Plus, I've finally settled on a title. What do you think of *After the Fall*?"

"Why not just *Winter*? It's simpler."

"I was thinking more like Adam and Eve."

"Ah, sin and loss of innocence. Perhaps remorse. Perhaps not. Let me sleep on it."

"OK. So, what did you think about the draft?"

"I like this one better, but it needs to delve even deeper. It's still not clear who Maggie is deep down, or what psychological forces drive her character.

CHAPTER 57

Marilyn

As my life ebbed away I looked at the photos on the dresser across from my bed. There they were: all in a row. Art, Gadg, and Jack Kennedy. The photo of Joe on my nightstand beside me was bigger and brighter, but I couldn't summon the strength to turn my head to see it. I wish I could have. Instead, the last images I saw were the men who'd let me down, the men I'd let down, and that unleashed a final surge of unhappy feelings and memories.

I somehow found the energy to summon the familiar anger I'd so often turned against myself. "I hate you, you piece of shit. You repel everyone who's ever loved you. Art, Gadg, Mommy and Daddy, Jack. And why not? How could anyone love you after they got to really know you? Why would anyone stay once that monster rears its ugly head?"

CHAPTER 58

Art

"I see Maggie as a barbarian. She comes from a poor, broken family and is almost totally uneducated. Everything she's learned, she's learned the hard way. Her life's been tough; she's endured a lot. That's made her strong in some ways, but it demolished her self-esteem. She feels inherently worthless, and the only way to appease her inadequacy is to get men to fuck her. But it's not the sex she craves, it's the feeling of being desired. And then she becomes famous, and everyone desires her. But deep down she doesn't believe it. So, her arc in the play is quite simple. She goes from victimhood to a viciously commanding egotism and then back to victimhood."

"I can see that."

"Of course, her evolution compels a corresponding change in Quentin."

"I always wondered why you chose that name. Were you thinking of Quentin Compson, the lost soul who drowns himself in *The Sound and the Fury*?"

"They resonate, don't they? Each is consumed by his need to save the woman he loves but is overwhelmed by her self-destructive nature. Of course, my Quentin is unencumbered by incestuous longing. He seems so strong and capable and in command at first but ends up, as you say, a

324

lost soul. He transforms from the older, wiser, successful professional who adores Maggie's child-like innocence and brings stability to her chaotic life, to a beaten man with no self-esteem and no self-respect. In his second phase he has abandoned his own core values and prostrated himself before the monstrous needs of Maggie, the great star."

Kazan finished off his drink. "Yes, you communicate Quentin's deep capacity for groveling very well."

I downed the rest of mine and poured us both another. "Finally, as Maggie falls back into victimhood, Quentin flees in order to save himself. But he incurs enormous guilt. Part of him feels he has abandoned Maggie when she needs him most. Another part knows that whatever he does, Maggie has always been drawn to her own self-destruction. He knows that if he doesn't flee, she will take him down with her. And his instinct for survival, for self-preservation, is too strong for him to permit that."

"So, he's a survivor. That's good. But torturing himself over it, that's ridiculous. Besides, the story of the respectable man who debases himself for a rootless woman has been told before. *Carmen. The Blue Angel.*"

"They were *femme fatales* who trapped men with their sexuality. Maggie was like that with most men too. But it's not her sexuality that captures Quentin. It's her genuineness. She has never felt the need to apologize for who she is or for anything she's ever done. He respects that in her. In fact, he envies it and wishes he had it for himself. She rejects the masks that he finds so essential. That's a big part of her attraction for him, along with her vulnerability, her sense of being lost and abandoned. Her neediness."

"Quentin the Rescuer. OK, but that has to come out stronger. And we need to see why he casts himself in that role. Why must he be the Rescuer in order to be loved and accept love?

CHAPTER 59

Marilyn

"Art, you said you loved me. You said you'd always stay. Liar! What about me? All you ever cared about was yourself."

I tried to focus on his picture but keeping my eyes open was an effort. "You shit!" I tried to scream, but the words were barely audible. "You pretended like it was about me, but it never was. It was always all about you. You know it was.

"Gadg, at least, was honest about it. He never pretended that I was anything more than a lay. He never pretended about anything. But you, you hid behind your mask of honor and integrity. Honor, my ass. You're just a scared little Jewish boy craving adoration. That's all you've ever been.

"And I'm just a scared Christian girl hoping someone will see me. Someone, anyone. Jesus never did. I thought you did for a while, Art. But I was wrong. You just looked at me and saw yourself magnified in my eyes.

"And now you've married that Kraut. Don't think I didn't see her making goo-goo eyes at you on the set. Didn't take you too long to move on, did it? Didn't take you long at all to get over me. Let's see if you can fool her as well as you fooled me."

CHAPTER 60

Art

"Let me be brutally honest, Art.   Do you mind if I'm brutally honest?"

"You always are."

"To me, this play is about morality and guilt, and I've never found those very interesting.   I think Quentin's boring. He's too introspective, too consumed by his need to find himself guilty and then somehow receive absolution.   But Quentin can never totally accept absolution, even when it's granted to him.   Characters like that make me uneasy. They're weak and pathetic, not tragic. I don't think they make for great theater."

"I don't see it that way.   Quentin's afraid he can't love. He's never been very successful at it before. So, he's afraid to give up on Maggie because he'd be surrendering his own desperate need to become a truly compassionate person, and in that way finally connect to humanity.   And perhaps even to himself.   But what if he has latched onto the wrong person? Might that destroy him instead of resuscitating him?   I'm sorry you find him dull. I think his dilemma is compelling."

"You would."

Gadg had always been brutally honest about our work, but his personal observations were more frank and more cutting than when I'd last worked with him a decade earlier. They hurt a little, but I'd always been committed to knowing myself as fully as possible and exposing my self-deceptions; so, I told myself I'd think about what he'd meant by *You would*. Was my preoccupation with always doing the right thing and bearing responsibility for my actions really some kind of neurotic rationalization for torturing myself? I didn't think so. I thought Quentin's dilemma was legitimately compelling. But I vowed to entertain the possibility that maybe it wasn't.

"Still, try to cut back on the introspection and self-flagellation," Gadg grumbled.

"OK, I'll see what I can do. What do you think about the second act? It's less introspective, more focused on Maggie."

"I like that much better. But go deeper. Show them provoking each other. Discovering each other's hidden vulnerabilities and exploiting them. What happens when Maggie suddenly recognizes that Quentin craves adoration, and that's what he's been getting from their relationship? She's worshipped him like a god, and he loves it. He's addicted to it. And in that respect, he and Maggie are the same at the core. They both crave the love of others because they cannot love themselves. That's their ultimate connection to each other."

"You've given me something to work with there. You know, no one can help me think a character through better than you. Not even Inge, and she's damned good."

329

I looked Gadg in the eye. "How are you with Mickey? You haven't said anything about him."

Gadg met my gaze. "The informer? You've obviously based him on me, just as you've based Quentin on yourself. And Maggie on Marilyn. I can see that you tried to show some sympathy for his position, and I appreciate that, I suppose. He still comes across as scum. But, if that's how you see things...."

"I need him to be capable of betrayal in order to bring out Quentin's ambivalence and his own sense of guilt."

"Because, after all, where would Quentin be without his guilt? I never understood it. His or yours. I do what I can, but *I am not responsible*. Why do you heap such a pile of responsibility on yourself all the time? Maybe it's your desire to be God. After all, if you are all-seeing and all-powerful, then how can you not be responsible? But Art, you are neither."

"I never said I was God."

"Look, when you're in a no-win situation, you can't win. So, what's wrong with surviving? Isn't that how we're designed? To survive at all costs."

"Some of us seem designed for survival. But others for sacrifice, and still others for survivor's guilt."

Gadg gave a wry laugh. "Some are born with guilt, some achieve guilt, and some have guilt thrust upon them. I have never understood survivor's guilt. You play the hand

330

you're dealt. And if you get lucky and a few unexpected breaks come your way, all the better. And if someone drowns beneath your churning feet while you're treading water to stay afloat, well that's a shame. It truly is. But it's not your fault. You didn't write the rules or set the terms for survival."

I didn't really see any point in discussing survivor's guilt any further, so I asked Gadg who should play Maggie.

"What about Barbara? She's a barbarian too."

"If you think Barbara's good for the role, then by all means, set up a reading."

"She's pregnant, so she'll probably need to read sitting down. But that won't matter. You'll see that she can handle it. Excel in it."

"She's going to have the child?"

"Yes. Barbara wants it, and I respect her choice."

CHAPTER 61

Marilyn

"I never even had a child to love," I sobbed. "No little girl to dress up and play with. Or share secrets with. Oh, Art, why didn't our babies live? They never even had a chance to be born."

Then my thoughts returned to Gadg. "Why didn't you like me more than Molly? More than all those other girls? Why didn't you love me? How could the sex be so great and your feelings so detached? I'm prettier than all those other girls, Gadg. Sexier too. I bet you pretend you're with me when you're screwing them. Don't you?"

CHAPTER 62

Art

Gadg was silent for a moment, then he added, "I was thinking of having Barbara wear a Marilyn Monroe wig."

"For the reading?"

"And the performance as well."

I tried to picture Barbara Loden in a platinum blond wig and the kind of body-tight dress Marilyn sometimes wore when she wanted to look really voluptuous. It worked.

"Sure, give the wig a try."

"I'll have Ralph dig one up for her."

CHAPTER 63

Marilyn

I lapsed into a momentary state of unconsciousness, but somehow I shook myself out of it. When I awoke, I found myself staring at my photo of the President.

"Jack, you like me better than Jackie, don't you? Your mousy little wife with her fine breeding and tiny ass. The President of the United States loves me, Jackie. Not you and your high-society pedigree. But Jack, why don't you want me anymore?"

"I do want you, Marilyn," I heard Jack say in my mind. "I want you more than you can know. But I am the President of the United States, for God's sake. If our secret love ever became public, it would ruin me and destroy the country. Khrushchev would smell my weakness and pounce like a tiger. Nuclear Armageddon in an instant! Everything explodes! *KABOOM!*

"No, I am like Wotan, chief of the Norse gods. To succumb to my desire and bring joy to my heart would bring about nothing less than the destruction of the entire human race."

"What's wrong with me?" I cried as I felt myself slowly slipping away. "What's wrong with me? Why does loving me always lead to the end of civilization? Why did God choose me

334

as His forbidden fruit? Jesus, can you answer me that? I'm succulent. I'm tasty. That's the way you made me, and I love it. But take one bite and we'll all be hurled from Eden. And then what? What comes after the Fall?"

My eyes closed and I fell asleep once more.

CHAPTER 64

Art

Gadg looked at his watch. "It's almost eleven o'clock. Time for me to go back home before Molly blows a fuse."

He started to rise from the couch when I stopped him.

"Gadg, I had an inspiration today. That's why I insisted you come by tonight, so I could tell you about it. I want to kill off Maggie."

"Kill her off?"

"Early in Act One I'll have Quentin reveal that Maggie has committed suicide just a few weeks earlier. A drug overdose. I think it will put everything that happens afterward into a stronger dramatic context. The audience will relate differently to Quentin's inner conflict if they know Maggie's eventually going to do herself in. It will intensify both his sense of betrayal and his need to escape her. What do you think?"

Gadg sat back down again. "Well, there's a certain ambiguity in leaving her alive at the end that I like. Alive but lost."

CHAPTER 65

Marilyn

I suddenly woke again, and I knew I was dying. But surprisingly it didn't scare me. In my drugged state I actually thought it was funny.

"I guess this is like a birthday," I giggled. "Except in reverse."

And then I began to sing myself to death. "Happy birthday to you. Happy birthday to you. Happy birthday, Mr. President. Happy birthday to you. Happy birthday, Mr. Playwright. Happy birthday to you. I love you, Mr. P- "

CHAPTER 66

Art

"But I can see advantages to killing her off early too," Gadg conceded. "For one thing, that would foreground her self-destructiveness. Do we think Quentin could have ever saved her, or was she doomed from the start, without ever any real hope for salvation?"

"Exactly."

"Killing her off gives us a lot to work with. Go ahead and see how that plays out."

THE END

ACKNOWLEDGMENTS

Although *Collaborators* is a novel, and I often created conversations and actions to suit the dramatic requirements of the story, I tried to remain as historically accurate as possible. The most outlandish and unlikely moments are all based on autobiographies and biographies of the principal characters. For instance, Kazan, himself, describes the photograph of Miller that looked down upon him and Monroe from a shelf above the bed in which they made love; he also writes that she came to his room immediately after agreeing to marry Joe DiMaggio, and initiated sex with him after she told him her good news. The photojournalist Mara Scherbatoff really did die before Monroe's eyes after her car crashed into a tree while she was chasing Miller and Monroe, and soon after, Monroe really did discover the hurtful things Miller had privately written about her in his notebook. To my knowledge, Miller and Kazan did not meet on the evening that Monroe died, but Miller later wrote Kazan that the day before her death he had decided to kill off Maggie, the character based on her. The account of Monroe's death, including the injection of a sedative via enema, is based on the very plausible research of her biographer, Donald Spoto, who was a source of many details in my novel, including Monroe's relationships with John and Robert Kennedy.

The HUAC testimonies of Kazan and Miller are largely transcriptions of their actual testimonies, although, especially in the case of Miller, I added some statements that they did not make but that seem consistent with their positions. For the accounts of blacklisting during the Red Scare I drew on some of my own published research on Cold War history and Cold War-related culture. Following are the primary sources on which I based *Collaborators*.

Autobiographies
Elia Kazan, *A Life* (1988)
Arthur Miller, *Timebends: A Life* (1987)
Marilyn Monroe with Ben Hecht, *My Story* (1974)

Biographies
Martin Gottfried, *Arthur Miller: His Life and Work* (2003)
Norman Rosten, *Marilyn: An Untold Story* (1967)
Norman Rosten and Sam Shaw, *Marilyn among Friends* (1988; a photo essay)
Richard Schickel, *Elia Kazan: A Biography* (2005)
Donald Spoto, *Marilyn Monroe, The Biography* (2014)

Historical Background
Eric Bentley, *Thirty Years of Treason* (1971; transcripts of testimonies before HUAC)
Richard A. Schwartz, *Cold War Culture* (1998)
-----, *Cold War Reference Guide* (1997)
-----, "How the Film and Television Blacklists Worked" (1999)
        Available online: http://comptalk.fiu.edu/blacklist.htm
-----, *The 1950s* (2003)

Made in the USA
Columbia, SC
26 January 2023

11105076R00205